Troubled Spirits

by

Sandy Wolters

Spirit Voices, Book One

Troubled Spirits

Cover Art by *RJ Morris*

The Wild Rose Press, Inc.
PO Box 708
Adams Basin, NY 14410-0708
Visit us at www.thewildrosepress.com

Publishing History
First Fantasy Rose Edition, 2017
Print ISBN 978-1-5092-1448-8
Digital ISBN 978-1-5092-1449-5

Spirit Voices, Book One
Published in the United States of America

"Excuse me. What did you say?"

The familiar reaction had Jody's heart sinking. She had to admit she did feel the tiniest bit bad for him. He'd had no clue the direction this discussion would take. Forcing a smile on her face, she knew it wouldn't be long before he ran in the other direction. He'd end up bailing on her just like everyone else she'd been interested in had done.

She could pinpoint the exact moment his mind turned suspicious. His gaze penetrated as he visually examined every inch of her. When his expression softened and the warmth returned to his demeanor, she knew he'd probably devised some logical explanation for what she'd just said. At least that had been the pattern in the past with the men she'd been interested in. Maybe he attributed her comment to exhaustion. Maybe he just thought he'd misunderstood her. She'd have to speak concisely so her words wouldn't be misinterpreted.

"I woke up last night to find a distraught four-year-old girl in bed with me." *No sugarcoating.* She'd be straight up about her abilities, and he'd walk out. She hadn't had time to get attached to him yet, so nothing gained. But for some reason, her heart sure felt like something had been lost.

"I don't know when she died, but she's determined to find her parents and talk to them."

The color drained from Jared's face.

Kudos for Sandy Wolters

A rough draft of the first scene in *Troubled Spirits* won a WIP contest sponsored by the PRG (Paranormal Romance Guild) Book Club in May 2015.

Dedication

I dedicate this book to my husband, Michael,
for all the love and support you've given me
throughout the years.
Your encouragement has kept me going
through thick and thin.
You are my heart.

Chapter One

Startled from a deep sleep, Jody opened her eyes to find a young child's misty form sitting on the bed—tears streaming down her face. As it often happened with kids that cry for any length of time, the poor little girl's sobs were punctuated with hiccups.

Groggy from sleep, her first instinct had her reaching out to embrace the small girl and offer whatever solace she could. Tendrils of unease spiraled through Jody's body when her fingers unexpectedly encountered cold air instead of warm flesh. Her mind roused instantly. She knew at once this child was dead. Spirits had none of the warmth of the living—though they possessed all the same passions.

As she rose to a sitting position, her heart couldn't help but break for the tiny, cherubic girl who somehow had found a way onto her bed. The heavy weight of the child's despair settled squarely on Jody's shoulders. As the realization of the spirit visitation hit home, she found herself in the unenviable position of having no clue how to appease the little girl. She'd just have to stay the course and watch as the child exhausted her pain-laden tears enough to calm herself and speak her mind. Maybe that was all the little angel wanted from her.

Waiting through the weeping and hiccups proved to be agonizing. Several tense minutes passed until finally this beautiful little girl with auburn hair raised her cobalt blue eyes to gaze into Jody's soul. *"I'm Fiona. I want to talk to my mommy and daddy."*

Stricken by the sad message, Jody's breath caught in her throat. Her hand instinctively covered her heart, trying unsuccessfully to repel the grief radiating from this tiny apparition. The emotional turmoil Fiona expelled dampened Jody's soul and weighed heavily on her. Anxiety rolled off the child's spirit in waves and crashed into her body. Each new surge of emotion left Jody feeling battered as if being caught between an angry ocean and steep rock cliffs with no means of escape.

Warning bells blared in Jody's head. Her empathic abilities were on high alert. Under these conditions, she'd never be able to distance herself from the onslaught of the little ghost girl's crippling emotions. Unable to separate herself from the child's grief made coming up with the appropriate response to soothe Fiona impossible.

"Oh, baby, I'm so sorry you're hurting." Her heart broke for this child as well as the mother and father who had lost her. She couldn't imagine how parents found the strength to cope with the loss of one so young and sweet.

"I sit with my mommy all the time, but she can't see me. She can't hear me. When I try to touch her, she doesn't feel me. I've tried to talk to my daddy too, but he's so worried about mommy that he...he..." The poor little girl couldn't continue.

Fiona's bottom lip started to quiver as she fought valiantly to control her tears. Witnessing the sheer determination in that small gesture made Jody's pulse race. The ghost girl caught her lip between her teeth to quell the tremors. The show of absolute strength in that gesture was duly noted. The young child trying her best to suppress her emotions alerted Jody to the importance of this visitation. It saddened her to see one so young digging that deep to gain the power needed to stabilize such debilitating emotions. The fortitude required for such a feat was impressive.

With no other option available, she'd wait patiently for Fiona to calm herself. Hopefully, it wouldn't be long before she could continue her story. But in the end, it didn't matter. She'd give this tiny slip of a girl all the time she needed to gather herself.

With a show of grit that Jody admired, Fiona resolutely brushed the tears from her cheek with the back of her hand. Taking what only appeared to be a deep breath, the child gazed into Jody's eyes as if she were her last hope. *"I'm scared for my mommy. My daddy's scared for my mommy too. She's so sad and cries all the time. I need to talk to my mommy right now!"*

As Fiona begged for help, Jody felt the crushing weight of the spirit child's words. Steeped with feelings of inadequacy, she had no idea what could be done to help this poor, downtrodden soul. "Oh, Fiona, I don't know what to say or do to make this better for you. I'm so sorry."

Caught up in the youngster's company, Jody realized the longer the child stayed, the more corporeal her spirit became. With each passing moment, this angelic little girl's resolve to get her message across became more emboldened—which apparently served to energize and strengthen the spirit sitting in front of her.

Her first glimpse of Fiona had been little more than a light mist. Now, however, she appeared as substantial as any living kid. Transfixed, she couldn't have torn her gaze from the child sitting next to her if she wanted to. Orange freckles dotting the tiny tyke's nose and cheeks caught her attention as the image of Fiona continued to be more robust. The smattering of freckles prompted a vision of this little girl with her fair complexion playing out in the sun too long. *What in the world happened to this child? She looks so cared for and so healthy.*

Considering the tremendous effort Fiona exerted, she understood how important this message must be to the sweet, baby girl sitting in front of her. No matter how emotionally and spiritually draining for Jody, she was determined to let the child have her say. Hopefully in doing so, Fiona would find peace.

The little girl scooted closer and held her small hand out. Touching a spirit was new territory for Jody. Never before had the dead demanded physical contact. Surprised by the action, and not having a clue what to expect, she tentatively reached out to the offered hand. The sensation of Fiona's touch closely resembled that of a living child. Now she wished the contact hadn't been allowed. The gesture only served to compound her stress level and intensified the grief she felt for little Fiona. The spirit's heartbreaking caress felt like a toddler who had been at play in the snow for far too long without gloves—solid but frigidly cold.

Jody gently stroked the back of the girl's hand with her thumb. The tender display had been a desperate attempt to not only ease the pain in the little one's soul but her own heartache as well.

Fiona slowly lifted Jody's hand, placing the open

palm against her deathly cold cheek. Mesmerized by this new experience and watching with unabashed curiosity, the child closed her eyes. Jody realized almost instantly she'd made a horrible mistake. A mysterious force, the likes of which she'd never known, whisked her away to some unknown destination. Realizing there was no control to be had over her body, her insides became paralyzed with fear. Feeling as though she'd been tossed down a long dark tunnel, she blindly tumbled through a darker than black void. Her arms and legs flailed out of control. Instinctively, her eyes slammed shut. Her breathing hitched as panic rose and wrenched a terrified scream from deep within her throat.

The freefall ended just as suddenly as it began. Too afraid to open her tightly clenched eyes, she childishly hoped the fact they were sealed shut protected her in some way. Jody allowed her other senses to open and gather information. Her skin prickled with the realization that nothing but stillness surrounded her. Having no clue as to where she'd landed, she instinctively understood this was the quiet before the storm. The sudden calm left Jody with a dreadful feeling of foreboding. Something terribly big and extremely ominous was about to happen. Everything within her braced for all hell to break loose. To protect herself, her body went rigid as she waited for whatever might come next.

While gathering the courage needed to see this through, her sense of smell started picking up on the unique scent only found in a hospital room. The distinctive odor of disinfectants flooded her senses shooting even bigger sparks of anxiety throughout her body.

Afraid but compelled to open her eyes, Jody scanned the small room in which she now found herself. The unbearable emotional pain had her flinching as the suffering of all those who had previously died in this room ambushed her senses. She glimpsed a nurse standing off to the side, her head slightly bowed, her shoulders hunched in mourning.

From the corner, Jody discreetly watched a woman wracked by sorrow. The grief-stricken lady haphazardly sprawled herself on the bed and cradled a small child in her arms. Jody's vantage point had the unknown woman's back to her, but the top of the child's unmoving head was clearly visible. Grasping the kid in her tight embrace, the grieving woman rocked back and forth as she cried into the child's neck. Jody felt physically ill when she recognized the beautiful auburn hair. Even without seeing her face, she knew right away that the little girl in the deathbed was Fiona.

As the scene started to unfold around her, it became apparent what she'd been drawn into. Fear, bigger and bolder than she'd ever felt before impaled her. Cold, stark panic encircled her, tightening around her body like a vice and labored her breathing. Fiona had taken Jody back to the moment of her death. Now an active participant in the tragic scene that played itself out in front of her, Jody had a front-row seat to the intolerable pain of a mother losing her child—that one earth-shattering, dreadfully private moment in time.

As if caught in some ghastly nightmare, her anxiety level increased so quickly she found herself wildly turning in circles and pounding on walls. *Oh God! Oh God! I can't stay here!* There had to be some way to liberate herself and find a hasty retreat out of Fiona's distressing vision. Eventually, the grieving woman's misery overwhelmed her and proved to be too much. Dread, dark and cumbersome, clamped its icy fingers on her as the realization sank in that there were no windows or doors to flee through. There would be no escape from the nightmare which held her captive.

The shrill scream from the woman on the hospital bed startled Jody and had her attention immediately focused back onto Fiona's fate. Horrified by the anguished cry, she covered her ears, but nothing would keep the woman's frantic plea out of her head.

"Don't leave me, Fiona! I can't go on without you. Baby, please, don't leave me. Fight, baby! Fight for Mommy."

Too much for Jody's senses to bear, the mother's heartbreaking sob broke the vision.

Jody's agonized scream reverberated through the room. She struggled to tamp down the sorrow by controlling her breathing. *Breathe in. Breathe out. Breathe in. Breathe out.* Repeating the mantra over and over, she hoped this small action would put her squarely back in her bed and release the tragedy of what she'd just witnessed. She focused solely on the words running through her mind until distance could be gained from the uninvited torment.

When Jody finally built up enough courage to open her eyes, she found herself back in her bedroom. Emotionally and physically spent, she had given all she could to the little girl. There wasn't anything left to offer.

Glancing up she noticed Fiona stood in the center of her bedroom doorway. *"I have to go and sit with my mommy now, but I'll be back."* The small girl disappeared in the blink of an eye, leaving Jody in an emotional tailspin. Being sensitive to spirits had always proved difficult, but when children were involved, her psychic abilities became almost too painful to abide.

Physically and emotionally drained from the visitation, Jody collapsed on her bed. In an effort to tamp down her anger at the Universe, she forced her fists against her eyelids and passionately called out to anyone who would listen, "I'm doing everything I can to help people with this gift you've given me."

Anger grew with each spoken word, allowing years of angst to flow out of her. "It's hard enough going to the grocery store or the park or anywhere else, only to find myself surrounded by people both alive and dead. I set myself up for ridicule every time I approach the living out of the blue to give them messages from people they've lost."

Visions of being slapped and cursed at by strangers ran rampant through her mind. People had even gone so far as to accuse her of wanting some sort of monetary benefit from them. "Is it too much to ask to be left alone in my own home? In my own bed?"

She followed the outburst with a deep, cleansing breath, trying to relax and release the tormented emotions she'd just witnessed. Not a moment too soon, a peaceful, warm sensation started at the crown of her head and shot rapidly through her body. A bright white light encompassed and touched every aspect of her being. The illumination, loving and warm, facilitated the complete release of the powerful, debilitating emotions Fiona had introduced. Embraced from deep within the depths of her soul, her audible sigh reflected the much-needed relief. Granted with the special gift of a powerful spiritual cleansing, a potent offering from a higher power, Jody couldn't be more grateful for the tranquility it produced.

Thankful for the peaceful intervention, she relaxed for the first time since Fiona's appearance. Even though this gift of conversing with spirits tended to be a strain on her emotions, she recognized the benefits it had given to many people over the course of her life.

"Okay. I admit it," speaking to her personal spirit guides who were always around offering guidance and support. "There are those special times when the living gives me the chance to speak for those that have passed. When that happens, I do see and feel the inspiration their deceased loved one's words have for them." Continuing to speak out loud, her convictions for helping others in her own unique way strengthened. "It's been my experience that messages from those long gone seem to transform the debilitating grief of the living into a sense of peace."

She couldn't let it go at that, though, and felt duty bound to voice her displeasure over the events that had just occurred. "Still, to send me this child in the middle of the night is cruel for both of us.

"There's nothing I can do to help her or her family at this moment. I have no idea who she is or who her people are. I beg of you, please don't put me through this family's grief for any longer than necessary. When I'm out in public, if I see Fiona standing next to her mother or father, I'll approach them, just as I've done for every other spirit. You have my word."

After saying her peace to the powers that be, she hit her pillow with force and rolled over trying her best to put Fiona somewhere back in the far recesses of her mind. Without a doubt, the time would come soon enough when she'd be face-to-face with the woman in that dreadful hospital bed. Until then there was nothing more Jody could do except hope and pray that Fiona would find solace until all the pieces fell into place. When that time came, Jody prayed Fiona's parents would be open enough to listen to the message their baby girl felt so obliged to give them.

Chapter Two

Ironically enough, Jody awoke to the alarm clock blaring *Stairway To Heaven*. Her sleep-fogged brain couldn't remember where she'd put the clock the night before. Not being a morning person made getting up and starting each day a struggle. Early on, she'd discovered the only way to get her tired ass up and moving each morning would be to change the location of her alarm each night. Doing so forced her to wake up enough to find it and ensured she wouldn't accidentally turn the alarm off and fall back to sleep.

On autopilot and eyes half shut, she sprang out of bed and ran toward the closet. Her leg clipped the reading table as she fumbled around the room. "Shit!" she screamed, grabbing the offended knee. Constrained to jumping on one foot, Jody struggled across the room to where she'd hidden the alarm the previous evening. Her foot tangled in clothing which had been carelessly thrown on the floor the night before. Not awake enough to keep herself from falling, her momentum propelled her into a heap only inches away from the alarm. A disembodied voice of one of her spirit guides yelled in jest, *"timber."*

Very funny. I'm surrounded by comedians. Jody ground her teeth together out of frustration. Yanking on the alarm's cord to jerk the plug from the wall effectively cut off the ear-splitting noise.

A contented sigh slipped through her lips as quiet filled the room. The pain in her knee forced her face into a tight grimace while she rolled onto her back and cursed the dawning day.

Upon opening her eyes, she found little Fiona standing over her brandishing a broad grin. The unexpected intrusion on her personal space had Jody's supine body instinctively jerking away. The back of her head slammed against the closet doorframe.

"Ouch!" she bellowed while grabbing her now throbbing head.

A few tense moments passed before Fiona bent down and whispered in her ear. *"Oops. Sorry, you bumped your head."*

Because of yet another invasion on her personal space by this headstrong child in such a short period of time as well as the full-blown headache she now had, Jody's anger bubbled over. With little Fiona's troubles momentarily forgotten, she couldn't maintain her civility and snapped. "Fiona! What are you doing here? You *can't* stay here." She shot the little girl her most intimidating stare.

Ignorant evidently to the anxiety her presence caused, Fiona sat on the floor beside Jody and made herself comfortable. *"I'm here because I want to speak to my mommy and daddy. Don't you remember?"*

Knowing there wasn't a thing she could do to help Fiona made her heart sink. Feeling like a total heel for her outburst and more than a little defeated, all she could manage was a groan as her head slowly fell back to the floor. Being hostile wouldn't help this situation at all. Trying to suppress the little girl's emotional pain, which threatened to overwhelm her, she stole a few quick moments to compose herself before responding. Still lying flat on her back, she dug the palms of her hands into her eyes. She could only hope the pressure would ease her headache and ongoing heartache caused by this child.

Jody gathered her resolve enough to hazard a glance at Fiona. Undoubtedly, the child didn't understand the rules of interacting with the living yet. Gritting her teeth again, she made the decision to be straight with the kid. Her intention wasn't to cause pain or hurt her in any way. The poor child had experienced enough suffering in her short lifetime. Somehow she had to make Fiona understand that by continuously showing up like this, Jody's sanity was put at risk. It wouldn't be possible to be subjected to the little girl's grief at all hours of the day and night. Such contact would prove to be a dangerous game of Russian roulette that would inevitably leave Jody's body and soul the clear loser. Surely once that fact had been explained to Fiona, the sad little girl would keep her distance until her parents were present.

Garnering her strength, she took a deep breath and sat up. To ease the sting of her response, Jody drew closer and gently held onto Fiona's hands. "Yes, Fiona, I remember. I know you need to speak with your mommy and daddy. But sweetheart, you can't stay with me. You have to go. Are there any family members on the other side that can talk to you about the rules of visiting from your side of the veil—from Heaven? The protocol is very important and must be followed. Too much contact between you and I would have a disastrous effect on both of us."

Guilt left her wincing as Fiona's bottom lip started

to quiver again. A large teardrop formed and fell from her eye, rolling slowly down her cheek. Imploring with unspoken words to let her stay, the child peered down at their clasped hands and then back into Jody's eyes.

The thought of being stern with the little angel sitting in front of her had Jody's gut twisting in knots. If she weren't careful, she'd start to hyperventilate from all the deep cleansing breathing Fiona had forced upon her. Chanting her mantra to remember to breathe seemed to keep the emotional chaos attached to this little girl at bay—barely. There had to be some way to gain control over these encounters without heaping unnecessary pain on Fiona.

Squeezing the child's hands to offer whatever comfort she could, Jody started to speak when her peripheral vision picked up movement next to Fiona. An older woman appeared and glided up to the little girl—sadness and anguish apparent on the woman's face. Mesmerized, Jody couldn't look away as the woman stroked Fiona's hair.

"Come with me, child," the woman cooed. *"We'll make some cookies and have a nice talk."*

The beauty of the love emanating from this woman for Fiona stole Jody's breath. Because of her proximity, the older woman's affection when she embraced the little girl enfolded Jody in the overlapping warmth. She was left spellbound by the raw emotion surging through the air as Fiona obediently stood and gave the woman her full attention.

"Grandma, I want to talk to my mommy."

The grandmother bent down and placed a loving kiss on Fiona's cheek. *"I know you do, love. The time will be here soon enough when you will be able to do just that. For now, though, you need to come with me. You can't stay here. I've told you, there are rules we need to follow. I suppose we'll have to go over them again."*

As the apparitions slowly melted away, Fiona clung to her grandmother but managed to give a shy farewell wave to Jody. Still dazed from the force known as Fiona, the grandmother's intervention was a pleasant affirmation that the little girl would be reined in, somehow.

In a moment of pure self-pity, Jody forced her chin to her chest. Disbelief over the crazy situation she'd found herself in was acknowledged with a slight sway of her head. Her fingers crossed in anticipation that the child's grandmother would keep her word and teach little Fiona the rules of interaction and just how important they were. The toll already taken on her body had proved too great to allow a spirit like Fiona so much access.

Jody had no clue how or even when the time would come when all parties involved found themselves in the same place at the same time. They might not meet for days, weeks, or even years from now. As usual the timing would be left up to the Universe. For everyone's sake, she prayed everything that needed to happen would fall into place allowing the reunion to occur sooner rather than later.

Chapter Three

Delighted to switch her focus to the more mundane side of life, Jody unlocked the door to Fur Baby Groomers, her business and sanctum. Fur Baby was Jody's charging cord, a place to plug in and reenergize sapped energy that spirit manifestations depleted. Her workplace, for the most part, was a ghost-free zone. The daily reprieve from the inescapable chattering of spirits Fur Baby afforded her had turned out to be one of life's biggest blessings. Within these walls, the Universe had granted her a safe harbor where she obtained a much-needed break from the emotional and physical burden of talking to spirits. Even her ever-present spirit guides made themselves scarce here.

She'd always loved working with animals and had a special rapport with them throughout her life. Unfortunately, the special abilities she possessed had always precluded her from having pets of her own. Animals tended to get nervous around the stray spirits that were drawn to Jody. Grooming dogs brought her joy and provided a way to share her love for animals—even if only with other people's pets. She thought of every one of her cuddly, furry clients as her own.

Jody counted her blessings every day for the personable staff members she employed. Having Kim and Cassi around to deal with the pet's owners provided her with a firewall of sorts. They made the chances of a visitation even more remote.

She conceded the fact that occasionally a deceased owner would show up to check on their still living pets. This type of spirit sojourn didn't bother her in the least. The pets always seemed to recognize their loved ones and weren't skittish when they made their presence known. Her precious energy remained intact during this type of visitation. Animals didn't need her to prove herself through the vigorous authentication process which people generally required from her. Pets just seemed to have the innate ability to know and understand their loved one's messages all on their own which took the pressure off of Jody.

Flipping the lights on, she made her way behind the waiting room counter to turn the computer on and get the front desk ready for business. When the bell above the front door rang, she glanced up to find Brad Masters strolling in. As part of their morning ritual, he held a cup of coffee for himself and a cup of tea for her. She knew by the smug grin he brandished, he must have something engaging to share with her this morning. His jovial presence soothed her and helped release some of the remaining pent-up stress from the previous night's and early morning adventure with Fiona.

Brad was a gifted veterinarian who worked next door at the Be Well Animal Clinic. Jody enjoyed their morning chats as well as his company. The man's infectious laugh always brightened her mood and kick-started her day on a positive note.

Over the years, Brad had become a work associate on whom she could depend. Not just for her morning laughter, but for his vast knowledge of animals. It didn't matter if they had fur, or feathers, or scales—he cared about them all. On many occasions, she'd had the privilege of watching him work. His love for all living things was evident in his gentle touch and mannerisms.

As much as she enjoyed his company, though, she'd made certain they never socialized outside of the work environment. Through experience, she'd learned her extrasensory abilities weren't something to share with anyone new to her personal life if she wanted to remain friends for any length of time. She thanked her lucky stars every day he hadn't tried to cross the friendly workplace boundary. As business owners, they shared a comfortable symbiotic relationship. She recommended his business to her clients, who received excellent care for their pets at a discount. The same held true for his clients and her grooming business.

Moving to one of the waiting room chairs, she leisurely leaned back and accepted her cup of tea. Feeling almost giddy with curiosity about Brad's morning tidbit, she was pleased to discover the knots in her shoulders were already relaxing.

Signaling her eagerness to get started with their discussion, she did her best to let everything go and riveted her full attention on Brad. She presented him with a smile. He enjoyed reading weird news articles and sharing the especially funny ones with her. A good belly laugh was just what the doctor ordered to counteract the distressing emotions—emotions which for some reason, she couldn't quite shake on her own.

Knowing full well his intent was meant to torment her with anticipation, he took a long sip of his coffee while peering at her over the rim of his cup. "You're purposely torturing me, Brad. Out with it!"

A broad grin settled on his face as he set his cup down. That particular smirk meant he'd found an especially titillating article.

"Did you hear about the man who turned himself into the police for killing his imaginary friend?"

Jody suspected Brad had to be pulling her leg. God knows, he'd taken liberties with the truth many times in the past to get a laugh. A giggle escaped at the absurdity of the story, but her curiosity got the best of her. With a flourish, she spread her arms wide and implored, "Do tell." Relaxing against the chair's back cushion, she opened herself up to receive the full impact of Brad's tall tale. By the sound of it, she was sure to hear a real doozy.

Brad's head shook in mock dismay as he emitted a "tsk, tsk" sound with his tongue. Watching him tell his whoppers entertained her almost as much as the stories themselves. She likened his storytelling abilities to attending a stage performance of an elaborate one-man show. Never sure whether he made the narrative versions up himself or if they were actual events, made the listening experience even more enjoyable. Either way, he was perhaps the best orator she'd ever met.

"Yep. It's a sad story. Apparently, Darryl…" Brad reached out and lightly touched Jody's arm to emphasize his point, "Darryl is the imaginary friend whom he allegedly killed. Apparently, Darryl is a real asshat." His eyes glistened with laughter as he winked at her. "His word, not mine."

Jody's hands flew to her mouth trying to squelch the chortle before it escaped through her fingers. She failed miserably.

Seemingly unfazed by her snorts of laughter, Brad

continued with a deadpan tone. "They've been friends for years, and throughout that time the killer had been blamed countless times for his imaginary friend's indiscretions. But what was he to do? Darryl was the only family he had left.

"So when the murderer was wrongfully arrested and jailed for something his invisible friend had done, you can imagine how riled he became.

"But that wasn't what turned an ideal friendship into frenemy territory. No, the angry man still loved his imaginary friend—his brother from another mother. He admitted to police that if he were in Darryl's situation and could just disappear into thin air, he probably would've done the same damn thing. He just couldn't hold that against him. What chapped his hide was the fact his best friend had abandoned him in a time of need. The dirty, rotten bastard didn't even visit him in jail." Brad's finger poked the air for emphasis. "And *that* was the circumstance which started the downward spiral in their relationship."

Unable to restrain herself any longer, Jody threw her head back, guffawing at his preposterous tale. Stress melted away as her soul filled with laughter.

"The final straw that sent the murderer into a frenzy dark enough to kill happened when he got out of jail. Keep in mind, the killer was still pissed about not seeing Darryl on visiting days. Imagine, if you will, his irritation when he showed up at home after doing hard time to find Darryl passed out on the couch and the apartment completely wrecked. He said Darryl had treated his humble abode as if it were a pigsty. He just couldn't put up with his imaginary friend's behavior anymore. Darryl had crossed the line. He had to go.

That's when he strangled him and buried him in the community garden behind his apartment complex."

Both Brad and Jody laughed so hard tears rolled down their faces. Trying to calm herself, Jody took a sip of tea. She regretted doing so almost immediately when the hot drink choked her. To help Jody regain her breath, Brad unceremoniously thumped her on the back. Gasping for air, she grabbed a tissue to wipe the spittle away and offered one to Brad.

"The cops held him in custody while they converged on the garden where they found a freshly dug grave."

"Oh, my God!" Jody screeched. Her laughter quickly died as she considered the possibility that perhaps Darryl wasn't so imaginary after all.

"Yep. They called in their forensics team and carefully dug the grave up. When all was said and done, the only thing they'd found was an empty bottle of Jack Daniels. When they asked the man who had confessed to the murder and subsequent burial about the lack of a body, he told them he wasn't surprised they couldn't find Darryl. He was, after all, invisible."

Their thunderous laughter rang throughout the room.

"I want to smell those cups for liquor. What the hell could possibly be so funny this early in the morning?"

Startled by the unexpected sound of her employee's voice, Jody squealed with fright. Clutching her shirt above her heart, she gasped, "Cassi, you scared the crap out of me!" Her infectious giggle prompted smiles from both Cassi and Kim as they leaned on the counter. "Brad was telling me the funniest story, and I guess we didn't hear you come in."

A wicked grin lit Cassi's face as skepticism had her right eyebrow reaching toward her hairline. "I still want to smell those cups."

Jody couldn't wait to share Brad's story with the girls. "You're going to love…" Mid-sentence, a small, cold hand grabbed the back of her arm. Spooked, she almost toppled her chair as she jumped up. She had no time to think about her reaction and how the others would scrutinize it. Whirling around to confront a child, only she could see, her finger rigidly pointed at what everyone else in the room perceived as an empty space. Thankfully, her throat closed on the words before she could open her mouth to admonish Fiona. She could only hope silence would keep her from further embarrassing herself in front of Brad and her staff.

Chapter Four

To Jody's horror, her swift reflexes to Fiona's appearance caused a chain reaction. Time seemed to pass at a snail's pace as everyone scrambled in unison. Alarm crossed Cassi and Kim's faces as both women leaped back. Their startled shrieks lumbered through the air as if they were being played on an old stereo using the wrong speed. Kim landed on her butt in the middle of the floor. Cassi used Kim's body as a launching pad to bounce off of before landing solidly on top of a chair.

Alarmed, Brad quickly reacted by grabbing Jody's arm to maneuver her protectively behind him. His abrupt action served to remedy the time warp she'd just imagined. To Jody's dismay, he scanned the place where Fiona stood and found nothing that should cause such a reaction.

Trying to keep her face a blank slate, she returned her gaze to the little girl. Flabbergasted, Jody stood stock still. She had no idea how she'd be able to come up with a plausible explanation for her actions.

Her gift had remained a highly guarded secret from anyone associated with Fur Baby. To keep her personal life from interfering with her professional life, she believed her psychic abilities must remain undisclosed. The two just weren't compatible. There wasn't anything she detested more than deceit, but Fiona had left her no choice but to do some quick damage control. She'd have to lie her ass off. Not being creative enough to be a good liar, she didn't need a crystal ball to recognize she was in a world of hurt.

Trying to regain her mental balance, Jody forced herself to take a deep breath and closed her eyes. In her mind's eye, a vision of the Tasmanian Devil whirling like a tornado and damaging everything in its path popped up in rare cartoon style. She briefly wondered if the little devil referenced her current unbalanced state or just Fiona herself. Either way the premonition didn't bode well for Jody.

Feeling even worse about the situation now, she opened her eyes just in time to see little Fiona's chin drop to her chest. Her tiny body swayed back and forth as she wrung her hands together. Her first instinct was to rush to the kid and give her a hug, but she forced herself to stay in place. Even without children in her life, Jody recognized the little girl's body language as a telltale sign that she *knew* she'd done something terribly wrong. More importantly, she knew she wouldn't be getting away with the offense.

Her only hope was that the fear she felt for herself could and would override the compassion she felt for Fiona. If that couldn't happen, the consequences would be disastrous. The tenderness Jody felt for Fiona and her situation *had* to be put aside—for now. The little girl's presence caused an enormous red flag to wave where only peace and serenity should be found. The child's blatant disregard for rules and boundaries would ultimately cause Jody's whole world to implode.

Now, unfortunately, she would have to find a way to fast-talk herself out of this awkward predicament.

Above all else, she didn't want Brad thinking she had her very own Darryl. That would never do. He wouldn't be able to trust her again. Fear of the unknown would certainly have him believing she'd gone off the deep end and embarrass him in front of his clientele. Hell, he'd probably never refer another client to her again. From what she could tell, her actions had already sparked a good case of the hibbie gibbies in him. Careful not to give anything away, she watched him as he watched her. Though nonchalantly, he seemed to be carefully examining her as if she were one of his furry patients.

The best defense is a good offense, her mind shouted at her. *Be nonchalant,* it instructed. Maybe, if she was lucky, she'd get out of this mess by bluffing her way through. She could only hope whatever popped into her mind would be more believable than a make believe Darryl.

"Are you all right? What scared you?" As if the situation wasn't bad enough, Brad's face reflected genuine concern, making her feel like a real sleaze ball for the lies she was about to tell.

Her eyebrow shot up questioningly. Offering a puzzled expression, she snorted a little louder than anticipated. "Of course, I'm all right."

A flashback of a pet rat that made a run for freedom from the veterinarian's office next door and ended up in her waiting room crossed her mind. Everyone, including customers, had found high ground on the closest available waiting room chair. They'd all remained atop their perches until the little furry escapee had been caught. *Nope. That won't work.* She dismissed that excuse as fast as it crossed her mind. Cassi and

Kim would insist she shut down the business until they found the pesky little critter. Clients were due to arrive any minute now, and she didn't want to lose their business.

With her mind a complete blank, no response befitting her outburst revealed itself. *Dammit!* Trying to remain outwardly calm, every ounce of energy she had left focused on keeping her eyebrow from nervously twitching. That embarrassing little tick was a dead giveaway when she dealt with too much anxiety.

When the uncomfortable silence had Brad's facial features scrunching up, she had to force herself to remain calm and not make a run for the door. Her lack of verbal response had started to grate on his nerves. She didn't need to have a spirit nearby to tell her how perplexed he was by her actions. His body language spoke volumes. "Something scared you," he remarked, expecting some sort of reasonable answer.

She bit her upper lip, trying to think of something, *anything*, to tell them that would ease their concerns. Doing everything she could to ignore Fiona standing there as bold as you please had her focusing all of her attention on Brad's shirt. Her inability to think of a reasonable response was quickly leading her right smack dab in the middle of a full-blown panic attack. In an effort to get her body under control, she glanced down at her hands which wouldn't stop shaking. That was the moment she realized her finger, still at attention, continued to point at the child no one else could see. Hoping no one noticed the offending digit, she lowered her hand as unobtrusively as possible as the heat of embarrassment covered her face.

As the quiet seemed to stretch on indefinitely, the

tick-tock of the wall clock shouted at her to come up with a decent lie. Her co-workers brushed themselves off and waited for an answer. She only wished she could think of one. *She had nothing!*

Brad leaned in close to Jody and examined her pupil reactions. She could almost hear his doubt for her sanity running through his mind. *He thinks I've lost my marbles. Who could blame him?*

Since a lie—any lie—refused to surface, she had no choice but to prolong the awkward silence. As he continued his examination, she kept her secret locked behind her tightly shut lips. There was no outward indication that her mind currently reeled at a thousand miles a minute. Trying to come up with a believable explanation for her behavior had her brain feeling as though it would overload at any moment.

Brad finally took the initiative and spoke up. "I didn't notice before, but you have bags and dark circles under your eyes. Didn't you sleep well last night?"

A whoosh of breath she hadn't realized she'd been holding liberated from her burning lungs. Jody had to restrain herself from jumping up and down like a lunatic. She could've grabbed his shirt and kissed him for giving her the excuse that had so completely eluded her. *I'm such an idiot! No sleep. That's perfect.*

Trying not to show her relief, she took a brief moment and glanced away before finally turning her attention back to Brad. He scanned the area in question one more time before his gaze came to rest on her once again. "You're starting to scare me. What's going on? Please answer me."

The tone of Brad's voice told her in no uncertain terms that her non-responsiveness had quickly shifted his concern to impatience. She opened her mouth to let the fibbing begin but clamped it shut again before she could answer him. Her heart suddenly sank as a thought tickled the back of her mind. If what had just popped into her head proved to be correct, the fear of her secret being exposed would be a moot point. There'd be no option left but to reveal the truth. Panic held her in the uncomfortable silence a little longer.

Scrutinizing the three living people in front of her, she had to figure out how to broach the subject of Fiona. If her theory proved wrong, she'd need deniability. *Please let me be wrong about this.*

Since Fiona had shown up at her workplace, the child might have some connection to one of the people standing in front of her. That association would certainly explain the little girl's appearance, here, of all places. As much as she hated the thought of unveiling her abilities to these people in this way, for the kid's sake, she had to take the risk and ask.

"Do any of you, by chance, know a little girl by the name of Fiona?" Mentally crossing her fingers, Jody hoped she was grasping at straws. Fiona hadn't paid any particular attention to the people in the room, but the chance she had some kind of association with one of them was a definite possibility.

The confusion crossing their faces told her everything she needed to know. Fiona wasn't connected to any of them. Not even distantly. Now all that was left to do was backtrack and get herself out of this mess. At least, with Brad's help, she had a plausible explanation.

Feeling like all the drama could finally be put to rest, she tried to ease everyone's fear for her with a lopsided smile. "I just had a…" Unfortunately, when

Fiona heard her name, the little girl perked up and considered it her invitation to speak. Rushing over to Jody, the kid's tiny fist started pelting on her already sore knee time and time again. *"I want to talk to my mommy and daddy. I want my mommy!"*

Chapter Five

Oh, God! Trying her best to ignore Fiona's outburst, she slammed her eyes shut. Her hands clenched. Her teeth ground together, leaving her face in a painful grimace. Doing everything in her power not to give Fiona's presence away, the muscles in her neck bulged from the strain. *Please! I'm begging! Just let me keep myself together until I can get rid of Brad and go to the back room, safely away from Cassi and Kim.*

"Oh my God! She's having some sort of fit! Quick! Kim, call 911!" Cassi's piercing, panic-laced cry instantly pulled Jody out of her internal struggle.

Horrified the situation had gone from bad to worse so quickly, Jody screeched, "No! No! I'm fine!" If she didn't pull herself together soon and give them a plausible explanation, she'd find herself in a straight jacket.

As the little girl continued to bang on her leg and cry, she did everything she could think of to refocus herself. Gauging by the expressions on everyone's faces, the confusion, and concern for her well-being had grown by leaps and bounds with every moment that passed. And why wouldn't they be upset? She was acting like a freaking fruitcake! She had to end this and get the hell out as fast as possible.

"I just had a bad night last night. I didn't get much sleep, and I'm a little distracted today. I hurt my knee and bumped my head this morning when I tripped over some clothes on the floor." As if to prove her injury, she agilely rubbed her head at the crown. "And I've got a terrible headache. I think it might be a migraine coming on." Pleased with herself and her acting abilities, she added a little groan to make her whopper more believable.

Moving quickly, Brad nudged her down onto the chair and examined her scalp. "I don't feel a bump, but let me take a closer look at your eyes." He pulled a penlight out of his pocket and tilted her head up. Shining the light in each eye, he seemed happy with what he saw.

"No concussion," he announced, as he stood back and took in her whole face this time. Only then did he seem satisfied.

Kim chimed in. "You work too hard, Jody. Cassi and I are here. You need to go home and take the rest of the day off. Plus, you have that art gallery show tonight for your friend. You need to feel better for that."

Jody sucked in her breath. Feeling as though the world had just crashed in on her, her hands cradled her face in horror. "Oh, my God. I forgot about the art show tonight." The panic she'd felt earlier just doubled. She had no idea what to do about the show. She *had* to go to support her dear friend, Terry. He'd always been there for her when she needed him.

If she showed up in this condition with Fiona in tow, she'd more than likely end up committed—or at the very least, heavily medicated in some depressing hospital room. Forcing herself to be objective, she recognized the fact she wouldn't be able to control the little girl. She certainly hadn't been able to up until

31

now.

It wouldn't take a big leap of faith for the art gallery patrons to believe her odd behavior resembled textbook mental instability. The thought of showing up and embarrassing Terry at his very first show left her mortified. Feeling beaten, she allowed her chin to drop heavily to her chest as her head swayed.

Misinterpreting Jody's actions, Kim sidled closer and took her hand. Speaking with an edge of authority, she declared, "I'm not going to let you cancel that party tonight. Your friend is counting on you to be there. You've mentioned what a big deal this show is for him. Remember? So if you're going to be a good buddy to him, you have to make an appearance. You need to be there for him."

She started tapping Jody's hand, punctuating each word as she spoke. "Whenever you make plans to go out and have a little fun, you always cancel at the last minute. If you ask me, I think you're afraid to be in public. How the hell are you supposed to meet new boyfriend candidates? How are you finally going to put that asshole that dumped you in the past for good if you keep yourself hidden away like this?"

At the mention of her latest disastrous attempt at a romantic relationship, an involuntary jerk twitched through Jody's body. *Could this fucking day get any worse?* Even after a year, she still felt the sting of failure. Her co-workers didn't know the real reason for any of her breakups. She couldn't and wouldn't hide her gift from someone she dated. All of her experience had proven that too much energy was needed to conceal all the dirty little secrets when men were involved. You're damned if you do and damned if you don't because spirits always managed to get in the way. They had a habit of mucking things up with men, even when she'd been up front about her gift.

She'd learned the hard way that constant disruption of her attention was just too much for any man—interested or not. That reason alone effectively doomed her future with a significant other. The last breakup had taught her that the scars left behind were too deep to justify the temporary high the romance itself had provided. For that reason, she'd sworn to herself never to get so intimately involved with a man again. Ever.

Tired of having the boyfriend conversation thrown in her face, Jody's features grew stern. "Kim, I told you before, I'm no longer open to romance. I've learned to live without dating. I'm happy alone."

Trying to soften the message, Kim clutched Jody's hand tighter. Her warm touch conveyed strength and nurturing making it difficult for Jody to stay mad. "Everyone's open to romance, sweetie. You're a woman. You can't live without it."

"Bullshit!" Cassi screeched. "Don't listen to her, Jody. She's got the concept all wrong. You can't live without *sex*. We're all big girls here and know that hot, sweaty sex has nothing to do with romance."

Sneaking a peek at Brad, Jody saw just how uncomfortable this girl talk made him as he grimaced and inched his way back a few paces. *Poor guy.*

In an attempt to keep the peace, Cassi gently shoved at Kim's shoulder. "She's had some hard knocks. Give her some space."

Showing more irritation than Jody had ever seen from her, Kim shook her head emphatically. Growling softly under her breath, the older woman's hand flew into the air with authority and declared, "Whatever!"

Jody had to stifle a laugh. Her love life had been an ongoing discussion between her two staff members since the last ugly breakup. Of course, their advice never really worked for her situation since they had no clue the problem laid squarely in her baggage—not the men who had dumped her.

Turning her full attention back to Jody, Kim stated, "Regardless, you're pretty jumpy today. We both know animals can sense stress and nerves."

And spirits. They can sense spirits. If she couldn't convince Fiona to leave Fur Baby, the kid would end up distressing all the animals.

"Go home and get some sleep. You'll probably feel one hundred percent better after you do."

At this point, knowing the only way to save face would be to leave, prompted her to give in. "I suppose you're right. I'm too tense. If I stay, the dogs will just get all worked up and won't have any fun."

Kim squeezed her arm and pulled her in for a hug. "Promise me you won't miss that party tonight. You simply must go. Your friend is expecting you to be there for him."

Jody squeezed Kim a little tighter. "You're right. I promise. I'll go."

Cassi picked Jody's purse up and held the bag out to her. "Get some sleep. We'll be okay here."

Jody nodded as Brad steered her out the door and got her into the car. "Do you need me to drive you home?"

Guilt over her deception crawled through her body and made her want to run and hide. She silently shook her head, hoping he'd just go away.

"Okay. Call me if you need anything."

Fearing he'd see right through her, she couldn't make eye contact. "Thanks, Brad, I will." She hoped her voice didn't sound as shaky to him as it sounded to her.

Continuing to hold the car door open, Brad appeared to have something else to say, but thankfully thought better of it and just walked away. But it was impossible for her to relax, even a fraction, until he had disappeared inside his clinic.

Finally alone, she laid her head on the steering wheel. She just needed a moment to relax before starting the car for the drive home—just one brief, peaceful moment of quiet.

Fiona's grief-filled voice piped up from the backseat. *"I need to talk to my mommy and daddy right now!"* The child's demanding cry had Jody's body cringing as if she'd been tied down and forced to listen to fingernails scratching on a chalkboard.

Chapter Six

Terry waited anxiously as the young men unloaded the most important piece in his collection. Nerves twisted his gut, and he tossed back another antacid. He'd just finished pouring his soul into the portrait two days ago, and it wasn't contracted—yet. The show opened tonight, and he'd fight tooth and nail to have his prized canvas included.

In his heart, he knew this portrait would be the pivotal piece in the show—that one important statement which connected all of his other artwork together. *Solitude* would leave people talking about it and him for weeks, if not months, to come. He just had to nudge the gallery owner a bit more to see the logic.

He'd spent countless hours on the phone with Julianne, owner of Beauty in the Desert Art Gallery, saying and doing everything he could think of to get her to agree just to take a look at *Solitude*. He'd poured his heart out, and when that hadn't worked, he'd done a good bit of groveling. Finally, even at this late date, he'd been able to persuade her to at least see the canvas, albeit reluctantly. Winning the first battle had him breathing a little easier, but he still had a long road ahead of him to get *Solitude* in the show.

Under normal circumstances, getting the gallery owner to agree to his terms would be an almost insurmountable hurdle. But *Solitude* could never be considered normal by any stretch of the word. Julianne had grumbled about adding the canvas to the collection for a multitude of reasons. But after he'd informed her that *Solitude* wasn't for sale, her decision to leave his masterpiece out had solidified.

Being honest with himself, he could understand her position. After all she was in business to make money. Even though she hadn't come right out and said so, he knew there were other concerns as well. Her art gallery was considered one of the up and coming, hot new businesses in Scottsdale. She wouldn't want to garner a reputation which made her appear weak. He understood if she gave into him she'd be fearful of opening herself up to being trampled by future artist's whims. *We can be difficult.* The more he thought about her concerns, the more his stomach hurt. He popped his last antacid. Trying his best to remain optimistic, he felt sure all he had to do was let her get a good look at *Solitude*. Once she saw his masterpiece, she'd understand the importance of the canvas and relent by including it.

Terry had always prided himself on diversity in his craft, working in many different mediums and styles. He'd never tied himself to a particular type of paint or technique. Doing so would prove too restricting and only serve to squelch his creative nature. With each new piece, something from deep within spoke to him. That inner voice always guided him in the right direction to capture the full potential of the subject matter.

Many times over the last few months he'd lost himself inside *Solitude's* canvas. He'd sit down to work and hours later he'd be roused back to consciousness. Every time this happened, he'd find the portrait closer to completion. Elation prevailed as he realized his ego had stepped aside and allowed his soul to take over. This method had left him with a breathtakingly stunning result.

Solitude showcased the raw emotion he'd poured into his entire collection, but elevated his art to a whole new level. He was positive no one would be able to walk away from this portrait without being touched by it in some way. Art was, after all, something to stimulate the viewer's senses and move them, good or bad.

The time had finally arrived. *Solitude* was about to be unveiled for the first time. Closing his eyes, he said a little prayer to the art gods. The next few minutes would be his make-it-or-break-it moment. Anxiety had his heart rate jumping as the back door of the gallery swung open allowing the men admittance.

****

Julianne stood in front of the covered canvas, wringing her hands.

"You're putting me in a very difficult situation, Terry," she said, practically snapping at him. "And I don't like it at all. Please remember, my word is final when it comes to showing this canvas." He started to object, but she shut him down with a raised hand.

"I know this piece means a lot to you, but the show is tonight, and I haven't even seen it yet. Since you're being so stubborn about not selling this portrait, I have the right turn it down." Her eyebrows rose, silently asking if he understood.

"You'll show it."

His audacity never ceased to amaze her. She had to give him credit. The man certainly didn't lack confidence. *Artists!* Julianne couldn't stop her eyes from rolling. *They're all egomaniacs.* Flustered by his persistence, she felt more than a little harassed because Terry had requested—no, demanded a place of prominence in the show for this particular canvas.

What was she going to do? The man had more talent in his little finger than any other artist her gallery had ever shown. She had to admit to herself, though, this canvas piqued her interest. As much as that fact irritated her, Terry's tenacity over the last few days had paid off for him. Curiosity had finally gotten the better of her.

"Artists know how to create, but *I* know how to show those creations. You're stepping on my toes here, and I don't like it one bit."

Terry opened his mouth to speak, but she stopped him short. "I know. I know. You're sure that once I see this portrait, I will fall to my feet in hysterics and drool. I'm telling you it's too late to center the show around this piece. If I like the canvas, we can put it over there." She waved noncommittally to a spot in the corner.

"Julianne, it's not my intention to tell you what to do with the show. You're the expert here. All I'm asking is that you keep an open mind until you see the portrait. I'm positive that once you do you'll change your mind about the significance of this piece. *Solitude* is too important to be put in a corner like an afterthought."

Artists were passionate people. Julianne knew that and still Terry's conviction for this canvas unsettled her. *What in the hell am I going to do if I don't like what he's created?* They were getting nowhere fast. "We're getting ahead of ourselves. Let's just see what we have here first, shall we?"

As the final barrier slid from the portrait exposing it to the outside world for the first time, Julianne audibly gasped. When her mind finally registered the image on the canvas, she became completely still.

Terry held his breath in anticipation. The moment of truth had arrived. The first reaction to art was always the most powerful. His gaze stayed riveted to her face, her body language, and all the small nuances which couldn't lie to gauge her response to this unique piece of his work.

When her eyes widened, and her mouth dropped open, he relaxed a bit. When her hands covered her heart, he mentally fist pumped. Seemingly mesmerized by *Solitude*, she absently took a step closer to the canvas.

Holding her hand out to him, palm up, her gaze was glued to the canvas as she continued to study it. Her voice a mere whisper. "Provenance?"

He retrieved the photographs from his pocket and handed them to her. He'd taken the photos of himself working on the portrait at various stages of completion. With this type of art, the public demanded proof in which the artist had indeed painstakingly created every line, every little nuance, and every shadow.

Quickly shuffling through the pictures, she verified the authenticity of the work.

"What do you call this piece?"

"*Solitude*."

As if enthralled, she nodded her head absently. "Yes." Her voice was laced with admiration. "I see…no, I *feel* that, and yet…" Her head tilted slightly as if the portrait had whispered to her. "And yet, there's a warmth, a feeling of hope for future sociability engulfing her. My God, Terry! It's as if this portrait is a living, breathing entity."

Talking to herself more than actually positing a question, she uttered, "How in the world were you able to get such an otherworldly quality to such a realistic visual? Amazing."

Pleased and more than a little relieved by Julianne's observations Terry grinned like a proud parent. She wasn't expecting an answer, so he didn't offer one.

While creating *Solitude*, Terry had been consumed with doubt. Being so close to the sentiment behind the portrait, he wasn't sure if he'd be the only person able to feel the emotion within it. Julianne's compelling reaction served to reassure him—no, far beyond that. Her visceral response had soothed him more than the bottle of antacids he'd eaten for breakfast.

He thought back to that magical moment when he'd snapped the picture of Jody, which inspired the canvas before him. The pain of a broken relationship had crippled his best friend. Her heart had been shattered, left in tattered pieces by some jackass who couldn't see past his insecurities. To help her healing process, he'd allowed his artist's eye to capture what he'd seen and felt in that very special moment. She couldn't see the illumination of hope surrounding her, but he could. Without Jody and the deep, loving, spiritual bond they'd shared since childhood, he wouldn't have been able to pour his heart and soul into his creation. Without her openness and inability to disguise her feelings from anyone who paid attention, this portrait would never have come to life. Everything had to align at exactly the right moment to create such a piece of art. The canvas represented a culmination of the perfect emotional storm between two people, one hurting and one willing to heal. Without all of those things coming together in perfect harmony, *Solitude* would still be beautiful, but it wouldn't be inspiring to its audience—it wouldn't be extraordinary.

Julianne studied Terry as though she'd been star struck. "The portrait is outstanding. I want *Solitude* for my personal collection. I'll buy the canvas for any price you name."

Validated once again by her reaction, he shook his head and smiled. "As I said, *Solitude* is not for sale."

Obviously still under the portrait's spell, she returned her gaze to the canvas. "I hope you didn't sell your soul to the devil to create this, but if you did, it was worth it."

Terry threw his head back as the laughter erupted from deep within him. The thought of bargaining with the devil to craft such a divinely inspirational work of art was outlandish.

Julianne rose on her tiptoes and kissed his cheek. "I want to thank you. I will be the first gallery in Scottsdale to show this new form of art, and what a spectacular specimen it is!" Excitement glowed in her eyes.

Her attention quickly focused back on *Solitude*. Terry's trained artist's eye could read her like a book. He recognized her distraction as her eyes glazed over. She'd stopped viewing the portrait as an observer. The time had come to put on her gallery owner hat. He assumed all the problems and technical minutia created by adding *Solitude* to the show at the last minute now had her undivided attention. She'd have to find the proper lighting, the proper placement, and the proper staging to do the canvas justice.

He'd just won the war. *Solitude* was in good hands.

Chapter Seven

At some point during the drive home, Fiona had disappeared from the backseat making the rest of the ride blissfully silent. Grateful for the reprieve, Jody focused on relaxing her taut muscles. The delightful peace within the car aided her efforts immensely.

Slowly pulling into her driveway, Jody came to a stop. Despite the peaceful respite, the constant bombardment of the energetic little girl's unfamiliar energy had left her verging on hysteria. A cackle fraught with panic escaped her lips. The nightmarish sound so creepy, it sent tremors of dread running down her spine. *Oh, God help me! I'm losing it.* Genuinely afraid for her sanity, she tried to regain control by forcing her fists tightly into her eyelids. She understood what was happening to her and around her, but had no clue how to stop the momentum.

The little girl seemed to be holding her hostage, sapping more of her strength with each encounter. Her experience with Fiona had taught her quickly that the price for being dragged into a constant altered state was more than she could afford to pay. She had no idea how to escape the danger of being so far removed from the rational world so frequently. Something had to happen soon to stop Fiona's interference in her life. If the intrusion didn't cease, she feared she'd no longer have the strength to separate herself from the thin veil that kept the dead at bay. She could end up lost in the mist between worlds. Ultimately, she feared she'd lose her ability to distinguish between the essence of the mundane and esoteric. She wasn't fooling herself. She understood *that* would mean the end of life as she knew it, mentally and possibly even physically. For the first time in many years, her gift had now placed her in grave danger.

People often believed that when someone was capable of speaking with the dead, any and all answers to their questions were at their disposal. That was simply crap—the biggest cosmic joke of all. If that were the case, Jody wouldn't be in the trouble she was in now. She'd learned early on that the Universe works in mysterious ways and provides help not when wanted but only when needed.

Clutching the steering wheel, she squeezed her eyes shut, and started her breathing mantra. She would use all the techniques in her arsenal to regain a little control over her life. "I can do this," she stated with resolve and tightened her fingers on the wheel. "I'm strong." *Breathe in. Breathe out.* "There's a reason this is happening, and everything will work out in the end." *Breathe in. Breathe out.*

After allowing herself a few more moments of positive reinforcement, she pivoted to step out of the vehicle. The car forcefully jerked forward, jolting her back to reality. Slamming her right foot on the brake, the realization hit that she'd not only failed to put the car in park but hadn't even turned it off.

"That's just great!" she yelled, violently hitting the steering wheel with the palm of her hand. The angry outburst did more to calm her frayed nerves than anything else she'd tried so far. Once again, Fiona had proven to be too much of a distraction. She had to gain the upper hand soon, or she'd end up hurting herself, or even worse someone else.

Using the force of her anger to slam the car door, she effectively sealed herself inside. The hot interior of the vehicle wasn't an ideal refuge, but at least peace and quiet could be found here. Her objective was to take full advantage of the calm while she could.

To separate herself from her psychic abilities, she stilled her nerves and focused what was left of her energy on allowing her ordinary, everyday senses to take over. This exercise was a type of reverse meditation that served to ground her when she felt out of control.

Becoming more conscious of her hearing, a mockingbird's beautiful trill calling its mate crept slowly into her awareness. Listening to the sounds of her neighborhood, she worked to visualize everything she heard, playing it like a movie in her head. In the distance, a dog barked. Her sense of touch and smell started to respond as the breeze picked up and kissed her skin. The sweet scent of honeysuckle wafted through the car and tickled her nose. She immersed herself in the tranquil reality of the world around her.

To her surprise, a butterfly joined her in the car. There was something mystical about the beautiful creature sharing the same space. No matter how infinitesimal, she welcomed the sense of serenity with open arms. She'd take what she could get.

Calmer now, Jody reflected on how her abilities had impacted her throughout her life. She tried to find a correlation in her past which would help her hurdle this new uninvited snag. Even going as far back as her childhood when nothing had been in her control, there'd never been an experience like this one with Fiona. Good spirits or bad, they'd contacted her and then always moved on, never to be heard from again. Because their visits were brief, only a minute amount of her energy had been stolen. No spirit had ever attached itself to her before. This was new. There was nothing in her past that would help her deal with the dangerous complications Fiona now forced upon her.

Somewhere in the distance, children's laughter caught her attention and had her feeling a little lighter. She tried to imagine her body stretching to the limits and joining in their joyful play. In doing so, she felt a slight pull at the corners of her lips as they rose in a grin. She took solace in the fact the world continued to go on around her as if all were well and normal. The world outside her car gave her hope. But she couldn't quite shake the feeling that a come-apart of gargantuan proportions would soon blacken her horizon.

Over the last twelve hours or so, she'd learned beyond a shadow of a doubt that this situation wasn't going to go away on its own. She'd have to go far beyond her comfort level to figure out how to help Fiona move on. At this point, she was willing to beg, borrow, and steal to get the information needed to make that happen.

The Universe obviously had a change of plan in store for her. She didn't have a choice. She'd have to man up, stop the bellyaching, and stop fighting the transformation, whatever that may be. Like it or not, her only way out of this situation was to charge through full speed ahead. Since she didn't have a clue where to start or what course of action to take, the time had come to ask the big guns for help.

Allowing her reverence for the enlightened, higher powers to shine through in her voice, she started her entreaty. "Please guide me in this situation with Fiona. Provide me with the wisdom and knowledge to do what must be done to help her." She closed her eyes, picturing her spoken plea being carried off on the warm desert breeze. *Well, that's it then.* All she could do now was wait for intervention on her behalf.

Exhausted and thinking only of the nap she planned to take, Jody dragged her tired butt through her front door. When she found Fiona making herself right at home, her surprise at the little girl's intrusion had her silently cursing. Nothing should surprise her anymore.

The reason for her meltdown sat on the living room couch, occupying herself by lifting her legs and then letting them fall. With each upward pass of the child's feet, Fiona's little Buster Browns kicked the underside of the coffee table making everything on top jump. She wanted to laugh at how normal this act would be if Fiona were still alive.

With the kid so close by, Jody felt faint even before the door closed behind her. Bone-weary fatigue that Fiona's presence always seemed to cause immediately kicked in. As yet unnoticed by the little girl, she stood in place and weighed the benefits of sneaking out the door and hiding for just a bit longer.

Just as Jody started to turn and leave, dizziness enveloped her. The air seemed to ignite with flecks of light as if someone had twirled a lit sparkler in front of her face. As she delighted in the glistening spectacle around her, an unexpected surge of adrenaline traveled quickly through her body. The boost of spiritual power was a shot of pure, bright white energy. A special gift had been bestowed on her the likes of which could only be granted from Heaven above. The impact surged through her like a bolt of lightning. Not only did the offering serve to renew some of her hollowed strength, but it also left her with the first inkling of how she could get through this mess. As the hair on her arms rose and stood at attention, little pricks of excitement built deep within her.

This entire mess boiled down to the simple fact she'd been fighting for control. Her ego had gotten in the way. She had to stop looking to the past for answers. They weren't there. Up until this point, Jody had believed she *couldn't* help Fiona until everything fell into the proper place. Business as usual. All she had to do was change her way of thinking. No longer having the luxury of waiting for fate to deliver Fiona's mother and father to her, the situation now called for her to take charge of bringing them all together.

Jody would have to think outside the box when working with the little girl who'd become a problem child. To survive this quagmire, she'd just have to accept the change and move forward accordingly. Liking her new role in the needed change wasn't a requirement. As this revelation hit her, she couldn't help but roll her eyes at her stupidity.

Even though her feelings about this new path were somewhat conflicted, the time had come to abandon her comfort zone. Light at the end of the tunnel had just appeared where Fiona was concerned. That was indeed an excellent turn of events.

Because she hadn't had to face the unknown in

years, she couldn't help but feel a little unnerved. Change was always a tricky prospect. *Her* unknown could very well be fraught with spiritual *and* physical danger. Jody couldn't help but chuckle at her foolishness. *I'm already in hell. How much worse can my life possibly get?*

Before acting on the new course of action, she took a moment to silently thank the higher powers that be for providing her with the needed answers.

Change was no longer on the horizon but right here in front of her and currently sitting on her living room couch. If she took too much time to think about what was to come, she'd be too scared to continue. She'd just have to dive right in and hope the learning curve wasn't too steep.

The time had come to sink or swim. Let's hope I don't drown.

Chapter Eight

Jody's confidence rapidly grew as she set her bag down by the front door. With her energy partially renewed and a new direction in mind, she expected this mess to be cleared up in no time at all. Her newfound advantage had her sprinting across the room with purpose, her gaze never wandering from Fiona. *I can and will do this.*

Deciding to speak plainly, she sat across from the little girl. Sure, she understood Fiona was young and would probably find answering questions about her life difficult, possibly even painful. But her plan wouldn't succeed unless the kid stepped up to the plate and gave her the needed information. A lot rested on the outcome of this conversation, but Jody kept her hopes high. Before laying the details out for Fiona, she worked out what to say in her head. Knowing as little as one misspoken word could lose the little girl's interest had her biting her lip to restrain the urge to start questioning the child.

"Fiona, I want you to listen carefully to what I'm saying to you. I haven't been able to help you because spirits typically don't seek me out until their loved ones are right there with me. That's how my gift has always worked in the past.

"Even though you're here and able to speak with me, it's not possible for me to communicate with your folks because I don't know who they are. I know you're desperate to talk to them, sweetheart, so I've come up with a plan. Some of the things we have to discuss may be difficult, but you and I are going to work together to get this problem resolved. We're going to try to figure out who you are, and how I can get in touch with your parents, okay?"

Fiona's reaction was immediate. The air around Jody crackled, and the temperature dropped. To keep from shivering, she folded her arms around her body. Hope, manifesting as jubilance, rushed off the child's spirit and enveloped Jody like a cool, January breeze. Experiencing Fiona's exuberance for the first time, she couldn't help but smile. The child's excitement was just as palpable as her other, more sorrowful emotions.

Celebrating this breakthrough, Fiona clapped her hands together as she butt bounced on the couch. The kid's whole spirit seemed to shine brighter.

Sending a silent call out to the Universe, Jody prayed she wouldn't disappoint the little girl. Never having to seek out a spirit's loved ones before had her a bit nervous. For that matter, she's never had to question a ghost, either. In the past, spirits simply told her what to say to the loved ones that needed to hear their messages. For both their sakes, she mentally crossed her fingers and hoped this crazy idea was possible.

"I know you don't understand how this works, but I can't magically transmit your message to your parents. If that were possible, I'd do it in a heartbeat for you, Fiona. But, as I said, I don't know who your people are and don't have the faintest idea where you lived or even when you lived. The type of contact you and I have is all new to me, so we're both just going to have to be patient while we try to figure this out together."

Studying the child sitting across from her, Jody realized by the intensity of Fiona's expression that her words had finally started to sink in. Just because she wanted to talk to her parents, didn't mean it would be easy or even possible. This plan may work, or it may not, but trying was a whole lot better than doing nothing. Only time would tell what kind of success they'd have.

"I'm going to ask you some questions that will help us find your folks. I can't promise this idea will work, but we're going to give it our best shot."

There was a distinct tug on Jody's heartstrings when Fiona's face brightened with eagerness. The child's willingness to do anything to talk to her parents, no matter how scary all of this must be for her, inspired Jody.

Being in such close proximity to the little girl had her empathic abilities working on overdrive. The kid's emotions were all over the place. She felt the full weight of Fiona's underlying deep sorrow at being separated from her family as if it were her own heartache. Layered with the little angel's suffering, joy at the possibility of finding her parents left Jody's eyes brimming with tears of happiness. While having no idea what Fiona's message would be once she could finally pass it along, she knew in the end, that wasn't what mattered. The most important thing was bringing peace to this child's soul.

As those thoughts ran through her mind, she was suddenly struck with an epiphany. This situation wasn't just about closure for her parents—it was Fiona's journey as well. Even in spirit, the poor baby would never be at peace until her mother and father knew she was safe. The love this child had for her family, even at such a tender age, bowled Jody over.

More than anything, Jody wanted to make this family meeting a reality for Fiona. Her heart told her this reunion would be the only way the sweet baby girl would have the ability to move on and attain any semblance of peace.

The thought of little Fiona being stuck in this wandering state, endlessly searching for her parents, ripped through Jody's soul. Under *no* circumstance could she allow that to happen. That kind of tragic outcome served to solidify Jody's determination. Despite anything which had come to pass and no matter how physically demanding, she'd go to hell and back if that would help Fiona's cause. After all, while she still had a life to live, that part of the child's existence was over. Sadly, this new course of action felt like the little girl's last chance for closure. Jody swore to Heaven above not to fail her.

An interesting thought crossed her mind as she opened her mouth to speak. This little girl's journey might be what Jody's abilities had been preparing her for her entire lifetime. This task felt *that* important. She cringed as the selfish thoughts of personal gain crossed her mind. Those feelings should never commingle with her gift. Even though the thoughts were self-absorbed and she knew them to be wrong, she couldn't help but think that by assisting Fiona, she might get some closure herself. Instead of being a catalyst of change to her abilities, maybe the little girl was her vehicle leading to closure—an end to her gifts.

All of those off-the-cuff readings, all of those spirits from the past, maybe, just maybe, led her to this one point in time. Perhaps she would be free of this so-called gift once this last arduous task met with completion. That reasoning could explain why this situation had been so trying for her.

How many times had she heard the climax to any trial or journey in a person's life often ended with a bang? Many times! This baby girl sitting in front of her could be her bang! Maybe whatever penance Jody owed the Universe would be paid in full, and she'd be able to live like a normal person. She could potentially have friends outside of her inner circle again. Maybe even a man to focus her attention on rather than spirits. It wasn't clear how much more her mind and body could endure while being connected to the spirit of this little girl, so she had to get her ass in gear.

With renewed purpose, Jody lovingly squeezed Fiona's tiny hand to get her full attention. If she couldn't calm the child's staggering emotions, she'd be overwhelmed herself, and they wouldn't get anything accomplished.

"Fiona, how old were you when you died?"

She held up four fingers and wiggled them. *"I'm four years old."*

It would be a waste of time asking how long ago she had died. Her experience with spirits in the past taught her time meant nothing after a soul crossed the veil. The child could have been dead a year or ten years. Fiona would have no way of knowing.

"Do you know your last name?"

Fiona's head tilted slightly. Her eyes glazed over signaling her focus had turned inward. The kid was trying her best to remember. As difficult as it was, Jody waited silently for the child to go through her memories. She prayed the little girl would remember this vital piece of information. Fiona's gaze eventually fell back on Jody's face.

After what seemed like a lifetime, the child finally broke her reverie and spoke. *"My mommy always used to tell me I have McCarthy blood in me."* As she conveyed her family heritage, Jody felt Fiona's contentment as if it were her own. *"She said no matter where I went, I'd always have family nearby."*

She was momentarily mesmerized by the beautiful smile that blossomed on the child's face. As unshed tears of pride pooled in Fiona's eyes, Jody went numb with a sense of childlike yearning that only a mother could fill.

"My mommy was right. I'm surrounded by family, and they're all really happy to see me. They all love me, and I've never, ever met them before!" Her hand rose to her mouth, but not in time to stop the unexpected giggle that escaped. Leaning forward and conspiratorially whispering, Fiona spoke as if telling a great big secret. *"The boys are all wearing skirts."*

"That's good, Fiona."

Jody was thrilled to get some of the answers she needed to track the girl's family down. Having more success than she could've ever hoped for boosted her optimism that things were finally turning around for them. All of her anxiety started to disappear as she thought of poor little Fiona being able to rest in peace sooner rather than later. Knowing the child might soon be able to speak with her parents had her heart feeling as though a heavy weight had been lifted. Hopefully that sought after discussion would end the torment in which everyone involved must've felt since her death.

With a clear mission, Jody ran from the room and returned with her laptop. Barely able to contain her excitement, she searched Google for the name *Fiona McCarthy*. A squeal escaped her lips when several hits popped up. But as she scanned the results, her enthusiasm took a big hit and left her feeling as though she'd just splattered against a brick wall.

Apparently, the name Fiona McCarthy was more prevalent than she'd originally realized. *Dammit!*

Fiona's young age made it easy to skim through those links which had nothing to do with the child. There were pages for authors, psychologists, Facebook accounts with that name, Twitter accounts, and on and on. Her only hope was to find an obituary or perhaps newspaper article about the little girl, but nothing relevant jumped off the page. Her little Fiona was nowhere to be found on the Internet.

Knowing she was on the right path, Jody refused to let this setback discourage her. She refocused her attention on Fiona. "Do you know what your mother's name is?"

"Mommy."

Wishing she had more experience questioning small children, Jody stifled a chuckle while chewing on her bottom lip. "Something other than Mommy. Think, Fiona. What did your dad call your mother?"

The child's face lit up. *"Sugar."*

Jody grimaced with disbelief. "Your mom's name is Sugar?"

"Yep. Daddy calls mommy Sugar Momma." Fiona nodded with certainty.

"Okay," Jody replied, even though this wasn't exactly what she wanted to hear. Maybe Fiona could help her out with other information.

"Did your mommy ever teach you how to use a telephone?"

Fiona excitedly nodded and clapped her hands together.

Jody secretly crossed her fingers. "That's great! You *are* a big girl! Did your mommy tell you what your telephone number was?"

"Yep! 911."

Jody wanted to laugh at the giddiness Fiona displayed. She was certain the little girl thought she had scored a whopping one hundred percent with her answers. Fiona continued to bounce around.

"My mommy taught me how to punch 911 on the phone."

"Hmm. Okay." The words trailed out slowly. Jody couldn't help but smile at the adorable little girl.

"My mommy said if I ever needed help, I could call 911. She said there'd always be someone there to help me." Out of the blue, the child's head suddenly bowed, and her bottom lip disappeared between her teeth. *"I don't think that's true, though. I've tried calling 911, and they can't hear me either."*

Jody's heart went out to the little munchkin. She'd apparently tried everything she could think of to talk to her parents.

"Your mommy is a very wise woman, Fiona. Unfortunately, calling 911 only works when the person is alive."

The little girl's features relaxed, and Jody could see her relief as she learned her mommy hadn't fibbed. Her response was a sweet, toothy smile and an understanding nod.

"Did your mother ever tell you what city you lived in?"

The child's face scrunched up as she pondered the question. Her tiny finger punctuated her thought process by tapping her chin. *"She used to say she was proud to live here."*

"That's good. Did your mom ever say where 'here' was?"

Fiona thought long and hard and then did a happy, little butt-bounce on the couch. *"Yes! We live in Merica."*

"Merica?"

Fiona's head pitched forward. *"Yep. Merica."*

Jody held her groan inside. "Do you mean America?"

Fiona jumped from the couch and did a high-spirited victory dance. *"Yes! America! Let's go talk to my mommy and daddy now!"*

Trying her best not to let defeat claim her, Jody leaned back against the cushions and rubbed her eyes. She had to figure out the best way to approach these questions. Apparently, her sleuthing skills were sorely lacking. She had no experience questioning or even talking to young children, which had become obvious by the way this conversation was going. Her inability to ask the right questions the right way had turned her idea of getting the answers she needed into a big, fat zero. Worse, with each moment that passed, Fiona got more excited which only served to drain her precious resources further.

"What about the name of a town or a state? Do you

remember if she ever mentioned Phoenix, Tempe, Scottsdale, or maybe Arizona? That's where I live."

Fiona inserted a finger in her mouth and chewed on her nail. Clearly, the child was struggling to remember any small detail about where she lived.

Jody didn't think pushing her any further with these kinds of questions would yield any usable results. The little girl just didn't know. At least she had a name and an age with which to start. Even though she'd failed to find any useful information online, Jody was sure Nathan would be able to help her. He'd be at the art gallery tonight for Terry's show. With his police background, he'd certainly know where to start. She'd just have to be patient and beg for his help later.

Relaxing her body, Jody tried to think outside of the box. Was there anything else that could be done right now? An image of Fiona in the hospital bed flashed into her mind, prompting an idea. "Fiona, do you remember when we first met, and you took me to your hospital room?"

The child visibly shrank in front of her. Dropping her head, the sweet baby girl's gaze focused on her lap. She nodded affirmatively but clearly didn't want to discuss her passing again.

"You told me that you visit with your mommy. Do you think it would be possible for you to take me to your home where your mother lives the way you took me to the hospital?"

Before Jody had a chance to think further about what she'd just asked, Fiona jumped up and quickly ran toward her. The impact felt as though she'd been hit by a speeding truck. Her breath left her body, and she found herself freefalling through what appeared to be a deep, dark tunnel. She scrambled to gain some purchase before crashing at the bottom. Her equilibrium destabilized as her body rolled and pitched out of control. Being propelled at such a high rate of speed prohibited her from knowing which way was up or down. As dizziness overtook her, she had to concentrate on not passing out. God only knew what would happen if she lost consciousness.

Landing with a resounding thump, Jody immediately wondered if any part of her body had been broken. Struggling to regain her senses, she noted Fiona's nervous giggle. She immediately questioned why the little girl's uneasy laugh was heard in her mind instead of with her ears.

Focusing her attention outward, she found herself staring at Fiona's cute little shoes. It took a moment for her brain to catch up but as it did, her body started to quake from shock. Only then did she realize, her visual viewpoint was from the child's perspective, not her own. *What the—*

"*Sh-h-h!*"

Horrified, she watched Fiona's finger disappear from view then move in an upward arc toward her own face. As if Jody had been the one to brandish the shut-up gesture herself, she felt the pressure of the little girl's finger at her own mouth.

"*My mommy doesn't let me say those kinds of words.*"

Uh-oh, Jody thought before panic could take root. Everything she saw was through Fiona's field of vision. Some piece of her was now somehow a part of Fiona. She glanced at the black toaster and then the checkered tablecloth. It didn't matter where she looked, all of it was seen through the child's eyes, not her own.

Careful not to speak aloud, Jody thought, *"What in the hell is going on here?"*

Fiona giggled again.

Aghast, Jody asked without speaking, *"Can you hear what I'm thinking?"*

"Of course, silly. I jumped inside you and brought part of you with me."

Agitated, Jody refused to allow her thoughts to linger on what Fiona had just said. She'd have plenty of time later to figure out what had just transpired to protect herself from this experience ever happening again.

Jody couldn't stop worrying about what was happening with her body while her soul was here with Fiona. Visions of her physical body moldering without the soul to keep it alive zipped through her mind, making her more than a little tense. Having no idea how long she could remain within the child's spirit spiked the need to act quickly. It became imperative to find something with an address. As soon as that task had been completed, she'd figure out how to get the hell out of Dodge, or in this case Fiona, and back into her own body.

They continued to sit on the floor while Jody formulated a plan. Distracted, she couldn't help but watch through Fiona's eyes as the little girl playfully tapped her toes together. *Click, click, click.*

If she had control over her own teeth at the moment, they'd be gritted with tension as the image of Judy Garland flitted across her mind. She tried to erase the thought of ending up in Kansas, fearful it might actually happen.

"Where does your mom keep the mail?"

Fiona jumped up, making Jody queasy and feeling as though she'd throw up from the motion. Clearly not in control, she didn't like this situation one bit which turned her attitude surly. Attempting to distance herself from her fear, she focused instead on a feeling of urgency. Since the child could hear her thoughts, maybe she'd be able to pick up on her emotions as well. Hopefully, this action would light a fire under Fiona and get her to pick up the pace to find an address.

Trying her best to get used to seeing through Fiona's eyes, Jody decided to concentrate on her surroundings. Everything appeared so big and tall. Across the room, she spied what looked like a stack of mail on the kitchen counter.

Sensing Jody's thoughts, the little girl sashayed toward the countertop and raised herself up on tiptoes. Her tiny hand disappeared over the countertop as her arm stretched as far as it could go.

Jody could feel the girl's fingertips barely touching the corner of the envelopes. Out of frustration, she spit out, *"Can't you just float up and get them?"*

Fiona's little curled up fists landed on her hips. *"This is not my fault. You're heavy! I can't lift us both."*

Jody couldn't help but chuckle at the situation. She could feel Fiona's frustration as if it were her own, and who knew? Perhaps it was. The absurdity of being swept up in a four-year-old's body was a situation she wanted to escape as soon as possible. The only way to make this bizarre experience worthwhile would be if she could get her hands on a piece of mail to find an address.

"Calm down, Fiona. This shared body experience

is all new to me, too. What if you and I both think about jumping at the same time? Maybe if we jump together, we'll be able to grab some of the letters and knock them to the floor."

Fiona's delight at being helpful was unmistakable. Jody could barely handle the giddiness being relayed to her directly from the little girl's soul. She suddenly felt a strong desire to skip around the kitchen island. Since she hadn't skipped anywhere for years, she acknowledged the child-like compulsion more than likely had been influenced by the little girl who'd somehow kidnapped her spirit.

"I can count to three," Fiona exclaimed excitedly. *"Looky! One."* She held her pointer finger out so Jody could see it. *"Two."* She added her middle finger. *"Three."* Her ring finger popped up.

"That's good. You count to three, and we'll jump together."

"One. Two. Three," Fiona called out. Together, they jumped, and Fiona's fingers landed on the corner of the mail. As gravity took its course, they held on as best they could while falling back to the floor. The envelopes flew through the air around them, scattering everywhere. Jubilant from their success, they mentally high-fived each other as letters rained down on them.

Bending down to the now scattered pile of mail, a loud gasp sounded from behind them. "Who's here?" The woman's terror laced shriek filled the room.

Fiona spun toward the voice leaving Jody dizzy and seeing stars. They each caught a glimpse of a woman's bare feet running from the kitchen. With each heavy footfall, her scream faded into the distance.

At the same instant, a deep, penetrating fear swept

through Jody, paralyzing her. She used every last ounce of energy she had to stifle her scream. Had Fiona's mother seen the little girl, or had the mail being propelled across the room frightened her? In those brief seconds before everything went black, she recognized the gut-wrenching fear she'd just felt wasn't her own or Fiona's, but that of Fiona's mother.

Chapter Nine

As Terry circulated through the throng of people and listened to the art show patrons critique his work, their reactions thrilled him. From what he'd been able to garner, his paintings were a resounding success. The buzz around the gallery led him to believe that several pieces of art had already sold.

Throughout the evening, he'd purposely kept his distance from *Solitude*. Since his passion for the piece extended to the extreme, if people didn't react to it as he'd hoped they would his heart would break. If anyone dared to offer any negative remarks, he didn't want to hear them. The portrait laid his heart and soul wide open on the canvas. People judging *Solitude* meant they were judging him, not on a professional level but on a purely personal level. To hear someone tearing the portrait apart would be too difficult and may result in bloodshed.

Still, his curiosity got the best of him. He kept nervously glancing over at the crowd surrounding the portrait. Throughout the evening, people gathered around *Solitude* and scrutinized it with intensity. The patrons would gaze upon his masterpiece until Julianne stepped in signaling the time had come to move on to other pieces of art. She would gently nudge them out of the way to make room for new viewers who'd patiently waited for their opportunity to see the canvas. *That had to be a good sign.*

Julianne deserved kudos for doing a magnificent job showcasing *Solitude* in such a short period of time. The canvas, while in a place of prominence, was angled in such a way the viewer had to walk around to see it. This approach created a unique kind of unveiling experience for each person. The spotlighting highlighted the piece with an exquisite soft glow, effectively adding another layer of mystery to the portrait. She'd also surrounded the canvas with the images he'd provided showing it in various stages of completion.

Although Julianne invited people to get a closer look, he noticed she stood guard over *Solitude* like a soldier in front of Buckingham Palace. Her unswerving presence ensured no one forgot their place and reached out to touch *Solitude*, which invariably they all seemed to want to do.

Lost in his visual eavesdropping, Terry jolted back to reality when he felt the weight of a heavy arm land on his shoulders. The shock of this intrusion on his personal space caused him to flinch involuntarily, spilling his champagne in the process. He'd never been a touchy-feely type of person, in fact, just the opposite. Always protective of his personal boundaries, he'd only felt comfortable with shows of affection between his close, life-long friends, Jody and Nathan.

Expecting to meet another art scene groupie who had no problem at all invading his personal space had him bracing himself. Plastering a smile on his face, he swung around to greet the most recent masher. Instantly, his phony smile transformed into a genuine grin as he found himself face-to-face with Nathan, the second musketeer in his intimate group of friends. Terry allowed Nathan to pull him into a familiar, warm hug, one so full of love only dear, old friends would dare display in public.

Nathan, Terry, and Jody had started out as childhood friends who remained as thick as thieves over the years. Good or bad, sickness or health, they were always there for each other. Despite the fact they knew one another's deepest, darkest secrets, the love they shared broke all limits. They'd spent the majority of their lives proving their devotion by dropping everything when needed and being there for support or whatever else the situation called for. The comradeship and love between them had deepened and became even more treasured with each year that passed. They were family, not by blood, but by choice.

"Dude, hell of a show! I'm impressed," Nathan bolstered.

Terry slipped out of his friend's embrace. "Of course, you're impressed. My craft touches the soul." He waved his hands in a grand, dramatic gesture. "Just ask anyone here," his voice comically haughty.

Nathan laughed as he accepted a glass of champagne the waiter had dutifully offered him. He held his glass high and teased, "You're the man!" He downed the sparkling wine in one gulp. The timber of his voice lowered conveying his sincerity. "Seriously, Terry, what I've seen so far is breathtaking. I'm really proud of you."

Puffing his chest out with pride, Terry allowed a broad smile to light his face. His biggest critics had always been his best friends. If they liked what they saw, he knew they'd tell him. They'd also be the first to say his art was shit, and he needed to go back to the drawing board. Literally. Heat borne from pleasure radiated through his face with his friend's sincere praise. "That means a lot coming from you, Nathan. Thanks."

Terry scanned the people standing around Nathan. "Did Jody come with you?"

"No. I tried calling her, but I figured she was too busy getting ready to put all the other women here to shame to answer my call." He traded his empty glass for a full one. "I'm sure she'll be here soon."

From the moment he'd decided to include *Solitude* in the show, Terry had been antsy. He should've gotten Jody's permission before showing the canvas. Not having her consent weighed heavily on him. Truth be told, he'd acted like a selfish prick, and that fact ate him up inside. He knew if she had objected and asked him not to show the canvas, he would've gone against her wishes for the first time in their lives. Jody hadn't even been aware he'd used her likeness. The thought of his best friend seeing the portrait for the first time in such a public setting had his heart skipping a beat. What would her reaction be? Would she love *Solitude*? Would she understand he'd created the portrait out of love for her? Would she forgive him for displaying her very raw emotions in such a public way? *Oh God. What have I done?*

Showing his annoyance, Nathan snapped his fingers in front of Terry's face. "Where'd you go? I've been talking to you, and you're completely ignoring me."

Guilt caused him to wince involuntarily. "I'm not a good friend. I haven't told Jody about the portrait I did of her. I hope she doesn't kill me."

Nathan waved him off. "I haven't seen it yet, but don't worry your pretty little head off. I'm sure it's a beautiful piece of work. If I know Jody, she's going to love it."

His best friend poked him hard on the shoulder. "So did you surprise me with a portrait?" He made a show of craning his head while looking at the paintings in his field of vision. "I'm a god. I should be immortalized."

Grateful for the subject change, Terry laughed and handed Nathan a third glass of champagne. "You may be a god, but you're ugly as hell. Your portrait would scare the crap out of people. Small children would have nightmares. I can't have the art gallery patrons running in all directions screaming about how awful the subject matter of my work is, now can I? The press would crucify me. People would ban me from parties." Continuing with the lighthearted banter, Terry pretended to be apologetic by exaggerating a shrug. "I'd probably never get laid again. You wouldn't want that weighing on your conscience, would you?"

"You're an ass," Nathan said with a chuckle and a quick shove. "By the way, I brought my partner. You should be impressed. I don't think he ever goes out socially." He glanced around at the people surrounding them. "I don't see him at the moment, but I'll introduce you when we come across him." He took a sip of the cold, sweet, bubbly wine and made a show of letting it roll around in his mouth. "Damn, that's good champagne."

Nathan leaned in closer to Terry. "The guy is exorbitantly wealthy, but I wouldn't expect a sale from him. Your work is emotionally stimulating, and he's purely cerebral. He seems to like art but responds better to more of an architectural aesthetic. I don't think he'd know what a genuine emotion was if it sashayed right up and bit him on the ass."

Taken aback by his friend's unflattering remarks, Terry shot his eyebrow up questioningly. Nathan rarely talked about the man who'd convinced him to retire from the Phoenix police department. Spurring his curiosity, he wanted to hear more. "Really? That surprises me. Why would you go into business with someone like that?"

Nathan chuckled. "Well, there are several reasons, but I'll give you the two most important. First, he's filthy rich, and I get whatever I need without much fuss. Second, his personality is perfect for being a private investigator. He's analytical to a fault and about as cold as they come. He doesn't let emotion alter his judgment. That's a good thing because I don't think he'd know what to do if he suddenly displayed such a *girly* aspect to his persona. He's a man's man. He might crumble and fall to the floor in little pieces if he actually felt any type of honest emotion.

"I swear he's the reincarnation of John Wayne, or at the very least one of his more memorable, take-no-shit, old-time western characters. The man doesn't let anything get in his way. He's tenacious and never gives up the hunt no matter how difficult. Besides, people don't say no to him, ever. He just turns those steely, dark eyes in their direction, and the world drops at his feet. If you're unfortunate enough to be on the other side of that piercing, intimidating glare, you're a goner. In great part, he's the best in the business because he's composed and relentless. People don't hire him because they like him. They hire him because they know he *will* deliver whatever dirt he can find on the asshole he's got in his sights.

"When he asked me to leave the police force and head the new security division of his company, I couldn't say no to him. You remember how frustrated I was while on the force? A cop always has to be careful not to step on anyone's toes for fear the case will fall apart due to some trumped up legal technicality."

Terry made a point of nodding his head affirmatively, happy his friend had found a way to deal effectively with the criminal element he detested so much.

He'd always idolized Nathan's superhero mentality. He was born to be in law enforcement. He was aware of how frustrated his friend had been during his time with the Phoenix police department. Not only did the bad guys always seem to win, but the justice system provided them with all the rights. That fact left the victims of crime feeling abused and victimized all over again, effectively making him lose his passion for police work.

While most people thought of Nathan as being an intimidating tough guy, Terry knew him to be quite softhearted. Because of his sympathetic nature, the justice system had left him disillusioned many times.

"J.D. is a force to be reckoned with, never breaking the law per se, but skirting the edge of it to get whatever he needs to crack his case. He always finds a way to apprehend the bad guys which allows him to make a real difference in the world. The rules are far more lax for private investigators than they are for cops, and he has no qualm about pushing those boundaries to the limit."

It'd been Terry's experience that every time Nathan thought back on his life as a cop, his mood turned sour. The inadequacies of the justice system had started to stress his friend out so he'd lighten the mood a bit. "When you say 'filthy rich,' are you talking Paradise Valley rich?"

Nathan scoffed. "After everything I've just said, *that's* what you zeroed in on?"

"Hardly." To prove his point, he listed what he'd heard, ticking off each personality nugget Nathan had covered with his fingers. "Filthy rich. Recluse. John Wayne. Bigger asshole than most. Badass P.I. See? I was listening." Terry laughed and playfully punched Nathan. "However, we *are* at my art show, and my work is for sale. That just seemed like the most pertinent information about him at the moment. So, how rich is 'filthy rich'?"

His ploy worked. Nathan's mood visibly lightened. "Okay. I see your point. What I mean by 'filthy rich' is an isolated mansion on top of Camelback Mountain with a private jet, personal pilot and crew rich."

The impressive list of assets had Terry's mouth dropping open. "I think we need to find him and give him the personal touch when showing him my art. Surely there is something here he'd like."

****

Trying to release all the knots in her body, Jody groaned through her stretch. She slowly swung her head to loosen the muscles and reached up to massage her neck. *Why the hell does my neck hurt so bad?*

Her mind still muddy from sleep, it took a great

deal of effort to open her eyes. Feeling befuddled, she scanned her living room, but for the life of her couldn't figure out why she felt so confused. Rubbing the grogginess from her eyes, she strained to sit up. "I must have taken a nap. Damn. I've got to get a better couch. Sheesh! Feeling this bad after a good rest is ridiculous."

Trying to get her bearings, Jody sat stock still. Glancing at the windows across the room, a prick of alarm hit her square in the gut when she realized darkness had fallen. *That's impossible. When did I fall asleep?*

An unexpected feeling of dread washed over her when she noticed the computer sitting on the table in front of her. Staring at the laptop as if it would reveal some important secret only served to intensify her distress. A wisp of a thought niggled somewhere in the back of her mind trying to get her attention, but she just couldn't grasp the problem. Her brain, still in the process of coming back to life, didn't allow for rational thought. Considering everything in her field of vision, she tried to determine what was out of place. *Something* wasn't right here. Her gaze shifted back to her coffee table and zeroed in on the computer again. She bolted upright, reaching out to the laptop without actually touching it. "Why is the computer…"

As the memory of Fiona jumping into her body and kidnapping her spirit seeped slowly into her mind, Jody's eyes widened in horror. Without thought, she jumped to her feet. "That must have been hours ago! How long have I been out?" Her legs wobbled and felt heavy like she'd just run a marathon. Every ounce of energy had been drained from her body leaving her weak as a kitten. Unable to stay upright, she flopped down hard on the couch, trying desperately to piece the recent events together in her head.

The memory of the bone-crushing landing at the end of the tunnel had her examining herself to determine if any damage had been done to her physical body. Her hands busily ran up and down her limbs. She touched every place she could reach and found no injury other than tired, sore muscles. *Thank goodness.*

As the memories of her out-of-body moments started coming back to her, her cell phone rang—the noise cutting through the quiet like a slap in the face. She shrieked with fear as if something had just jumped out and screamed *boo*. Clutching her head, she tried her best to get a hold of herself.

Straining to stand, she cursed the weakness in her legs. Focusing all of her attention on putting one foot in front of the other, she crossed the room to find her phone in her purse. When Nathan's number popped up, she started to answer but stopped short.

"Oh my God! What time is it?" She glanced at the clock on the wall and almost fainted. Dropping the phone without answering, she hustled toward the kitchen. Her body needed some sugar, needed that quick rush to get herself moving. She tried to summon every ounce of strength she had left while stuffing her mouth with Twinkies and a banana. *Sugar will just have to do until I can drive through someplace and get a burger on the way to the show.*

Putting the events of the day aside, she couldn't miss Terry's art exhibit. The show was too important to him which made it important to her. She would be there to support him come hell or high water, or even little Fiona.

Chapter Ten

Disgruntled, J.D. found a painting with the least number of people around it and planted himself there in the background. He wanted to kick himself for saying he'd come to this event. In the span of fifteen minutes, the evening had proved to be exactly what he thought it would be—a big, fat, fucking waste of time. *What the hell was I thinking?*

When Nathan invited him to come, J.D. had intended to say no, but his instinct kicked in and urged him to accept. Something had drawn him here tonight. He only hoped he had the patience to hang out long enough to determine what that something turned out to be. So here he stood, getting more agitated by the moment, suffering through the high-dollar perfumes and the oohs and ahs of the partygoers. Annoyed at himself, he couldn't keep from rolling his eyes and wondering how his gut could've been so faulty.

Even though J.D. had grown up in wealth and, as an adult, continued to add to the family coffers, he'd learned very early on that money didn't transform people into better versions of themselves. However, affluence could indeed corrupt them and nine times out of ten did just that.

For the most part he preferred his own company. Seclusion guaranteed there'd be no chance of getting blindsided by someone else's agenda. In his humble opinion, most people living the so-called upper-class lifcstyle were unreliable and potentially as dangerous to the public as psychics were.

Throughout his years as a P.I., he'd had the great misfortune of having to deal with too many of the elite, uber wealthy as well as the parasitic fortune-tellers. His investigations had proved the filthy rich and lowly soothsayers were all out to make a buck, usually off the backs of poor working stiffs.

In the case of psychics, the mark could be rich or poor; everyone had a big bull's-eye on their back. All grieving people were ripe for the picking and would pay anything for the chance to hear or see their loved ones again. *Idiots.* While each case was different, he'd been successful at proving they were all parasites and took great pleasure in waving as they were carried off to jail to pay for their thievery.

While he made a habit of doing pro bono work for the less fortunate, he would always jump at the chance to take money from the upper class for an investigation. His only criterion for new cases being, the work had to spark his curiosity and have the potential of a lengthy jail term for a greedy asshole.

Two women interrupted his internal bitching as they made their way to the portrait in front of him. "I swear, Claire, this artist is fantastic! Just look at how he uses the colors on canvas. The sea is boiling as if it's alive, actually tossing and turning. You can almost feel the storm deep down in your bones as it sends shockwaves of fear straight to your heart."

To keep his groan from escaping, J.D. pinched the bridge of his nose. *What pretentious crap!* He had seen the painting, and yeah, it was pretty—a word he seldom used, but 'shockwaves of fear straight to your heart?' *Give me a fucking break.* Sometimes a painting was just a damn painting.

He loathed the arrogance of the rich. Their exaggerated seriousness about intellectual pursuits only served to piss him off more. Tonight, he'd been forced to listen to their wild imaginings being ascribed to this artist as if they had some secret understanding of his creative intentions.

Needing a distraction from his growing irritation, J.D. scanned the area for a waiter. He'd have a few more drinks, look around a bit longer, and then head home to watch some baseball. *That* was his idea of relaxation.

Even on those rare occasions he found himself in a social environment, J.D. never broke character as a private investigator. Always able to blend in with his surroundings, he kept his mind alert and his skills keen. He was considered the best in his field, begrudgingly known as the chameleon by the long list of prestigious criminals he'd had the privilege of bringing to justice.

Being inconspicuous made it easy for J.D. to avoid participation in tedious conversations. Going unnoticed made his eavesdropping on private discussions a piece of cake and a handy tactic to have in his line of work. He'd picked up many juicy and valuable tidbits of information this way. After a few glasses of wine, people let their guard down with friends. Believing their conversations were private, they spilled all sorts of confidential information. He smirked to himself. *Nothing's private.*

As J.D. made his way toward the exit, his ears perked up at the constant repetition of the name

Solitude. Everyone seemed to be struggling to describe their reaction to one of the paintings on exhibit. At first, he assumed the chatter was just more of the typical pretentiousness he'd had to endure throughout the evening. Each new conversation he'd heard about the struggles to describe a simple painting, served to pique his curiosity. *Perhaps there was something worth seeing here after all.* Placing his glass on the tray of a passing waiter, he decided he could afford to spend another fifteen minutes to find a canvas called *Solitude* before heading home.

Scanning the room, J.D. noticed a group of people in the process of leaving a large canvas. Their heads were tilted back to get one last view of the artwork as they ambled away. From his position, he wasn't able to see the painting itself. Carefully working his way through the partygoers, he moved efficiently across the room to see the mysterious portrait which ostensibly had everyone in attendance confounded. As he got closer to *Solitude*, the crowd dispersed, seeming to clear a path for him. *Perfect timing.*

As soon as *Solitude* came into view, J.D.'s eyes locked onto the portrait. For the first time in many years, his situational awareness failed him. His field of vision faded to black, disappearing altogether, leaving only him and the woman of *Solitude*.

His body betrayed him as he gazed at the canvas. It never crossed his mind to question the sensation of being pulled into the portrait. Hell, he allowed it to happen. He wanted it to happen.

The woman of *Solitude* stood before him, somberly staring through the rain-streaked window panes as her essence drew him to her. So lifelike, and in so much pain, he was certain at any moment she would turn and see him. Somewhere deep in his mind, he envisioned her slowly lifting her hand out for him to clasp. She called to him, begging to be held, comforted, and kept safe. She wanted—no, she *needed* the warmth and love restored that had so brutally abandoned her. If he obliged her, in turn, he knew she would give him warmth and unconditional love for the first time in his life. The world as he knew it disappeared. His hearing sharpened as he listened to her gently calling him.

He didn't have a clue as to the tragedy that befell her in the moments before this rendering. Nor did he or could he understand the gravity of her loss in that one moment in time. But instinctively, he knew whatever the cause had been it had provoked a life-changing event.

Something or someone important to her was now absent. Whatever or whomever she had lost affected her to the point of grieving. He wanted to be the person to wrap his arms around her and hold her until she felt his warmth and strength. He wanted her heart to know he would be the one to make everything all right for her.

Solitude's effect on him was profound, to say the least. His body unwillingly started vibrating with something to which he couldn't put a name. The portrait forced him to feel with his inexperienced emotions, making him extremely uncomfortable. Confused and more than a little concerned by this insane reaction, J.D. tried to force his rational mind to battle for control—control over what he didn't have a clue. But in the end his rational mind was no match for whatever this was he found himself experiencing.

He tried to take a step back, but his legs wouldn't

cooperate. Instead, the canvas drew him forward toward an inexplicable chain reaction. While this situation should have left him running in the other direction, instead he felt, surprisingly enough, comfort and peace. Two blissful states of mind for which all the money in the world hadn't been able to provide.

A hand grabbed his arm, rudely shaking him from his trancelike state. It took all of his willpower not to jump at the intrusion.

"I'd love to tell you about this piece if you'd like to learn more about it." A woman slid a brochure in his hand and luckily, his fingers were able to hang on to it.

He could only stand and stare at the portrait in front of him. As the long-winded woman beside him continued to speak, he tried every trick he knew to regain some semblance of composure.

"Everyone who has seen this piece has felt an emotional connection to it. This type of art is called Hyperrealistic Portraits. The artist takes a snapshot, either color, or black and white, and creates an exact duplicate with pencils or pens on canvas. The effect is so lifelike that viewers have difficulty seeing the difference with the naked eye between the original digital picture and the completed handcrafted version. It's hard to believe anyone would have the skill to make an ordinary picture from a camera come to life in this manner. The artist tasks himself with adding what a camera can't catch—the emotion of the subject. It's an incredibly difficult skill, but, as you can see, one which has been done flawlessly with *Solitude*.

"Pens and pencils—just everyday items we all use. The average person is incapable of realizing the beauty these simple objects can unleash when held in the proper hands."

Thankfully, the woman seemed to have run out of breath, finally shutting up. J.D. had regained his senses enough to convey in no uncertain terms his commanding, no-nonsense mannerisms before he spoke.

"I want to buy it."

"I'm sorry, but this piece isn't for sale. I can show—" The hushed noise as his hand crushed the brochure she'd given him produced the desired effect. She stopped the incessant chatter. He put the crumpled paper in his pocket.

Never before had he thrown his money around to get what he wanted, but the time had come to pull out all the stops. He couldn't leave without *Solitude*. There were no tenable words that could explain why this was so, but he knew it would be like leaving a piece of himself behind. Later, he'd take the time to reason it all out. Right now, he was prepared to do battle for *Solitude* and the woman within the portrait.

Calling upon his most intimidating manner, he purposely ground his teeth, clenching his jaw muscles tightly to demonstrate his displeasure. Even with people that didn't know him, this action spoke loud and clear.

"No. I want this piece. Everything's for sale. Name your price."

"I'm sorry, but the sale of this portrait is not up to me. The…"

He finally turned to her showing the full force of his intent. It pleased him that she took a protective step back. "Get me the gallery owner."

Her muscles constricted tightly in an attempt to dampen her displeasure with being talked to in such a manner. *Good. I have her attention.* She tentatively stepped forward with her hand extended. "I'm Julianne Warren, owner of Beauty in the Desert Art Gallery."

He glanced down at her hand with mild disgust and then back to *Solitude*, effectively dismissing her. "If you can't help me procure this portrait, then I want to speak directly to the artist. Find him for me."

From his vantage point across the room, Terry had watched the interchange between the large, raven haired man and Julianne. The man had a poker face and wasn't giving anything away. Well, nothing other than the fact he seemed furious about something. The longer he watched from afar, the more he recognized the extremely effective display of intimidation tactics. From this distance, Terry wasn't able to tell what the man thought or what the topic of conversation was. But Julianne was becoming more agitated by the minute, so he decided now would probably be the best time to intervene.

Terry sauntered up to the man and stood next to him waiting patiently for an acknowledgment of his presence which never came. Finally he decided to take the lead. "Is there some sort of problem here?"

He glanced over at Julianne, who held her hands up in surrender. She visibly relaxed and slid a short distance away to give them some privacy.

Still staring at the portrait, the man stated in no uncertain terms, "I'll give you ten thousand dollars for *Solitude*."

Upon hearing the man's take-no-prisoner voice, Terry allowed a sheepish grin to cross his lips. *Now* he understood the problem. The issue of *Solitude* not being for sale was something he could handle. "It's not for sale."

"Twenty thousand."

"No."

"Fifty thousand."

Anger quickly reared its ugly head between the two men. Flattery over someone willing to pay that kind of money for something he'd created had been the only thing keeping Terry from punching this ass. The privileged attitude he exuded only served to piss Terry off. *Who the hell does this guy think he is?*

No longer willing to spar with him, Terry turned to face the man whose gaze remained glued on *Solitude*. He'd seen the money-can-buy-anything type before. Granted, not quite to this extent. The only effect this kind of behavior propagated was to irritate the shit out of him. He didn't like this asshole, and he'd give *Solitude* to Goodwill before he sold it to him for any amount of money. "Look, dude, I will *never* sell this portrait. I don't care what you offer me. This piece of work means more to me than any dollar figure you propose. I'm *not* selling it."

When the bastard finally stepped back and faced him, they were nose to nose…well, more like nose to Adam's apple since the man was at least a full six inches taller. Terry had to dig deep to find the courage not to turn tail and run. *This is one fucking scary man.*

"I *will* have this portrait." Each word had been spoken through clenched teeth, making his statement sound more like an angry demonic hiss than human communication. If Terry wasn't so pissed off and, he had to admit, intimidated, he'd laugh at the temper tantrum.

The men stood there in a standoff, staring daggers

at each other, silently willing their opponent to flinch.

Camera flashes erupting throughout the room drew J.D. out of the aggressive stare-off. Everyone in the gallery had their phones lifted and pointed in his direction. Angry at having his picture taken, he swiftly twisted around to admonish the gallery owner. As he turned, he found his gaze boring into the stunned and all too real face of the woman in *Solitude*. The first glimpse of her beautiful face left his body trembling.

J.D. realized almost immediately, the art enthusiasts had recognized the woman and wanted a piece of her for themselves. Their personal photos of her would act as a concession of sorts. A souvenir for them to remember this highly sought after portrait which seemed to be unattainable to anyone else but him. Because he *would* secure *Solitude* for himself. Of *that* he was certain.

His argument with the artist was already forgotten. Unaccustomed to being led by emotion, he made a conscious decision to follow and *feel* whatever was happening to him. He'd dissect the details later.

J.D. focused on the tears welling up in her big green eyes while staring at the model for the painting. His angry features softened, and his gut started to churn with something he could only guess was sympathy.

The woman's pallor concerned him. His heart broke when he noticed her bottom lip quivering. Starting to sway as if she were about to faint, her hands flew out to act as a stabilizer and kept her from hitting the floor. J.D. took the opportunity to grasp her delicate hand, gently cradling it between both of his to offer support. He slid closer so she would feel the nearness of him. As his body touched hers, he felt sure she'd recognize that he'd be there to catch her if she fell.

When the artist had the balls to approach the woman and grab her unattended hand, anger raged within J.D. Couldn't this joker see *he* was there for her? The man had brilliantly captured her on canvas. He'd had his fifteen minutes with her. She belonged to him now, and he wasn't going to let go. He'd just claimed her for himself, and no one would stand in his way.

The depiction of her in *Solitude* had awakened something in him he hadn't known existed. Now that he'd found her, he wouldn't back away from her. He couldn't.

Claimed her? When his mind finally caught up with his emotions and realized where they had taken him, a tremble shook his body. J.D. knew he needed time to figure out how this woman had gotten under his skin before he went off the deep end completely. Unfortunately, with the artist around, he just didn't have the luxury of time on his side. All he knew for certain was he wouldn't leave her in the care of any man, let alone the artist who'd captured her likeness so intimately. *No way in hell.*

Something snapped inside him when he noticed the gentleness of the artist and woman's combined touch. Their caresses so familiar, it seemed to be an everyday occurrence. The artist obviously knew her very well, but he'd be damned to hell if he let the likes of him comfort her. The jerk wasn't good enough for her. He was an *artist* for Christ sake! Over the span of his career as a deadbeat painter, he'd probably captured the likeness of hundreds of other women. He could have one of them.

She was his, and there wasn't a chance in hell he'd

lose the battle for her. From this moment forward, J.D. would be the one *and only* man she would entrust with her safety. He would see to that. He'd just made it his mission to put the artist squarely in her past where he belonged.

Infuriated, J.D. glared at the artist. A slow, dangerous growl, just loud enough for the jerk to hear, escaped his throat. The wordless demand to release her was loud and clear. After that warning, only an idiot would refuse to step away.

The artist, clearly a fool, and now in danger of losing a piece of his body, did something J.D. hadn't experienced in a very long time. The bastard ignored him.

He recognized the liberties the artist took with the woman proved they were *very* close. He had to restrain himself as the asshole leaned in and whispered loud enough for J.D. to hear.

"Jody, baby, do you like the portrait?"

J.D. was ready to break the man's neck. *Baby?*

His heart rate picked up when he felt Jody lightly squeeze his hand. That small action had been enough to redirect his attention. He would take the sweet gesture as a sign that she needed him. Mesmerized by her and the emotions she generated, J.D.'s eyes never left her beautiful face. Tears which had previously been held back now freely ran down her cheeks. She continued to hold tight to both men. J.D. knew their support was her only hope to stay upright.

"I don't understand. When did you…" Her words faded away, but her voice left an unfamiliar longing within J.D.

"You were so sad that day. Do you remember?"

Her head inclined once to acknowledge the artist, but her gaze remained on her likeness.

"You were so beautiful standing there by the window, but at the same time, wracked by such deep heartache. I knew I had to capture the emotions surrounding you. I couldn't just leave it at that though. I had to show you what you couldn't and wouldn't see on your own at the time.

"Do you *see* what I'm talking about, Jody? Can you *feel* the joy within the heartache?"

She relaxed her hands and withdrew them from each man. Hand extended, and on wobbly legs, Jody slowly drifted toward *Solitude*. The gallery owner stepped forward to stop her from touching the portrait, but the artist intercepted her effectively impeding her progress.

Jody tentatively reached out and gently stroked the canvas. J.D. quickly closed in on her to keep her steady. Annoyance sparked within him as the artist followed suit.

"I was heartbroken over the broken engagement. I knew then that I'd never find the kind of relationship I'd craved my whole life. At that pivotal moment, my future had become clear. That kind of happiness just wasn't meant to be for me. When I looked out the window, I couldn't stop crying. As if the Universe felt my pain, the sky opened up and cried with me."

Her fingers gently grazed over the canvas. They glided from the rain streaked windowpane to directly behind where her likeness stood in the portrait. J.D. became concerned when her breathing became erratic.

"I didn't realize at the time, what you captured here in the brightness of the flash behind me. My mother, in spirit form, was embracing me when I needed her the most. You were able to capture the essence of lost love and eternal love all in the same space of time." Emotion got the better of her and she started to softly sob. To J.D.'s surprise, she leaned into him for support and his heart melted.

The buzz in the room around them had suddenly grown to a fever pitch as more and more people heard the model for *Solitude* was viewing the portrait for the first time. The crowd started to converge on them and J.D. knew he needed to get her someplace safe, someplace he could take care of her.

Suddenly, and none too gently, J.D. was nudged in the ribs with a stiff elbow. Before he knew what was happening, Nathan had swooped in and scooped Jody up. He tucked her face into his chest and started toward the office area of the gallery. "Don't worry. I'll get you away from these vultures."

Chapter Eleven

Quietly closing the door behind them, J.D. kept his distance from the others in the room. All of his senses were on hyper alert. Within the span of sheer moments, he'd felt an irresistible attraction to Jody. And her voice? He couldn't explain it, but her first utterance had imprinted the sweet tone somewhere deep within him. If all of that wasn't bad enough, the only reason he knew her name was because the dirt bag artist had whispered it in her ear loud enough for him to hear. The fact he'd followed her name with 'baby' continued to fuel his anger.

Somehow, she'd broken through the barriers to J.D.'s hardened heart. He knew beyond a shadow of a doubt that she was his. None of this made any sense to him. Even if his life depended on an explanation, he wouldn't be able to articulate the why or the how of it. They were simply *meant* as his grandmother used to say. His grandmother—the only person who'd ever loved him, and she hadn't crossed his mind in years. Jody had reminded him of that long forgotten, treasured memory and how being loved unconditionally had made him feel a lifetime ago.

She was the reason he decided to attend this event. He could feel the rightness of that fact down to his bones.

Not being the sort of person to act so irrationally,

J.D. needed to back down, if only momentarily. He wanted to learn more about her to figure out what his first move should be. To accomplish that, he needed some space to observe.

Being so far out of his comfort zone had his body feeling stressed. His fists clenched tightly—leaving his fingers feeling the burn from the strain.

It didn't take his deft powers of observation long to recognize Nathan and the artist were both protecting her, and *that* fact burned. Watching her intimate interaction with them play out had his gut twisting with resentment.

I should be the one holding her! As that thought flew across his mind, annoyance followed closely behind. *What the hell is happening to me?* Everything inside him screamed to make an advance, carry her out of here, and take her to his home where she belonged. Being this out of control left him in a position of weakness. His first order of business required getting a tight hold on his feelings before he did something stupid.

If he acted too quickly, whatever advantage he had would be gone. As of yet, he had no clue what kind of edge he would have, but when the opportunity presented itself, he'd find it. He always did. At this point, the only thing he could be certain of was the queasy feeling he had from being trapped in this emotional wasteland.

Having to stand silently by and watch as Nathan sat Jody down on the couch to soothe her, had his ire flaring. He wanted nothing more than to kick his partner's ass for comforting the woman who only moments ago he'd claimed for himself. Nathan sat next to her, tucking her into his side for an affectionate embrace. The outward show of adoration caused a lurching sensation in J.D.'s heart. He strained to keep his mouth shut. Apparently, the artist wasn't the only one with deep feelings for his woman. *Observe, dammit! Don't show your hand.*

"You okay?" Nathan gently prodded, speaking in a soothing tone to the woman who had stolen his heart.

Although painful for him watch, J.D. wasn't able to tear his gaze from her as she held a firm grip on Nathan's suit coat. The intimate contact between them appeared to provide her with much-needed strength. Nodding her head in the affirmative, she nuzzled his neck for comfort. While he didn't have all the facts yet, J.D. was sure this scene had played itself out before. All the participants were comfortable—all the participants except for himself, of course. He planned on rectifying that soon.

Nathan angrily looked to the artist for answers. "What the hell was that all about, Terry? Those people treated her as if she were some sort of superstar. None of them were going to be happy until they got their hands on a piece of her. You know how much Jody hates being the center of attention."

So the artist's name is Terry. That's a perfect name for a man who plays with paints for a living.

Ignoring Nathan's question altogether, the artist focused on Jody. He slid forward on the table, and then the asshole placed his hand on her knee as if he had a right to do so. Trying to curb the outrage this intimate gesture provoked, J.D. breathed deeply, hoping each flare of his nostrils would curtail his anger. His commitment to self-control weakened more with every minute that passed. *He's got a fucking death wish! If that bastard doesn't get his hand off of her in two seconds, I'll take it off for him and leave a bloody stump behind!* Unaccustomed to the green-eyed monster of jealousy, his fervor shocked him. As the unfamiliar riotous feelings continued to grow, he sank deeper into a murderous mindset. He didn't have a clue how to bridle the destructive emotions.

"Jody, I'm so sorry about including *Solitude* in the show. I should have shown you the portrait and asked your permission first." As the artist continued to speak, she scooted out of Nathan's embrace and slid to the front edge of the couch. "After all, it was your emotions I exposed to everyone. I put your private hell on exhibit for everyone to see." Terry's lips pursed as he paused, almost as if he were afraid to ask the next question. "Can you forgive me?"

J.D.'s breath caught in his throat when she drew Terry's face near her own. Her small hands caressed his cheeks, as she offered a smile which held nothing but love. Watching the interaction between them left a cold void in his chest where his heart had just been crushed. He wanted to turn around and bolt out the door, slamming it shut to free himself of whatever had overcome him this evening. But he couldn't leave. She had him glued to where he stood. No matter what the circumstances, he knew he'd never be able to turn away from her, especially with the likes of the other men in the room. She was his, plain and simple. She just didn't know it yet.

"Terry, the portrait is beautiful. I'm so honored you would memorialize me that way." She bent forward, and her lips touched his nose. J.D.'s mind came to a full stop as he watched the intimate scene play out in front of him. "It's…" she paused trying to find the right words. "It's arresting. It's extraordinary!"

In one fluid motion, the douche bag pulled her onto his lap, and rocked her. His relief evident by the way he burrowed his face into her neck. J.D. couldn't bear the pain of seeing her in the artist's arms any longer and turned away.

"Jody, if the portrait isn't what has you so upset, what's wrong?" Nathan's voice served to refocus J.D. and aid in resuming his eavesdropping efforts. It was evident, even to J.D., she was about to give some sort of lame excuse. He'd seen his clients with that expression more than once. He felt a tug at the corner of his lips as he grinned. *She's not a good liar.* That's good to know.

Saving her from having to lie, Nathan held his hand up to stop her from denying the problem. "Don't tell me nothing's wrong. Your eyes have dark circles, and you look as though you haven't slept in a month. You seem… I don't know. Maybe fragile is the word I'm looking for. It's like you've been on a long, arduous trek through hell and haven't quite made it back yet. It's obvious to both me and Terry that something is terribly wrong."

She nodded and bit her lip. "Why don't we talk about this later, after the show? Terry needs to get back out—"

Nathan interrupted her. "Whatever is bothering you *is* important." His eyebrows furrowed, reflecting his worry for her. When she didn't respond immediately, he barked, "Now!" J.D. vowed to kick his ass for speaking to her like that.

Seeing she was close to caving in, clued him into the fact his time for observation was nearing an end. Whatever bothered her had weighed her down enough that she couldn't hold it in any longer.

"I need you to do a favor for me, Nathan."

"Of course. Whatever you—"

Everyone's attention shifted in J.D.'s direction when he loudly cleared his throat. With full awareness locked on Jody, he strode toward her, every muscle rippling with tension. As he cleared the distance between them, he felt the full force of the possessive wall Nathan and Terry had erected around Jody. Hell, the air was so thick, the barricade could be felt as if it were a real, unmovable object. He silently vowed to break that wall into tiny shards by any means necessary.

"Terry, I'd like you to meet my partner, J.D."

Ignoring the introduction, J.D.'s intense gaze remained locked on Jody, who now stood across from him.

Terry scoffed. "Well, now I understand." He turned to Nathan with a look of disgust. "You were right. He is an asshole." Nathan waved off the remark.

"This is Jody." Her hand tentatively inched out toward J.D. Almost afraid to touch her again, he gently took her offered hand in both of his. As had happened before, his body's reaction to her was immediate and filled him with wonderment. For the first time since entering this room, he felt calmed by nothing more than her simple touch.

"Jody, this is J.D."

A shy smile deepened her dimples and lit her face, leaving J.D. hypnotized. Before he knew what was happening, he gave her more than he'd ever offered another living person. "Please, call me Jared."

His demeanor, while gentle, was confident and commanded Jody's full attention. His eyes sparkled like a piece of shiny obsidian glinting in the sunlight. When he finally allowed his smile to reach out and touch the rest of his face, she almost sighed from the beauty of him. Beauty—not a word typically used for characterizing a man, but Jody instinctively knew this man was anything but normal. He had the rugged male good looks that women swooned over and displayed what she perceived as a controlled supremacy. The sheer power emanating from him was nothing like she'd ever felt before.

He wasn't a man to be trifled with, either in business or love. She wasn't fooling herself. He carried a sense of fierceness about him. Something deep, dark, and feral resided within him. The force of his presence made the woman in her wonder how she could tame him. And didn't that just ring of stupidity?

Jody was shocked at how quickly she fell under his spell. Being in his presence made her realize he was the type of man she could easily see herself falling for head over heels. But then he'd have so much power over her he'd end up destroying Jody when he left. And he would leave, of that, she had no doubt. If she had to live through a loss that devastating, she'd never survive. The failure would be the end of her.

She cringed when she realized how easy it would be for her to give into her baser needs where this man was concerned. She had to do something to back away from him before he had her completely under his spell. But gazing into his eyes left her powerless. Magic resided in those beautiful dark eyes.

"Whoa! Wait just a damn minute here!" Nathan declared.

Regretfully, Jody returned her attention to Nathan. Antagonism rolled off his body in waves and zeroed in on J.D. The sudden tension surrounding the men made her extremely nervous. Animosity grew quickly between the business partners, and for the life of her, she couldn't understand why.

"What's wrong with you?" she asked, genuinely shocked by her friend's behavior. If she didn't know any better, she'd think he was jealous.

Ignoring Jody, Nathan spoke through clenched teeth, a tactic he'd learned from J.D. "I'd like to talk to you outside, *Jared*, if you've got a moment," clearly not positing a question but delivering an outright demand.

J.D. ignored Nathan's aggressive request. "I think I'll stay for a while. I believe Jody was just getting ready to tell *us* what's bothering her. I'd like to help if I can."

The man's obvious advances on Jody prompted Nathan's heartbeat to race. Neither he nor Terry had ever had a romantic relationship with Jody, so his feelings didn't stem from jealousy. She was closer than a sister to him. With all the heartache she'd been through in her life, she didn't need someone as dark and ominous as J.D. moving in on her now. For her sake, he had to stop whatever this was between them from happening before it began.

Nathan had known J.D. for several years. He'd been his business partner for just over a year now. In all that time, he'd never socialized with him outside of the professional environment. The man was a secretive bastard who kept to himself. He'd be surprised if the number of people with whom J.D. had shared his given name could be counted on more than one hand. Hell, he saw the man every day and hadn't even known what his given name was. J.D. didn't like people and would never dream of granting anyone the intimacy of addressing him in such a manner.

So what was up with all this warm and fuzzy stuff? *How dare he make a move on Jody!* Nathan had no doubt J.D. would bring her nothing but pain. He'd never seen his business partner show even a passing interest in a woman before. As far as he knew, the man had never before lowered himself to chase a woman. Grinding his teeth together resulted in a shooting pain in his jaw. Partnership be damned. He'd be the one to put J.D. in his place. Jody was much more important to him than any job.

Nathan's anxiety clearly presented itself to all in the room as he became bolder in his attempt to separate Jody and J.D. He needed to end whatever was happening between them immediately. Sparks of fear for the consequences Jody could face with a man like him in her life ran through his body, leaving him jumpy.

"No. You and I, we need to talk." He tried to keep the timbre of his voice resolute but, it sounded jittery even to his own ears. "We'll go outside and—"

"Nathan!" Jody cut him off. "What in the hell is wrong with you? Stop this. Please, stop being so rude. I don't need this right now."

The pleading in her voice had gotten through to him, making him feel like a real shit until he saw J.D.'s face radiating with smugness at the small victory. That fucking smirk almost sent him over the edge of reason.

If he couldn't control his anger over this situation soon he might just punch his partner in the jaw. He had to restrain himself for Jody's sake. She'd never forgive him if he crossed that line.

Nathan almost boiled over when J.D. again took her hand in his and even added a goddamn caress.

"As I said *before* we were interrupted, please, call me Jared."

"Jared it is."

Shit! Nathan watched in horror as his sweet, little Jody smiled innocently at a man whom he'd called a cold-hearted bastard no less than a dozen times a day over the last year. He just wished he knew what was in J.D.'s mind.

J.D. hadn't heard anyone call him by his given name since childhood visits with his grandmother. He had to admit it felt good when his name rolled off of Jody's tongue and couldn't wait for her to say it again.

Enjoying the warmth of her hand in his, he continued to stroke her silky skin. "Why don't you sit down and tell me…" He felt a quick jab on his back and realized the forgotten artist had hit him with his elbow. "Excuse me. Tell *us* what we can do to help."

Nathan, still standing in the middle of the room, got everyone's attention as he groaned loudly. He swiped at his hair and, J.D. realized, accepted defeat if only for the moment as he crossed the room to join them.

Chapter Twelve

Ignoring all the angst of the last few minutes, Jody regrettably freed her hands from Jared's firm grasp and turned back to face Nathan. "I need you to find someone for me."

The way he puckered his face reflected his surprise at her unusual request. "What do you mean? Find who?"

"Excuse me," Jared cut in. "I do this for a living. I can find anyone. It doesn't matter where they are, or how deep into hiding they've put themselves. I can find them."

Jody restrained her giggle. *You can't get much deeper into hiding when it comes to little Fiona.* She internally chastised herself for the inappropriate joke when the temperature in the room started to plummet.

She'd hoped to be able to get her story out without too much interference from Fiona. After their whirlwind trip earlier in the day, she figured the little girl's energy would be too depleted to have much of an impact tonight. After all, she'd found herself in the regrettable position of having little to no energy to keep going. Unfortunately, the tension between Nathan and Jared had taken too much time.

She'd suspected the little girl would show up in some capacity sooner or later, and here she was much earlier than Jody had thought possible. She could *feel* her, but Fiona apparently lacked the needed strength for this meeting. Instead of a full-body apparition, Jody saw something akin to heat waves rolling off a hot surface. Wherever Fiona hovered in the room, the air around her became distorted. *That is one determined little girl.*

Nervously biting her lip, she thought about Jared's proposed help. "I don't know, Jared. I don't have much extra cash, and I know tracking people down can be expensive. Finding this person is critical. I'm only asking Nathan for help because I haven't had any luck locating the person myself."

"No need to worry about the fee, Jody." J.D. turned to the artist and offered him a devilish grin. "Terry and I have come to an agreement for payment in full. Haven't we, Terry?"

Jody felt like she was on a seesaw. Nathan had finally stepped back, but by the look of surprise on Terry's face, the tension in the room had now shifted between these two men. Jared seemed to be having an ill effect on everyone except her. Hoping to move past this and get to the problem of Fiona, Jody piped in, "I don't understand."

By the way Terry's jaw clenched, she could tell he had to restrain himself from pummeling Jared. *What on earth is going on between these men?*

After a few tense moments of glaring at one another, Terry's attention started to ping-pong between her and Jared. That was a dead giveaway he was quite upset and trying desperately to figure out what to do. Suddenly, his gaze came to a rest on her.

Terry made a show of relaxing his features. She wasn't sure if that was for her benefit or his own. "The fee is taken care of."

Confused about what just happened, Jody stared at her friend. "I don't understand. What's the fee?"

In a nonchalant manner, Terry's shoulder rose as if it were no big deal. "Before you got here, we were discussing a price for one of my paintings. I just agreed to sell it to him. No big deal. It's a win, win for everyone. Now, tell us who you're looking for and why, and let the ass—*man* get to work."

Not liking anyone paying her way or even making deals on her behalf, she was unsure if J.D.'s help was worth the apparent upset it had caused her friend. As the silence continued, Terry squeezed her hands and emphatically stated, "It's done. No worries. Nathan has told me how good J.D. is when it comes to finding people. You wouldn't have asked if it weren't important. So let's get started."

"Okay. If you're sure. Thank you. I really appreciate it."

Terry's words seemed to have a calming effect on Jared because he finally relaxed a bit. She'd have to remember later to ask what canvas he wanted so badly.

Momentarily distracted by a glimpse of red hair and a pink shirt behind Jared, Jody withheld her troubled sigh. Fiona was becoming more solid but still resembled a light mist floating aimlessly around the room. As she watched the little girl stumbling around, her eyelids suddenly felt very heavy, and her vision blurred as it does when a person fights off sleep. Trying to snap herself out of the haze, she purposely jerked her body. The reality was, the more visible Fiona's form appeared, the more exhausted Jody would become. To make an appearance, the little girl stole her energy at an alarming rate. It wouldn't be long before keeping her eyes open would be an impossible task.

Jared scanned the room from where he sat. "Let me find a piece of paper and something to write with so I can take notes." As he stood and sauntered to the desk in the corner of the room, he walked right through Fiona. Jody found it interesting that his step slowed, and his hands spread out to his side. He stopped as if he were trying to ascertain what he'd just felt and finally just shook it off. Regaining his momentum, he found what he was looking for and returned to the group.

Finally feeling the time to address little Fiona had arrived, Jody turned to Terry. "I was hoping to convince you to sketch a picture of the person I need to find, so Nath—I mean Jared could have a visual of who I'm looking for."

"Of course, I'll do that for you. Why don't you start at the beginning and tell us why this is so important to you?"

Answering him with a slight nod, she leaned back into the cushions. Her eyes closed to help her gather the strength needed to tell Fiona's tragic story.

"I find myself in an unusual position." To calm herself, she reached out for the hands of her closest friends. Fiona's story was a difficult one, but she knew Nathan and Terry would understand. Since they were aware of her history, they'd recognize how traumatic this problem had been for her. More than anything, she needed their strength right now. "I'm afraid a spirit has attached herself to me."

Terry's eyes widened in surprise, and, as usual, Nathan wanted to get to the heart of the problem. "What? That's something new, isn't it? Are you in danger?"

"Well…"

Jared dropped the pen he'd found and quickly stood. With a deep frown creasing his face, he held a hand out in front of him to halt all conversation. "Excuse me. What did you say?"

The familiar reaction had Jody's heart sinking. She had to admit she did feel the tiniest bit bad for him. He'd had no clue the direction this discussion would take. Forcing a smile on her face, she knew it wouldn't be long before he ran in the other direction. He'd end up bailing on her just like everyone else she'd been interested in had done.

She could pinpoint the exact moment his mind turned suspicious. His gaze penetrated as he visually examined every inch of her. When his expression softened and the warmth returned to his demeanor, she knew he'd probably devised some logical explanation for what she'd just said. At least that had been the pattern in the past with the men she'd been interested in. Maybe he attributed her comment to exhaustion. Maybe he just thought he'd misunderstood her. She'd have to speak concisely so her words wouldn't be misinterpreted.

"I woke up last night to find a distraught four-year-old girl in bed with me." *No sugarcoating.* She'd be straight up about her abilities, and he'd walk out. She hadn't had time to get attached to him yet, so nothing gained. But for some reason, her heart sure felt like something had been lost.

"I don't know when she died, but she's determined to find her parents and talk to them."

The color drained from Jared's face.

Everyone could read his reaction just as clearly as if he'd shouted it at the top of his lungs.

"Are you telling me you're a *psychic*?"

Jody didn't miss the venom dripping from his last word. Somewhere from deep within her, she found the strength needed to face off with him. Allowing her anger and, yes, disappointment to shine through her eyes just as he had done, she stated as clearly as she could, "No. *Psychic* is a pretty broad term. I converse with spirits. I guess you'd call me a medium."

Jared's eyes narrowed to slits. She could see the wheels turning in his brain trying to figure out if she was a mental case or maybe just a charlatan. If she was reading his harsh expression correctly, she'd have to go with charlatan.

Fury raged within her. Lack of sleep and utter exhaustion had her wanting to lash out for being judged once again. However, before she could challenge Jared, Fiona sparked her annoyance.

Without giving Jared the opportunity to say anything, she jumped to her feet. Her mind registered that her quick movement had startled him when he took a step away from her. What seemed, to all in the room but her, to be a void space next to Jared, captured her full attention. Feeling as though she were about to lose her mind, her hands slid protectively over her cheeks as she bellowed at the top of her lungs, "Dammit, Fiona, stop that! Your interference is making it difficult to concentrate. I'm trying to help you. The least you could do is sit still for ten minutes!"

She hated losing her temper, but her nerves were being stretched to the limits. The little girl had been dancing around Jared as if he were a Maypole. In her current exhausted state, Fiona's shenanigans would make it extremely difficult, if not impossible, for her to focus on the importance of this meeting.

Chastised, Fiona trudged over to the empty chair and sat down. "*Sorry.*"

Jody pivoted back to Jared and pursed her lips. "I'm sorry about that interruption." She peered back at the chair. Once satisfied, she returned her attention to Jared. "It shouldn't happen again, but I can't promise it won't."

She would have laughed at his stunned reaction had it not hurt so badly. "Do you think I don't get this same backlash from most everyone I meet? I know what you're thinking, and frankly it's *your* problem, not mine. I speak the truth as I see it. You're just going to have to put your big boy pants on and listen to me. That is, of course, if you're still interested in helping me." The words snapped from her as if she were firing them from a fully-loaded machine gun. Based on Jared's angry stature, they'd hit their mark. By the expression on his face, no one had ever dared speak to him like that before.

After her tirade, Jody noticed that for the first time since the initial introductions, Nathan looked relaxed and smiled. Terry, on the other hand, was curious and obviously excited about the prospect of sketching a ghost. "What does the little girl look like? What did you call her? Fiona?"

Trying to work through her anger at Jared's reaction, Jody plopped herself back down on the couch before answering. She couldn't worry about what Jared thought right now. For some reason, she felt as though time wasn't on her side. From the time she climbed into her vehicle tonight, a sense of urgency to get Fiona home had been bombarding her. She needed to act as fast as possible. Jared would either help or not. He would either believe her or not. She couldn't waste any more of her precious energy worrying about it.

She glanced over at the chair the little girl was sitting in and couldn't help but smile. The kid was a giant pain in the ass, but precious as hell. "Yes. Fiona is her name. Oh, Terry, she's adorable." Enjoying the attention, Fiona jumped out of the chair and starting posing like a superstar model.

"Like I said, she's four. She's about this tall." She held her hand up in the air to show the men her height. "She has beautiful red hair, cut in a little page boy and bangs which are a bit too long. She wears a little blue barrette in her hair on her left side, just above her ear. She's got—"

Not taking being dismissed calmly, Jared's anger couldn't be more evident when he butted in. "Wait just a damn minute. Are you claiming that you can actually see this little girl right now?"

Jody jumped at the fierce tone of his voice and acknowledged him with a lone nod.

"Well, then, I've got an idea," the sneer of disbelief in his voice was clear as he strutted around the room like he owned the place.

Jody regarded Jared, not understanding why the harsh tone of his voice made her feel as though she'd just been struck. She'd heard all of the accusations from others a thousand times before. The blame laid squarely at her feet because she'd been an idiot and forgotten herself when they'd first met. She'd allowed the fairytale of believing they could have something on a more intimate level, even if temporarily.

Stupid! Stupid! Stupid! He may have been interested before her gifts were revealed, but now that he knew, he pulled no punches.

His impression of her spoke volumes. His anger had him trying to disprove everything she stood for. It saddened her to think of how compelling his physical pull was for her. When they first met, she felt she could've walked into his arms and never been scared or alone again. She had no reason to be angry with him. Her feelings had betrayed her, not him. *Why should he turn out to be any different than any other man I've met?*

She regretted the undeniable urge in which she'd liked to have gotten to know him better. In no time at all, he'd somehow gotten through all of her defenses. And that pissed her off.

No matter what her initial thoughts of him were, she'd finally had enough of his pompous ass strutting around the room trying to do nothing more than prove her wrong. His actions demonstrated him to be a bullheaded jerk, who obviously wanted to break her. No one deserves to be treated like this. *Not even me.*

Having everyone's full attention had Jared's lips curling with a menacing smirk. "If you can see her, then why don't you just take a picture of her? Wouldn't that be a lot better than a drawing?" His words came out silky smooth and tinged with arrogance.

Now, it was Terry's turn to be offended. "Hey, asshole, I don't *draw* pictures." His finger shot out and started jabbing the air as he spoke. "I—"

"What a minute," Jody interrupted. She stood and glanced at the chair. "Fiona, is that possible? Would you let us take a picture of you?" Jody had no idea if the camera could capture what most people couldn't see.

Taken aback by what he'd just heard, Jared's eyebrows rose so high they'd gotten lost in his hairline.

Fiona shouted with glee. *"Yes! I love having my picture taken!"*

Jody reached into her pocket and pulled her phone out. She engaged the camera, but before she could lift it, Jared interrupted her. "Wait a minute. *I'll* take the photo with *my* phone."

Purposely rolling her eyes, she waved her hand through the air. "Be my guest."

He held his phone up but had no idea where to focus the camera. Instead of verbalizing that fact, he sent Jody a questioning look. She responded with an annoyed *harrumph* and positioned herself slightly behind him. Leaning into him, she moved his arm into the best position with Fiona centered on the screen. The close contact left an unwanted thrill of intimate pleasure passing between them, making them both squirm.

"You ready, sweetheart?"

She felt Jared tense as she spoke to the child he couldn't see. "Right there," she said. She held his hand still so he could take the picture which would be responsible for changing his mind on the existence of spirits forever.

Just as Jared snapped the photo, his phone buzzed and the screen went dark. He was positive he hadn't captured anything with the camera. He couldn't have. But he didn't want to view the evidence with an audience so he excused himself. "I've got to take this call." Without hesitating, he opened the door and hurried from the room.

Jared rejected the incoming call and paced the small hallway. Stopping, he held the phone up and started to unlock it. His finger paused over the numbers. "I could leave right now. Put all this craziness behind me." He purposely nodded his head in the affirmative and started for the main room but stopped before exiting the hallway. "Dammit."

Pivoting around, he made his way back to the door and just stood staring at it. Swiping his hand through his hair, Jared tried to pull himself together. "Just look at the damn picture. Nothing's going to be there. I can walk right out of here without giving any of this further thought." Except he knew that wasn't true. It would be impossible to walk away from Jody.

Jared unlocked the phone and stared at the little ghost girl sitting with her legs crossed at the knees and hands primly held in her lap. The figure was misty, but there. Numb, he leaned against the wall.

Once the feeling had come back into Jared's body, he took a deep breath and walked through the door.

Jody held her hand out. "May I?"

He frowned and then gawked at the chair where the little ghost girl's image had been caught. Jared handed her the phone.

"Can I see?" Fiona asked, jumping up and down next to Jody. Dropping to her knees, they both reviewed the photo. *"Hey! How come I can see through me?"*

Jody's shoulders absently shrugged. "If I had to guess, I'd say you look like that because you've been so busy lately. You're getting drained, like me. You're not usually so transparent. Most times, you look as solid as every other person."

"Let me take another picture," Jared said. "Where is she now?"

Jody was down on one knee with Fiona propped up against her side. "She's right here." Since the little girl wasn't completely solid, they had to be careful not to distort her image as they posed. She put her arm around the child, and Fiona snuggled into Jody as best she could. They both glanced up at the camera and demurely smiled as Jared took the picture. Jody didn't bother to get up and glance at the photo. Without question, Fiona would be there staring back at Jared, and more than likely sending little freak-out tremors through his body.

"Fiona, it might be best if you go and find your grandmother. You need to get some rest if you want to have the strength to speak to your parents. I think we might be able to do that very soon. My friends and I are going to work on finding your mommy and daddy. It's going to take a little time, and you need to be patient. There's no need for you to stay."

The little girl hugged her and leaned in to give Jody a kiss. Jared caught that poignant moment with his camera as well.

When it became clear Fiona had departed, Nathan stepped forward. "Have you communicated with Fiona's grandmother? Couldn't you just ask her where Fiona's family is?"

"Unfortunately, no, I can't. I saw her once when she came to get Fiona. She never communicated with me. The woman only spoke with the little girl and has not come back since. I truly believe the woman would come to me if she could. So, for now at least, it's just us on the hunt."

Chapter Thirteen

After everything that happened over the past several hours, Jared was relieved he hadn't driven himself to the gallery. With all he'd learned about Jody, there was no way in hell he'd be able to concentrate on driving right now. In one evening, she and little Fiona had turned his world upside down by opening his mind and once frigid heart up to new possibilities.

He glanced out the car window as the empty streets of Scottsdale flew by, unsurprised by the deserted roads. He was in the heart of a town well known for its nightlife. The affluent city had the reputation of being the playground for the rich, the famous, and the wannabes. It was far too early in the morning for anyone to be out and about.

Reflecting back on the evening, he pulled his phone out and thumbed through the pictures of the little ghost girl. The four of them had ended up talking until the wee hours of the morning in the art gallery office. The all-nighter had opened his eyes to some pretty incredible things. While Jody took a brief cat nap, Nathan and Terry had casually shared information about ghosts, Jody, and her gifts as if that exceptional subject matter were the norm. He didn't often get blindsided, but it had happened twice last night—first with Jody and then with Fiona.

These first few moments away from the woman

who'd stolen his heart gave him the opportunity to review the past evening's events with a clear head. The realization in which the only woman he'd ever reacted to in such a deep-rooted, instinctive manner talked to dead people on a regular basis bowled him over. What's more, the fact he was okay with that left him chuckling. A scant ten hours ago, he would've scoffed at the idea that either thing could be possible. He allowed his head to fall back against the seat. *Love and ghosts. What the hell have I gotten myself into?*

He'd never believed in love or ghosts until he'd laid eyes on her. Jody had torn away barriers tonight which he'd painstakingly built brick by brick since his childhood. As those barriers crumbled at her feet, the possibility of something more in life, something very special, had now opened up to him. She was, at the very least, a pleasant surprise. Even with all of his wealth and power, he willingly admitted that new possibilities, as well as unknown revelations, had been few and far between in his lifetime. What he could potentially gain from her, both in knowledge and newfound love, was priceless. He couldn't wait to see her again.

Love. He let the word roll around in his mind. "Is that really what I'm talking about here?" He'd scoffed at the concept of love his whole life. But now, instead of being incredulous about experiencing the elusive emotion, he was convinced he'd missed out on something crucial without it. Something purely perfect and gratifying had been lacking every day he hadn't known Jody. They barely knew each other, and he'd already handed her the key to his future happiness. That one thought both warmed and terrified him.

His thoughts drifted away as the car took a sharp

turn. Momentarily blinded by a bright light, he realized the sun had just started coming up. Instead of going home, he decided to go straight to the office and look into the clues Jody had given him about Fiona. Unwilling to trust her information with anyone else, he'd handle everything himself rather than pass it on to his staff. From this point forward, he'd always put her wants and needs first. That thought produced a broad grin. Never before had there been anyone important enough to place before himself, and the fact he enjoyed the feeling so much, surprised him. Punching a button on the control panel next to him, he spoke curtly to the driver. "Take me to the office."

"Yes, sir."

Reflecting over the course of the evening, he'd been shocked to realize how many times Fiona had sporadically popped in on them and couldn't help but wonder if other ghosts did the same thing. Jody had assured him that, unlike little Fiona, most spirits made one appearance and then left never to be seen or heard from again.

Jared had learned some valuable information last night. Jody had been patient and given him her unique Ghosts 101 tutorial. With each of Fiona's visits, she'd taken the time to describe the shift in air pressure. She'd mentioned how he'd walked through the little girl's essence at the beginning of the evening. He remembered the goose bumps he'd gotten, as well as the sensation of the air turning dense and cold. With that knowledge and Jody's help, he'd quickly learned to feel when Fiona showed up.

He couldn't see her, and didn't think he wanted that experience, but after making the effort, he'd learned to use his other senses to pick up on the child being nearby. With each new visit, he became more adept at noticing the little electrical impulses assaulting his body. Those energy fueled charges resulted in a tingling effect which raised the hair on his neck and arms.

He'd carefully watched Jody as each of Fiona's frequent visits sapped a little more of her strength, and it scared the hell out of him. So much so that he'd made the mistake of offering up his energy instead. Jody had quickly put her hand over his mouth and chastised him about the consequences of giving permission for things he didn't understand. Apparently, he had a lot to learn.

Getting in touch with Fiona's mother and father was paramount. He intended to be the one to put the pieces together for Jody. He wanted to free her from this tragedy—to unburden her, so hopefully, she could see past his initial stupidity on the matter and perhaps forgive him. It wasn't her gratitude he wanted, though. He wanted *her* and being in her life had become a priority for him. He'd play fair but had no qualms about playing dirty, if need be, to win her over. She was too important to him to let her slip away.

First, he'd help her get through this. Once she was free of Fiona, he'd make her his. Even though he'd felt the heat between them instantly, something deep within braced him to move slowly with her. He knew if he rushed her, she'd bolt in a heartbeat.

Jared thought back to the moment he'd first laid his eyes on *Solitude*. Without even meeting Jody, seeing the vision of her in the portrait was the first instant he'd fallen in love with her. He made himself a promise never to be responsible for making her feeling the depth of sadness and loss which emanated from the portrait. Realizing how close he'd come to losing her over his initial reaction to her gift frightened him. He didn't want to be *that* insensitive man anymore. Instead, the positive aspects of the portrait became his focus. He'd made a conscious decision to pour all of his energy into giving her the peace and love which had also been present within *Solitude*.

Weary, he rubbed his eyes trying to focus on the elusive subject at hand. With so much unfamiliar emotion connected to his thoughts of Jody, he felt completely out of his element. He was a fast learner, however, and learn he would. Look at how far he'd already come. Just yesterday, he believed emotion to be a character flaw, something which could lead to the downfall of everything he'd ever created for himself. After all, in his profession, he'd been witness to that outcome many times. In his experience, love, or what people perceived as love, destroyed lives. Now that he found himself in a position to feel that powerful sentiment, he realized how flawed his original thoughts on the matter were.

Being an analytical person, Jared fell back on what he knew best. He made a mental checklist to accomplish his goals. The first and most challenging task would be to figure out how to be patient. For Jody's sake, he had to concentrate on making the meeting between her and Fiona's parents happen quickly. Their personal relationship wouldn't be possible until that was wrapped up. He wanted her full attention when he made his move.

She hadn't been able to get much information to go on in the search for Fiona's family. He had to give her credit for trying, though. Truth be told, if he were to put this case in perspective, his client was a young kid who probably still counted to five on her fingers. That alone made information gathering from the source difficult. Add to that the fact she was dead and finding answers became almost impossible. In any case, he shouldn't have too much difficulty finding a death certificate for a four-year-old child named Fiona McCarthy. As soon as he had what Jody needed, he'd take her the information and offer to escort her to wherever the parents lived.

A pang of unease clenched deep within his gut. He had a bad feeling about the impending meeting. Worry continued to grow as Jared glanced once again at the picture with Fiona by Jody's side. He put himself in Fiona's parents' position, knowing full well they were grieving a devastating loss. He realized that if someone approached him out of the blue and said they had a message from his dead little girl, he'd likely drop them where they stood. He'd have to be prepared to protect Jody should the need arise.

****

Several hours later, Jared had exhausted all of the available search tools to which he had access. Having had no luck in finding Fiona left him frustrated. For what must be the hundredth time, he turned his phone on and looked at the photos of the little girl.

"Could Jody be mistaken about your last name? She seemed confident it was McCarthy." Half expecting an answer from the little ghost girl, he sat there quietly and waited.

Getting nowhere fast, he needed more information. A slow smile crossed his face as he pushed himself away from his desk. "I guess since I'm at an impasse,

I'm just going to have to see my client. Maybe, with the right questions, she can provide further details."

An unfamiliar feeling of light-heartedness swept through him as he entered his office bathroom to take a shower. "It shouldn't be unusual for me to stop by and check in with my client. Although I've never done it before, she doesn't know that."

As he slid out of his shirt, he caught his reflection in the mirror. Surprised at the sight, he couldn't believe the difference in his appearance. The familiar hardness of his face which stared back at him every morning was no longer there. He liked seeing himself smiling and happy. He could quickly get used to that.

Maybe I'll stop on the way over and pick her up a flower. Women like flowers.

Chapter Fourteen

Jody's doorbell rang prompting Terry to holler above the din of frying bacon and eggs being whisked, "Come in."

Hearing a grunt of displeasure, Terry, wearing nothing but his boxers, whirled around to find a very perturbed Jared walking toward him. He carried a single red rose in one hand and a laptop case in the other. The look of disdain which crossed the pilferer's face left him chuckling. Restraining himself had never been a strong suit. He had to have a little fun at the thieving bastard's expense.

"For *me*?" Terry threw his head back and released a demented cackle. From the little he knew about Jared, he wasn't the sort of man to bring anyone flowers. He got great satisfaction from calling him out and making him even more uncomfortable with the gesture.

It would take some time to get over his annoyance at having *Solitude* stolen out from under him. But after the last few hours he'd spent with Jody, if the end result brought her some much-needed peace, he'd give the portrait away again in a heartbeat. Mentally crossing his fingers, he prayed Jared's reputation as a P.I. proved to be correct. This nasty business had to be concluded sooner rather than later. If Jody wasn't able to resolve this mess with Fiona soon, he feared they'd be burying her in no time at all.

"I'm here to see Jody," Jared stated the obvious through a growl.

"And here I thought you'd come all this way to see me," Terry snapped back knowing full well he displayed the petulance of a toddler. "It's a little early for a house call, don't you think?" He made a show of spreading his arms to bolster his state of undress while holding a frying pan.

Jared forcibly clenched his jaw to keep from spewing obscenities and valiantly fought an internal war to pummel the fucker.

He didn't like being the butt of any joke. Knowing full well he'd just suffered the brunt of this farce left him glaring at the man standing there in nothing but his undershorts. A streak of jealousy had him wondering how badly he'd get burned by yanking the frying pan out of the dickhead's hand and knocking him over the head with it. He'd had enough of the artist's games and hoped his tone of voice and notorious death look would put an end to them. "I'm here to see Jody. If you don't tell me where she is, I'll find her myself."

"She's still in bed." Terry smirked as the innuendo hung heavily in the air between them.

That's it. Jared had enough. Rising to the bait, he made a quick move in the artist's direction. Terry jolted back and seemingly braced himself to run for his life.

"Nope."

When Jared heard his partner's booming voice, he pivoted in place to find Nathan leisurely strolling from the back of the house. His hair still sopping wet and a towel carelessly tied at his waist. "She's in the shower."

Nathan's dazzling smile only adding to Jared's desire to punch one or both of these bastard's faces until their shit eating grins were just a distant memory.

"You're here early. We had a slumber party after the gallery. We thought Jody could use a little fun."

Jared's steely gaze scrutinized Nathan from head to toe. "From what I've seen so far, very *little* fun," he retorted dryly and meant every word.

Nathan burst out laughing. "A little short-tempered this morning, are we, *Jared*?" The exaggerated emphasis on his name that had just been revealed the night before irritated him.

Jared found it difficult to hide his disappointment at having to deal with these two idiots and their twisted sense of humor. He wanted—no, he *needed* to be near Jody and had tired of all the roadblocks. "Cut the shit," he said disgustedly. "Just get her for me. I need some more information to find Fiona."

Suddenly the room became silent. The only sound to be heard was that of the shower running in the back of the house. All jokes had ceased, and the air felt heavy as if weighted down with tension. The distressed glances that passed between Nathan and Terry sent a cold shiver of dread down Jared's spine.

"What's happened? Is Jody all right?"

"It was a rough night—well, morning. I was hoping you'd have the parents' names first thing today." Nathan's strained voice did nothing to calm Jared's anxiety.

Trying to tamp down his unease, he bit the inside of his cheek. "What happened after I left?"

"Quick. Come sit down before Jody comes out." Nathan prompted as he rushed past Jared. His hushed, urgent tone combined with worried glances grated at Jared's already raw nerves and had alarm bells blaring in his head.

With patience worn thin, he thought he'd snap at any moment. "Well?" If they didn't tell him soon, he'd beat the information out of them.

Nathan nervously glanced back at the hallway. "I can hear the water running in the shower, but we haven't got much time before Jody comes out. I don't want her to overhear what we're saying." The fevered pitch of his voice relayed the indisputable urgency he felt. "Terry and I have known Jody since we were kids. She's grown into this gift of hers. It's taken her years to become comfortable with her abilities. When we were kids, she used to be terrified of everything. Spirit's constantly surrounded her and never gave her a moment's rest. Being unable to sleep, and afraid to be alone—ever—can do a lot of damage to someone as sensitive as Jody.

"Over the years, she's found that if she shares the messages of the dead with the decedent's family members, she's able to cope. She's able to sleep and have some semblance of a normal life."

Nathan rubbed his bloodshot eyes before continuing. "Knowing all that, the last few hours we've spent with her we…were…" When he stumbled on the proper description of what he'd witnessed, he looked to Terry for help. Jared was on the edge of his seat as he glanced at the artist for an explanation. He couldn't help but notice the heavy burden of concern Terry carried for his friend within his bleak expression.

Terry leaned into the other men and whispered, "Over the years, we've spent many nights together. But last night was a fucking nightmare. I don't know how she's coped with Fiona's persistence. The little girl won't leave her alone. She can't sleep. She can't function on any level, and she can't find any solace because of it. She's hanging onto her sanity by a thread."

The genuine anguish reflected in Terry's voice heightened Jared's distress for Jody, but the man's next words made his heart falter. "This problem is starting to make her physically ill. She started throwing up. This whole situation is tearing her up on the inside as bad as it is on the outside. Any control she could hope to have is slipping away, and it's happening fast."

Nathan added, "I heard her in the bathroom last night crying. Fiona was with her, and she pleaded with the little girl to leave her alone, even if just for an hour.

"I'm scared if we don't get a conclusion for Fiona and her family soon, Jody may have an emotional or physical breakdown. This situation is getting worse by the minute. It's affecting her whole personality."

Everything he'd learned about Jody's situation shot Jared's mind into overdrive. Thoughts were filtering in and out so quickly, he had difficulty keeping up. Yesterday, he'd been a fearless man. Today, he was an emotional wreck. Nothing in his background had prepared him for the sentimental chaos Jody made him feel. The emotion she drew out of him tore at his very being and brought him to his knees. The unmistakable connection he'd instantly felt toward her intensified his awareness of his inadequacy in dealing with such things as fear where she was concerned. Perceiving that particular emotion on Jody's behalf seemed to compound his anxiety and overwhelmed him in the process. He had no idea how to protect her, let alone navigate through something he had no control over. To be strong for her, Jared had to find a way to get a hold of himself. She needed him, so he'd do whatever he could to make this right for her.

A door slamming in the back of the house broke the men's deliberation. Jody cried out, her words uncharacteristically laced with anger. "Nathan? Where'd you go? What the hell? You used all of my conditioner! How am I supposed to…" Upon entering the living room, she stopped dead in her tracks. Jared watched her closely as she scanned each of the men standing at attention in various states of undress.

Displaying her displeasure with a furrowed brow, her anger focused on Nathan and Terry. "Why are you two out here and barely dressed?" Jared could tell by her expression that mortification over the scene had her seeing murder. He didn't know much about women, but he knew when one was pissed off.

Just as she started across the room to kick some ass, she stopped mid-stride. While she stood in place, Jared recognized the exact moment when the anger within her disappeared and expectation took its place. Obviously overwrought and tired, Jody's mind had just clicked that he'd come with information.

She hurried across the room into his waiting arms. "Did you find Fiona's parents already?" Nathan and Terry jumped at the opportunity to scurry out of the room.

The outside world disappeared for Jared. The woman he hadn't been able to stop thinking about now looked at him with such hope in her eyes.

With her in such close proximity, it took a few moments to gather his thoughts. She stood in his arms, still wet from her shower, wearing a short, silken robe and smelling like Heaven. The top of the robe had slid open, exposing cleavage. A lot of cleavage. He would have had a difficult time ignoring that under normal circumstances, except these were *not* normal circumstances. The robe's material was soft and clung to her wet curves. Nothing had been left to his imagination, striking him momentarily dumb.

He appreciated the fact this was the first time he'd ever been alone with her. His arm tightened around her as he handed her the rose.

She accepted the velvety flower and graced him with a shy smile.

"I need to sit with you and get a little more information. I thought you might be more comfortable here than coming into my office."

Jody tried not to show her disappointment, but Jared read it on her face. Knowing he'd let her down tore him up inside. He swore he'd do whatever he possibly could to bring her smile back.

"I brought my laptop. I'll set it up while you get dressed. We'll find everything we need to know about Fiona in no time at all. I promise."

Unable to muster the strength to be anything more than polite at the moment, she forced a slight nod of her head. Pulling out of his embrace, she left the room without a word to make herself presentable.

Jody could feel herself falling apart, cell by cell. Fiona had passed the point of being a pest. Something had changed. The little spirit child had become desperate and seemingly more out of control with each visit. Fiona was now in full-blown tantrum mode and even more of a threat to Jody than she could have believed possible.

Returning several minutes later, she clung to her rose and readied herself to get to work. Sitting next to Jared on the couch, she couldn't help but sneak a peek at his laptop screen. She didn't recognize the program, but that didn't surprise her. She'd never been tech savvy and only used the Internet occasionally.

Trying to relax, Jody used a quick silent meditation. Feeling a little better, she scanned the room. The little girl was nowhere to be found. She breathed a sigh of relief at the temporary reprieve from Fiona.

"Okay, I'm ready. What do you need?"

"Can you give me some more information about Fiona's last name?"

Knowing she'd already given all the information she had about that to him, she shrugged her shoulders. "McCarthy is all I know. Why?"

"I don't think that's her last name. I believe McCarthy might be her mother's maiden name."

The disappointment she felt could be heard in her audible sigh. *Well, shit! That's a big problem.* Without thought, she lifted the rose to her nose and breathed in the flower's soft perfume. As she pondered what he'd said, the silky petals brushed her lips.

"Fiona said her mother told her she had McCarthy blood in her. Because of that, wherever she found herself, family members would always be around her. She told me there were many McCarthy's with her on the other side, and the men wore kilts." The memory of that conversation drew a faint smile from her. "Well, skirts—she said the boys were all wearing skirts. I took that to mean kilts."

Her hand rose in a perplexed gesture. "That was all she told me about her name. I didn't question her further because it felt like that was all she knew. It never crossed my mind McCarthy was her *mother's* family name." Allowing the dejection she felt show, her shoulders slumped forward. "I guess it should have."

Even to herself, her voice sounded dull. As despair seeped deeper into her body, Jody let her face go slack. She started to resign herself to the fact she'd never get closure for Fiona. In turn, closure would be denied for herself. She had to prepare for the very real notion she would fail at this important task. That knowledge broke her heart.

"What am I going to do?" her sorrow filled plea barely above a whisper.

Trying to calm her, he grasped her hand and hung on tight. "We can still find her. Let me start a different search. All I need to do is change a few parameters. We'll see what comes up. I'm not giving up, and I don't want you to give up either."

Her attention focused on Jared's tender touch and the strength in his voice. That, alone, would get her through. She didn't know how or why, but something deep inside her believed that fact to be the God's honest truth.

As he turned back to his computer, she became fascinated by the way his fingers danced effortlessly across the keyboard. Being such a large man, she'd had him pegged as the hunt and peck type. When he appeared happy with everything he'd just input, his long, graceful finger hit 'enter' to command the computer to reveal its secrets. Hopefully, they wouldn't have too long to wait before getting the needed results. As he started to get comfortable, his computer dinged, signaling a quick hit on his search.

Hearing the computer's sharp beeping sound contributed to Jody's tension, and her muscles painfully constricted. A lot rested on what he'd found. What if this information was another false lead?

She had to remind herself to stop worrying. Instead, she'd do her best to stay positive and keep her hopes up for some good news.

Moving closer to Jared, she gripped his arm for strength. "What is it?" her voice almost breathless with anticipation.

Satisfied with what he'd read, his broad smile told her everything she needed to know. He reached out and gently stroked her still damp hair. She felt herself melt into the warmth of his gentle touch and allowed herself a moment to enjoy it.

"I think we've found her."

Staring deep into his warm, dark eyes, Jody found the confirmation she was looking for. She couldn't help herself as relieved tears of joy ran down her cheeks.

"Let me tell you what I've got, and you can tell me if you think this is *our* Fiona." His thumb gently swept her tears away.

Our Fiona. Stunned by his statement, she couldn't take her eyes off of him. Did he have a clue as to how his choice of words moved her? Somehow those two little words left her feeling a sense of peace and belonging she'd never felt before. She wasn't alone in this. For the first time in her life, she truly felt as if she were half of a team—a genuine part of an '*our.*'

The sound of his deep voice broke her deliberation. "It looks like Fiona was born four-and-half years ago."

"Yes," she said, still trying to contain her excitement in the off chance this child wasn't their

Fiona.

"Red hair. Blue eyes. Height is thirty-six inches. Weight is twenty-five pounds." With those statistics at hand, Jody sensed little Fiona had just become a very real entity for Jared. She felt the moment sorrow for one so young and innocent took hold of him.

"She was such a small, little thing."

"Yes, she was."

Jared took a moment to absorb the sad truth of the facts they'd just learned and put them in perspective before he continued. She heard the grief behind his sad sigh.

"This says she died a month ago from meningitis." His words trailed off. "Jesus," he whispered. "Meningitis works quickly. One day the child is healthy. The next day she gets sick. The next day she's dead." His face was her window to his soul and held nothing back. His bewilderment from the depth of sorrow flowing through him was as transparent as glass. "My God. Those poor people."

Wanting to ease his pain, Jody gently caressed his cheek. "She showed me her death state in the hospital room. Her mother was begging her to come back to her." Feeling the strength of the bond between them, Jody laid her head against his shoulder for a moment of shared comfort. "I felt the woman's disbelief, her guilt over not getting Fiona to the hospital quicker. That was the most terrible and tragic event I've ever witnessed in all my years of doing this."

With the first obstacle in Fiona's journey completed, the urgency to start moving and finally put an end to this situation ramped up to an all new high. She still had no idea as to where Fiona had lived.

Thinking about what still needed to be done to make this meeting happen swamped her. If the parents weren't located in the Phoenix area, she'd need to set up travel plans immediately. Leaning over Jared's shoulder, she inquired, "What information does it give about her parents?"

He glanced back at the screen. "Mother, Sarah Hinton, twenty-two years old. Father, Dallas Hinton, twenty-four. Their last known address was in Fort Worth, Texas."

"Thank you." Relief flooded her and lightened the tumultuous load she'd been carrying for far too long. Drawing him into an embrace, she quickly kissed his soft lips. With a known destination at hand she couldn't linger. The time had finally come to press forward and end this. Her mind filled with details—reservations needed to be made. She had to pack. Her staff needed to be notified she wouldn't be in.

Jared could almost feel her brain reeling from the newly attained information as she crossed the room to the purse by the front door. Jody bent to pick her bag up but something invisible stopped her, freezing her in place. She remained there as if time had stood still, motionless and as breakable as any fine porcelain figurine teetering on a high mantel. Her beautiful face expressed nothing but a blank stare.

At the first sign of physical distress, Jared was up and running toward her. Just as he threw his arms around Jody, her legs collapsed and forced her to the floor. He rocked her in his arms as a grief-stricken scream filled with all of the torment Fiona had caused tore free from her lips.

In his line of work, Jared had seen this reaction

many times. Clients would work themselves up into an emotional frenzy as they were forced to wait for answers to whatever questions they had. When Jared provided those answers, good or bad, they were overcome. He knew the rush of the climax could be debilitating. He likened the response to running a never-ending emotional marathon, where a light finally appeared at the end of the tunnel. Something inside people, both mentally and physically, broke down after crossing the finish line. They were so exhausted, the result was a momentary loss of control, which more times than not, led to a total collapse.

Nathan and Terry ran into the room when they heard Jody's tortured scream. As the other men knelt beside them, Jared continued to cradle Jody. He gently kissed her forehead, whispering words of encouragement into her golden hair.

Insisting on being the one to provide her with the strength needed to conclude this journey with Fiona, he stated emphatically, "Listen to my voice, Jody. Fiona's journey is almost over. I need you to take deep breaths and try to calm yourself. Do you feel my warmth? Do you feel my arms around you? Do you feel the strength I'm offering you? Everything I have is yours, baby. Take whatever you need."

He kept the tone of his voice deep and soothing, imagining it would carry through the murky darkness and coax her back to reality. Back to him. He felt her cling to him as he embraced her, allowing herself to seize the much-needed warmth and strength he'd offered. As she regained awareness, he made sure that his concerned eyes were the first thing she saw. Making the moment even more intimate, she reached up and traced his face with her fingertips.

Drawing her into a bear hug, he tightly squeezed her body even closer into his. "Please tell me you're okay."

"I am."

Jared's attention turned to Nathan and Terry. He had to admit, this mess had left them all a ragged trio. They looked beat down and haggard.

Jody peeked out of Jared's safe embrace. "Nathan, I have to get a flight to Fort Worth. My credit card is in my wallet. Can you get me on the first flight out?"

"No." The fierce look Jared gave the two men left no doubt about who was in control. "I'll call and get my plane ready to go. We'll be in the air as soon as we can get to the airport."

Both Nathan and Terry acknowledged him with a nod. Jared allowed the two men to remove her from his tight grasp. They took her to the bedroom, helped her quickly pack for the difficult trip ahead, and then left Jody to get dressed.

Chapter Fifteen

Jody felt a little like a superstar as Jared ushered her onto his private jet. She had expected to board a little prop plane, not something as lavish as the flying hotel suite she now occupied. The chairs were huge and made from the most luxurious leather she'd ever felt. There were a couple of extra large screens, either for use of a TV or computer, maybe both, she couldn't tell which. A table had been set for a service with fine china and a beautiful bouquet of mixed flowers sat next to one of the windows.

Since Jared was discussing the flight plan with the pilot, Jody continued to stroll down the plane. She found a lounge with a large white leather couch and matching chairs, a fully stocked bar, and a TV the size of a movie screen. Beyond that, the next door revealed a conference room of all things.

The entry door to Jared's private jet slammed shut, securely locking them inside. Jody returned to the sitting area and found Fiona just as the busy staff made their rounds and prepared the plane for takeoff. The little girl's influence had the atmosphere in the aircraft crackling with excitement. She quickly moved from chair to chair, touching everything in her path.

Jared came up beside Jody and placed his arm around her waist. "You're tense. Why don't you sit down? This will all be over soon. I promise."

Fiona continued to run circles around the plane, never even bothering to get out of the way of the flight attendants. She just ran right through them.

"It's not that. It's Fiona. She's here and is having a ball playing with everything in sight."

An attendant moved toward them just as Fiona discovered one of the screens. *"Looky, Jody! There's two TVs!"*

"No! Don't touch…" But the little girl had reached the darkened screen before Jody could stop her. Jared and Jody watched as the computer screen came to life and then blinked out. A loud popping noise accompanied the power surge as Fiona unknowingly stole the energy. Her little body lit up like a Christmas tree.

"Wow! Did you see that?" Jared yelled, but he wasn't looking at the screen. He was looking at where Fiona stood.

"Can you see her?"

"I saw a bright orb of light. There was a brilliant flash and this beautiful, bouncing, bluish colored light appeared. It's gone now. Was that Fiona?"

"Yes. I'm afraid she may have fried your computer." Jody bent down in front of the little girl and placed her hands on the kid's shoulders.

"Fiona, we're going to see your parents today. Both of us need to be rested for the reunion. Why don't you go and sit with your mother until the time comes. Can you do that for me?"

Fiona threw herself into Jody's arms and embraced her, slowly disappearing until she had completely vanished. Thankfully, the child had been easily convinced to go but not before Jody had the full attention of the flight crew. Her giggle couldn't be contained when she'd realized they had watched her talking to, and interacting with thin air. Gauging by all the hushed whispers and raised eyebrows she'd caused quite a stir.

The crew's uneasiness become apparent as their belief of sharing a tiny space, very high up in the air, with a loon had hit home. They not only stayed a healthy distance away, but kept a close eye on what they perceived as a passenger with a few loose screws. This type of behavior was nothing new to Jody. What surprised her was Jared stepping up and having a private conversation with them. He'd immediately put a cease to all of the uncomfortable stares and chatter. She didn't know what he'd said to them, but he'd stood up for her. By doing so, he'd unwittingly made her feel safe and protected.

****

With the exception of a little turbulence, the first hour of the flight from Phoenix Sky Harbor to DFW had been blissfully quiet. Now that Jody knew who she'd be meeting and where, the few short flight hours had to be used to get as much rest as possible. Jared never once intruded on the silence between them with empty words, but instead offered quiet strength and support just by being there.

As the jet streaked through the darkening clouds, he sat idly beside her maintaining his stoic facade. Jody knew if she were able to crack his calm exterior, he'd be wound tight, ready and willing to swoop in and do whatever task she required.

It didn't escape her notice that even without the benefit of conversation, he seemed to be completely aware of her needs. It unnerved her to realize just how transparent she appeared to be when it came to him. If she were thirsty, a glass of water magically appeared in front of her. If the heaviness of the upcoming meeting started to weigh her down, to distract her mindset, he'd gently play with her fingers. The more Jody thought about his actions, it became clear they were somehow instinctive, as if this whole scenario was scripted somehow. He'd prepared and memorized his role as leading man, while she'd decided to improvise.

Thinking back on the memory of him learning about her abilities had her smiling. To say the least, he'd been a real ass. While he hadn't believed a word she'd said when they'd first met, he seemed to be taking her abilities in stride now. Except for Nathan and Terry, that was more than any other man had ever been capable of doing. Of course, she reminded herself, they weren't involved with each other. If he understood how constant interruptions by spirits wanting to get messages to family members put a damper on a romantic candlelit dinner, she was confident he'd run for the hills.

As Jody reflected on Jared, she allowed herself to sneak a sideways glance at his handsome profile. It might take a while, but once a person moved past his obvious physical strength, they'd be left dealing with his even more dominant self-assurance. The man oozed confidence. She had no doubt he'd be considered the alpha male wherever he found himself. That being so, he'd surely demand something she'd never be able to give him—a partner's complete attention. Spirits didn't care if she wanted some alone time with a special person. They were relentless when approaching her and stepped into the mix without a qualm.

Uncomfortable with the fact her musing seemed consumed with the man sitting next to her, she refocused and tried to see herself as others do. It was common knowledge that many people thought of her as scatter-brained. They had no reason to believe otherwise when her focus shifted away in a split second, sometimes even in mid-sentence. One minute she'd be absorbed in a conversation. The next, she'd be looking around trying to find the living person to whom the next spirit in line demanded addressing. Much of her social time on dates was spent preoccupied on channeling spirits which made men surly at best. Where men were concerned, she'd learned long ago that spirits were a real ego buster. Whoever happened to be unlucky enough to be a part of her life would inevitably feel second best. It wasn't a fair assessment of her or her feelings, but she certainly understood it. In any case, she didn't need a high IQ to know any man that found himself involved with her suffered a huge disadvantage.

Jody felt a slight shift as the plane started its descent, a physical sign confirming the imminence of the impending meeting. The closer the reunion got, the more uncomfortable she became. So much rode on the gathering between mother, father, and child. She didn't doubt herself or her abilities in the least. No. The real problem in this situation, as she saw it, was the countless unknowns. Unfortunately, she had no real control over any of them.

What if she couldn't get the Hinton's to listen to her? It had only been about a month since Fiona had died. That was such a short period of time, and it put her at a real disadvantage. Many people just weren't ready to hear from the dead so soon after their passing. Would Fiona be stuck in some kind of limbo if she couldn't get her mother and father to listen to her message? Would the little girl ever be able to move on and find peace? The stakes were high for both her and Fiona. If it didn't go well, she had no clue what would happen to either of them. Knowing Fiona wouldn't just disappear and go away quietly was the only absolute certainty in this whole situation.

Out of the blue, Jody lurched forward as nervous jitters punched her in the solar plexus. The blow to her midsection left her squirming. As the anxiety level rose, her breathing became erratic, leaving her gasping for air, a sure sign a colossal panic attack was imminent. *Oh God! No! This can't be happening in front of Jared!* Trying her best to control the situation and relax only made the anxiety stronger. Just as little pinpricks of light filled her vision, the dizziness hit. Miraculously, before she could slip away, Jared's hand found hers and held on tight. Never saying a word, he shifted his weight and gently put his arm around her.

"I'm here for you. It's going to be all right. No matter what happens today, we'll see this through together."

Jody clung to him as he pulled her from the brink of a major mental come apart. She felt a magical tidal wave of warmth roll from his body and envelop her like a warm blanket made for snuggling. With each breath she took, his heat soothed and mended every single crack in her shattered armor. Clenching her eyes, she focused on the gift of strength he'd graciously offered for the second time that day. Once again, she'd found herself wondering what she'd done to be so lucky to get his help.

****

On the drive from the airport to the Dallas Ritz-Carlton, Jody worked to relax her neck by slowly rolling her head and then allowing it to fall back against the seat. Trying her best to remain grounded, she focused on her surroundings as she glanced out the window of the rental car. In a perfect parallel to her melancholy mood, the sky boiled with heavily laden, angry storm clouds which were so familiar to Texans living in tornado alley. Instead of feeling welcomed, she had to do her level best to buffer the ominous feelings the cityscape projected.

Her actions would soon shake Fiona's parents to their core. Jody had suffered through the loss of loved ones herself. That being said, nothing could prepare her for dealing with the kind of suffering these people had lived through over the last month. If they'd just give her a chance to speak for their daughter and listen to Fiona's message, she prayed it would help the healing process begin for them. Maybe they'd be able to live their lives with some peace of mind. They'd know their darling baby girl was still with them and above all else, okay. That information wouldn't bring her back to them, but it should help with their grief. Best case scenario, Fiona's messages would make living each day a little easier for them.

Jared had to fight the Dallas traffic which became increasingly tangled and slowed their progress to a snail's pace. Knowing she was in good hands, Jody tried her best to stave off impatience by allowing her mind to shut down until they reached their location.

****

Entering the lavish two-bedroom suite, Jody dropped her bag on the floor and moved to the couch as if on autopilot. She'd been trying to put on a strong front for him, but as she crossed the room, Jared couldn't help but worry. Seemingly unaware of her surroundings, she sat on the overstuffed couch, wringing her hands in her lap. He didn't know how she had the strength to go on. She appeared to be lost in some kind of altered state in which he couldn't understand but wanted to help her through more than anything he'd ever wanted before.

For Jody's safety he'd tried to keep a close eye on her without being overbearing about it. Her mind and body seemed unable to assimilate anything around her. That scared the holy bejesus out of him. Her inability to understand the lack of awareness of her surroundings as a problem only increased his apprehension regarding her safety. While she physically sat in front of him, only a part of her seemed to be there.

Thoughts of her fragility had Jared swiping his hands through his hair out of frustration. After they'd landed, she'd been so preoccupied he'd had to lead her around, gently guiding her in the right direction. He knew with a certainty she would've walked in circles for hours had he not been there—ending up lost or worse. Thinking of how helpless she was in this state, through no fault of her own, had him questioning the wisdom of what she'd called the Universe and its guiding forces.

The urgency of the moment had him moving toward her. Jared sat and reached for her hands, feeling gratified pleasure when she tightly held onto him. He tried to relay a sense of calmness instead of the dread which had overtaken him since they'd landed.

"Are you ready for me to make the call?"

Those beautiful green eyes peered up at him with such admiration his heart skipped a beat. Slowly Jody's grim expression softened a bit as she finally answered with a nod.

Jared filled his lungs with a deep breath to calm his nerves, pulled his phone out and dialed the number he had for Mr. and Mrs. Hinton. The pressure was all on him now. He felt his hand shake uncharacteristically as the importance of this one phone call hit him. He silently prayed he didn't screw it up. He put the phone on speaker mode and steadied himself as it started ringing.

One ring. Two rings. Three...

"Hello?" The woman's voice seemed weak, almost a whisper.

"Mrs. Sarah Hinton?"

"Yes."

"Hello. My name is J.D. Bastion. I'm a private investigator from the Phoenix area. Your name and your husband's name have come up in a matter I'm investigating. I'd like to meet with you both to discuss a critical element of the case."

Jared started to sweat as both he and Jody listened to nothing but dead silence. He began to worry that Mrs. Hinton had hung up on him.

"Ma'am?"

"I don't understand what you're saying. What investigation?"

Hoping to get the woman whose daughter had been responsible for turning Jody's world upside down on board with his request, Jared poured on his professional persona. His only show of nerves had been when he'd started pacing as he spoke. He hoped the unease he felt didn't reveal itself through his intonation. As he talked, he made sure his voice commanded attention and offered compassion all at the same time. He tried to fulfill the personification of strength and authority people expect when dealing with a professional P.I.

"I'm sorry, Mrs. Hinton. I'm not at liberty to discuss the matter over the phone. I need to meet with you and Mr. Hinton as soon as possible concerning an important issue related to a case I'm working on."

Confusion laced her voice. "We live in Fort Worth, Texas. We can't go all the way to Phoenix to meet with you, especially since you won't tell me what this is regarding. My husband is a trucker and has a very busy schedule."

He facepalmed himself and shook his head at his stupidity. "I'm sorry, Mrs. Hinton. I didn't make myself clear. I'm at the Ritz-Carlton in Dallas. It's only about forty minutes away from you."

Mrs. Hinton's breathing became heavier as her voice edged with stress. "I don't understand what you're saying. Why would you come all the way from Phoenix to meet with my husband and me? What investigation? Why do you need to speak with us? What's this about?"

Trying to ease his building headache, he massaged his brow. This call had started to go horribly wrong. Jared felt Mrs. Hinton slipping away, and would never be able to live with himself if he were responsible for screwing this up for Jody and Fiona.

Jared and Jody's eyes made contact when they

heard a muffled conversation through the speaker. The next voice that spoke on the phone belonged to a very perturbed Mr. Dallas Hinton. "What the hell is this about? You've upset my wife. Who is this and what exactly do you want with us?"

"Mr. Hinton, as I told your wife, I'm a private investigator from Phoenix, Arizona. Your name and your wife's name have come up in an investigation. It's crucial I speak with you. I've set up a conference room here at the Ritz-Carlton in Dallas to meet with you both at your earliest convenience."

"Why would I—oh, wait a minute." The pause on the other end of the line seemed to go on forever but gave Jared hope.

"Does this have to do with Aunt Leona's death?"

Jared's surprise had him glancing at the screen of his phone in disbelief. He thanked his lucky stars for Aunt Leona. Somewhere in the back of his mind, he hoped he didn't go to hell for using her death as his way in with these people. "I'm not at liberty to discuss the details of this investigation over the phone. However, I *can* tell you the investigation does revolve around a family member's death."

Seemingly satisfied the secretive investigation had to do with his aunt's death and possibly an inheritance, Dallas Hinton acquiesced. "Okay. We'll meet with you. What time should we be there?"

Jared smiled and gave Jody a great big thumbs-up. "How about an hour?"

"Hold on a minute, please." Mr. Hinton had either muted the phone or covered it with his hand. "Thanks for waiting. I'll be there, but my wife isn't feeling well. She hasn't left the house since…" His words trailed off.

The unspoken conclusion to his sentence left no doubt what had kept her in the solitude and safety of her home.

"Mr. Hinton, I cannot discuss anything without your wife being present. It's imperative she come with you."

There was another muffled sound as if Dallas once again covered the mouthpiece. A moment later he responded. "All right. We'll both be there."

"Good. I'll be waiting. Just check in with the front desk, and the concierge will show you where to go. And please remember, I need to speak with *both* of you at the same time."

"All right. We'll both be there."

Chapter Sixteen

Jared marveled at Jody's ability to compose herself under such stressful circumstances. Up until this moment, she'd been a mental and physical mess. Somehow, along the way, the tables had turned, and *his* nerves were now on the brink of shattering. To keep himself from going stir-crazy, he paced the floor. Walking at a quick treadmill speed seemed to be the only way that kept the butterflies from swarming in his stomach.

As he completed his latest pass of the room, Jared glanced over at Jody's slight form as she sat seemingly unruffled at the conference room table. Like a beautiful statue, her hands were folded in front of her, and her eyes were peacefully shut as if she didn't have a care in the world.

When he realized her lips were moving slowly and purposely with inaudible dialog, his curiosity had him leaning toward her. Closing the distance between them, he heard her whispered words and felt oddly comforted when his name crossed her lips. She'd included him in what had been some sort of prayer for wisdom and protection, and it made him love her all the more. Her selflessness of thinking of him at a time like this overwhelmed him.

He watched what could only be described as a miraculous transformation came over her. No longer looking broken and on the verge of a collapse, somehow, she appeared completely revitalized as if she'd had a week's worth of sleep. Still seated at the conference room table, her sudden unflappable demeanor filled him with a sense of tranquility. Her prayers now completed, the only hint of movement around her were wisps of sun-streaked hair as they floated gently around her face on the air conditioned breeze. She took his breath away. He reached out to her with his senses and found nothing but serenity.

Absorbed in his observations, he jumped with a start when a light rap sounded on the conference room door. Jared sought out Jody's eyes and waited for a nod to signal her readiness. Having her consent, he took a deep breath and purposely rolled his shoulders to brace himself for what he'd find once the door opened.

Nothing could have prepared him for coming face to face with the two broken people that stood in front of him. He felt as though he'd been sucker punched. The burden of sorrow they carried on their backs spoke volumes. It wasn't necessary for the Hinton's to verbally express their anguish. Their grief surrounded them and moved with them as if it were a living, breathing entity, all the while sucking the life from them.

Sarah Hinton stood with her head down and a posture that all but yelled to everyone around her that she'd recently suffered a massive, personal beating. While a little stronger, Dallas Hinton's composure showed signs of being frayed beyond anything Jared could imagine.

He understood people grieved differently. He also knew most marriages couldn't withstand the test of the death of a child. It didn't matter how much two people loved each other before a loss that profound. Once guilt and blame started to surface in the back of their minds, it became too big and too difficult to surpass. If he had to guess, the two people in front of him were going to become another sad statistic making the loss of little Fiona even more heartbreaking.

It quickly became evident that the distance between the man and woman standing before him wasn't just a mere arm's length. A vast, deep, dark chasm filled with the murkiness of an immense personal tragedy separated the two. The space between them so mammoth and treacherous, he didn't believe it would be possible for them ever to find a bridge to cross and recapture what they'd once had.

Ready or not, the time had come to either bring a little peace to them or rip what was left of their hearts out. Feeling unsteady, Jared ushered them into the room. "Please have a seat and we'll get started."

Jared intentionally escorted them to the other side of the table. In the event they decided to bolt, they'd be further from the door making fleeing from the room more difficult. If warranted, he hoped the distance would provide enough time to stop them before they were able to gain their escape.

As the couple situated themselves, he noticed Jody's almost imperceptible nod. She'd given him his sign that little Fiona was indeed present and ready to go. *It's show time*. As he offered everyone water, his mind filled with the prayer he'd heard Jody offer earlier.

Never before being a party to something like this, he forced himself to remain calm and proceed as nonchalantly as possible. "Mr. and Mrs. Hinton, my name is J.D. Bastion. This—" his hand extended toward Jody—"is Ms. Jody Clarke. Thank you for coming." He paused long enough for Dallas Hinton to acknowledge him with a nod. "Ms. Clarke has some information for you so I'll turn the floor over to her." He nodded to Jody as he sat beside her.

Before the couple entered the room, Jody surrounded herself and Jared in a bubble of bright white light. Normally she didn't feel the need for this type of powerful intervention and only requested it through prayer when she felt serious trouble might arise while passing messages between the living and dead. In her experience, this spiritual tool seemed to have a calming effect on everyone involved in these types of situations. An added benefit was the potent protective light also afforded her a much needed energy boost, just as the spiritual cleansings she'd received in the past had. As long as the bubble around them held, they'd be protected from the intense emotions she knew encircled these people. This reunion would be impossible if she were forced to deal with all of the outside influences the Hinton's brought with them. Fiona had already proved to be more than she could handle. Relieved to find the protection was indeed in place and holding, she tried to relax.

The two people she'd been waiting to meet for what seemed like an eternity were finally sitting across the table from her. From the moment this meeting had become evident, the subject of how to broach the subject of Fiona with her parents had crossed her mind several times. If Jody made the mistake of hemming and hawing around too much, she knew they'd probably lose their patience quickly and leave. She'd decided the best course of action would be to blurt out her reason for being here right away. Rip the Band-Aid off all in one quick motion so to speak.

"Two nights ago, I was awakened in the middle of the night by a little girl crying. She said she needed to talk to her parents. She'd tried many times to get her mother's attention, but no matter what she did, her mother couldn't hear her. She expressed a great deal of fear for her mommy, and emphatically stated that she needed to deliver a critical message to her." Jody paused and watched the Hinton's reaction carefully.

As Dallas Hinton started to grasp what was being said, she felt his hostility lunge out from across the table and grab her by the throat. If the Hinton's couldn't be convinced soon that Fiona had been communicating with her, they'd leave. Everything she'd been through would've been for naught.

Not yet connecting Jody's words, Mrs. Hinton's head remained down, but Mr. Hinton's rage-filled gaze never left Jody's face. "She said her name was Fiona."

As expected, all hell broke loose. Sarah Hinton's head jerked up at the mention of her baby girl's name. Dallas Hinton stood so fast his chair toppled behind him. "How *dare* you!" he bellowed. Jared quickly rose and stood next to Jody. She knew he'd throw himself at Mr. Hinton if he made a move for her.

Turning crimson from anger, Dallas roughly grabbed Sarah's arm and jerked her up. "We're leaving."

Remaining calm, Jody looked at Jared and held her hand out. "May I have your phone. I'd like to show Mr. and Mrs. Hinton the pictures you took."

"I'm not looking at anything, lady. If you know what's good for you, you'll stay out of my way and never contact us again. I don't know what you hoped to gain by this, but it's cruel. Can't you see my wife is suffering enough?"

She remained silent while Jared quickly opened his picture file on his phone. The moment he found the three photos he'd taken of Fiona, he handed it to Jody. Moving rapidly, she skirted around the table to get to Sarah. She tried to hand the phone off to her, but Mrs. Hinton was too distressed to take it.

"Look, Sarah. You can't leave until you see these photos. They were taken last night in Scottsdale, Arizona. It's Fiona—it's her spirit." Jody held the phone out and watched as the haggard woman glanced at the picture. Sarah Hinton's body reacted before her brain could chime in. She quickly took two steps back, reached for her throat and started gasping for air. Upon realizing the misty image caught on the camera was indeed that of her little Fiona, the woman began to hyperventilate.

Jody didn't miss the blind rage within Mr. Hinton. Jared apparently recognized the anger as well because he still stood defensively at her side. Knowing he'd protect her at any cost, she did her best to stay focused on Sarah.

Mr. Hinton violently made a grab for the phone to see what had upset his wife so profoundly. When he saw the pictures, he reacted with fury borne of loss and fear. Jody couldn't be clear if it was fear of the unknown or fear for his wife's sanity.

A tortured grimace twisted Dallas Hinton's face. He shot a dangerous look at Jody, which relayed in no uncertain terms he was capable of murder. If he'd had a gun, she'd be in his sights. Jody understood the blame he placed squarely at her feet for upsetting his wife. Clearly, he'd considered her interference as an outright disrespect for the grieving they'd been through. It was obvious to everyone present that his first and only consideration was for his wife and her welfare. Sarah had been on a journey through a very personal hell. Because of that, Dallas had to be concerned that her progress through the grieving process had probably just suffered a huge setback.

As everyone tried to figure out their next move, Dallas reared back and forcefully threw the phone at Jody. Sarah Hinton let out a blood-curdling scream as she clutched at the air with both fists. She'd tried, unsuccessfully, to catch the physical evidence of her daughter's after-death appearance as the phone flew past her just out of reach. Jody's arms shot out to protect her head. As the phone, going the speed of a missile, hit her wrist, she suffered a nasty stab of pain.

Jared was on him in a flash. He restrained Mr. Hinton's arms behind his back and whispered something in the man's ear. By the grim expression on Jared's face, she knew his words were harsh and had only been allowed to move past his lips to stop the violence.

Dallas fought off the hold and crept dangerously close to Jody. "What the fuck is this?" He demanded as Sarah Hinton continued to scramble under the table where the phone had come to rest. "What exactly is it you're trying to do here? How dare you do this to my wife and me! I demand an explanation now." Never flinching, Jody firmly stood her ground.

Still on the floor, Sarah reached up and clutched at her husband's arm. "It's her, Dallas. It's our little Fiona." She shook him to get him to look at her. "Look, dammit! It *is* her!"

As if beaten, he wearily glanced down at the phone his wife held out for him. His face magnified his pain. Dallas started to visibly shake and cursed as he twisted away from the evidence the photo held. He stumbled to the window and stared out at the dull Texas sky.

Sarah pleaded with Jody. "Fiona, my baby— please, tell me why she didn't come to me herself. Is she angry at me because I didn't get her to the hospital in time? Please," bridled with remorse, the woman begged, "I have to know the truth. Does she blame me?"

Jody's heart clenched as Sarah Hinton broke down in a heap on the floor. "Does my baby girl blame me for her death?" she wailed through convulsive tears.

Sarah's tormented plea for answers softened Jody's defenses and allowed her to forget the pain in her wrist to focus completely on the task at hand. Jared backed off, but kept Dallas in his field of vision just in case the grieving man couldn't restrain his violent anger.

Jody carefully approached Mrs. Hinton, collected her off the floor and eased her onto a chair. Sitting next to her, she attempted to hold Sarah's hands and offer whatever tranquility she could.

"Please, let me start from the beginning. I've had quite a bit of experience talking to loved ones who've passed over. But in all my years, I've never had an experience like Fiona before."

Tears streamed down Sarah's face, and a proud smile lit from beneath them. "That's my baby girl.

That's my Fiona. There's no one else in this world like her. She's special."

Jody purposely nodded her head in agreement. "Yes. She is very special. I want to start out by saying that Fiona has gone to extraordinary measures to get us together so she could talk to you and your husband. She's been so worried about you that she attached herself to me. It's her way of getting me to do everything I could to find out who you were, and give her the opportunity to talk to you."

Still in awe of Fiona's spunky determination, Jody couldn't help but laugh under her breath. "Do you remember the mail flying through the air in your kitchen?"

Dallas spun around, shock reflected on his tear-streaked face at what Jody had just said. His stance made it clear he hadn't believed Sarah when she'd told him about that incident. He'd probably written it off as exhaustion, or maybe just wishful thinking due to delirium from the pain of losing their baby girl.

Sarah's hand covered her gaping mouth. Recognition bloomed in her eyes as she realized that on top of everything else she'd been through, she hadn't been going crazy at all. "I knew that was her!" Reverence punctuated her whispered voice. "I heard voices at first. It sounded like my little Fiona speaking with someone."

Given the absurdity of the situation, Jody couldn't stop her laughter. "She was. She was talking to me. We were both there. I'm not exactly sure how she did it, but she ran through me. The best way I can describe it is that she kidnapped me, so she could take me to your home and find your address."

"I don't believe a word of this!" The words were spit at Jody from across the room. The statement, fueled with so much fury, left Jody cringing out of fear. Dallas moved to his wife and fiercely jerked her arm to get her up. "Come on, Sarah. We're getting the hell out of here."

Jody stood and reached out for his arm to stop him. Dallas swung his body to block her hold on him, almost knocking her down in the process.

"Mr. Hinton!" Jody directed all of her attention to him and realized his message would have to come first.

Up until this point, he'd been the strong one in the relationship, helping his wife navigate through the grief while leaving his own unattended. Their roles had suddenly been reversed. Judging by his actions, it wouldn't be long before Dallas Hinton lost his fight with his misery. He had now moved into the uncomfortable position of needing the support that he'd been so generous with over the last month. His unease and fear of letting go were apparent. He didn't seem like the type of man who gave into his emotions often, and that fact could make the rest of this reading tough to get through, if not impossible. She looked him straight in the eye and said as confidently as possible, "Sunny Girl would like to talk to you too."

Jody saw recognition flit across Mr. Hinton's eyes. His expression, once murderous, suddenly softened. His body gently swayed until he couldn't hold himself upright any longer and collapsed at Jody's feet. She knew his daughter's pet name would shake him and figured that's why Fiona had insisted she use it.

Worried this may turn into a medical emergency, everyone rushed to the grieving man's side. Dallas couldn't breathe. Jody took him by the hands to offer whatever meager strength she had left.

"Fiona insists I call her Sunny when I'm speaking to you about her."

Dallas went dead still and locked eyes with her looking for any hint of deception. Jody willingly opened herself up to him and allowed him to see into her soul. His shock was apparent as he realized there wasn't anything devious within Jody. His beloved daughter's simple determination shone back at him through her gaze.

"Sunny wants you to know she has Rocko with her."

Tears flowed freely down his face. His grief, unable to stay buried a moment longer, had him crying out in pure agony. Sarah lovingly wrapped her arms around her husband's shoulders.

"Sh-h-h, baby," she cooed. "The time for crying is over. Fiona worked very hard to make this family gathering possible. We need to be clear-headed enough to listen to her." With a show of strength that belied her, Sarah maneuvered Dallas to the table and sat him in the chair next to hers. Pulling a tissue from her purse, she gently wiped his face, caring for him now as she hadn't been able to do over the last month.

Jody waited to continue with Fiona's message until the couple had settled themselves. The weariness Dallas displayed worried her. At least she'd been able to put his concerns about Fiona's appearance and communication with her to rest. They could finally progress with the business at hand.

"How did you know I called her Sunny? I'm the only one who ever called her that. I only did it at bedtime. And Rocko—you couldn't possibly have known about him."

"She told me just now. She wants you to know that she has Rocko with her. You don't need to worry about him anymore. She said she'd take real good care of him for you."

His sad smile removed any tension she'd previously seen on his face. "Rocko was my dog. He died about a year before Sunny…" he struggled with the words. He stole a moment to peer at his and his wife's joined hands before speaking again. "Before Sunny left us."

Jody's gaze was locked on a spot beyond Dallas. The expression that crossed her face could only be described as distasteful. She squinted and asked under her breath, "What the hell *is* that thing?"

She had the Hinton's full attention.

Fiona giggled. *"That's Rock'em, Sock'em, Rocko, my dad's dog. The best dog EVER!"*

Jody tried to cut her giggle off by covering her mouth with her hand. She'd failed. She locked her gaze on Dallas and said with a skeptical shake of her head, "She's bringing forward a dog that she's calling Rock'em, Sock'em, Rocko." She paused, her head still slightly rocking in disbelief. "I'm sorry, but I've groomed thousands of dogs, and I've never seen anything like this one. Rocko has got to be the…" Jody stopped just short of relaying her first reaction to the extremely ugly dog. She cleared her throat, stalling for time to come up with a nicer description for the beast. "Rocko is the most unfortunate looking creature I've ever seen."

Dallas and Sarah's foreheads came together with a

loving touch. Both giggled through their tears at the memory of the hideously ugly dog. "Yeah, he wasn't a pretty mutt, but what he didn't have in the looks department, he made up for with love. He'd follow Sunny Girl around from sun up to sun down." Looking deeply into his wife's eyes, they both smiled at the memory. "Do you remember, Sarah?"

She squeezed him close to her in a tight embrace. "Yes, baby. I remember. They truly loved each other."

The room went quiet. All eyes were on Jody again when everyone realized she was listening to something. Her demeanor changed. Her gaze shifted back to Dallas so he'd recognize the importance of what she was about to tell him.

"Fiona…" Jody jumped, surprising everyone at the table. "I'm sorry. I didn't mean to startle you. She still wants me to refer to her as Sunny when I'm speaking with you, Dallas. She's very insistent about that," Jody stated as she rubbed her side where Fiona had poked her. "She said she never told you, but she loved it when you called her Sunny and your little Sunny Girl. It was something special between the two of you. She cherishes it and carries the memory with her.

"Mr. Hinton, Sunny wants you to know she's not upset that you weren't there when she died. She knows you carry a deep guilt about that. She wants you to know she wouldn't have been able to leave if you'd have been there. That's why she left just minutes before you could get to her.

"She says to tell you she wants you to remember back when Rocko died. It made you sad, and you cried. She wouldn't have been able to go if you were there because she saw how sad you were when Rocko left. It was *her* decision to leave when she did so you wouldn't have to see her pass. She doesn't want you to feel guilty about it."

There wasn't anything more sorrowful than seeing a full-grown man sob from a broken heart. With each tear he shed, the guilt he'd been carrying around for being absent at the time of her death, the guilt that had weighed him down for so long now, was being lifted from his shoulders.

"It was a very special gift of love just for you, Mr. Hinton. She wants you to know that and understand it wasn't your fault."

Jody focused on the space next to Dallas and nodded. "She wants you to know that when you go out to the pond and talk to her..." Fiona's abrupt interruption made it difficult to keep a straight face. "Okay. Okay. She wants me to remind you the pond is where the two of you caught that *ginormous* catfish." Jody spread her hands wide just like Fiona had shown her, resulting in an outburst of laughter from everyone in the room. "When you go there and talk to her, she's with you and hears every word you say. She told me you're the best dad ever, and she loves you with all her heart."

Jody turned to Sarah and leaned in. *Now for the most difficult message.* "Fiona wants you to know it's not the right time for you to come and be with her yet. You need to stay with her daddy." The room went silent as the realization of her words dawned on the participants. Sarah gasped when her innermost secret wish for death had been revealed.

Shocked by this latest revelation, Dallas wrapped his arms around his wife and held on for dear life. He spoke to her through his sobs. "I can't lose you too, baby. You can't leave me."

Jody now understood why Fiona had become more frantic as time went by, never giving her a moment of peace.

"That first night Fiona and I met, she took me to her deathbed. I saw the two of you cuddled together. You were begging her not to go. You talked to her about how much you loved her and needed her to stay. She heard every word, but it was her time. It wouldn't have mattered when you got her to the hospital. She wouldn't have survived. She was being called home.

"She wants you to know she wouldn't have given her life up with the two of you for anything, even if it meant staying until she was old. The two of you always made her feel loved, and wanted, and safe."

Shocked by what she'd just learned from Fiona, Jody's eyebrows rose. She looked into Sarah's eyes and smiled. "You're pregnant." It was a statement, not a question.

Sarah vehemently shook her head. "No."

Jody nodded affirmatively. "Fiona says you are. She just told me you need to take care of yourself and eat good food like strawberries and apples. If it were up to her, you should probably stay away from broccoli." Jody laughed at the absurdity of the message and held her right hand up in the air. "I swear, I couldn't make this shit up if I wanted to."

Sarah threw her head back and laughed for the first time since Fiona had died. "My little Fiona hated broccoli. She would moan and groan to try to get out of eating it."

Jody snickered. "Well apparently, she's looking

out for her little brother. She's holding his soul for you until it's time for him to come. She's been telling her baby brother all about you two and how much fun he's going to have."

Jody's attention was once again distracted. The people in the room patiently waited for her to receive the coveted information from their baby girl. "Fiona promised her little brother that you would give him Thumper Bumper. She's told him all about the stuffed, green bunny. She says he's expecting to see it right away, so don't forget it when the time comes.

"She also says he's going to look just like her daddy. His hair is light brown and curly."

Jody leaned in to add her two cents. "If I were you, I'd go to the doctor. She seems pretty certain about this pregnancy."

Jody started to see hope for the future, as well as healing of the past in the faces of Fiona's parents. Their demeanor had changed dramatically. Fiona had lightened their heavy load. They'd been holding on to each other since almost the beginning of Fiona's messages. Their sweet, little Sunny Girl had given them the gift of bringing them together again. She'd given them what they each needed to move on and look forward to in the future. The Hinton's were going to make it. Jody was sure of that.

"Fiona's showing me something, but I'm not quite sure what it is. It's a small piece of black fabric. It has what looks like a silver helmet at the top, with green and gold leaves flowing from it. In the center is a white shield with a picture of what looks like a deer." Unclear about what she was seeing, Jody shrugged her shoulders. "I have no idea what this is, but she's waving it in the air like a flag and wants you to know she has it."

Sarah's voice cracked. "I put it in her coffin before it was sealed. It's the McCarthy coat of arms. I told her to find our people, and they'd keep her safe."

Jody's smile brightened the room. "She's with them! Before we found you, Fiona wouldn't give me any peace. She didn't understand the rules of engagement between the living and the dead. A woman appeared and told her to go with her. She told her they'd make cookies and have a little chat about bothering the living." Jody laughed at the memory.

"Fiona identified the woman as her grandmother. I'm surprised she didn't come through today, but it feels as if everyone has taken a step back to let Fiona have her say."

Jody studied the couple sitting across from her. She was thrilled for them. Fiona's visit had given them a new chance at life. They were smiling and laughing through their tears and holding each other's hands.

The weight of this meeting had started taking its toll on her, though. She'd have to end this soon. "I have something for you." She picked a package up off the floor and set it on the table before them.

"I know Fiona touched many lives when she was alive, and that hasn't stopped in death. This is a gift from one of those people, a friend of mine who's an artist."

Sarah opened the box to find a beautiful portrait of Fiona drawn in charcoal. Terry, who'd never met her in life but had fallen in love with the spunky little girl in death, had sketched her.

Overcome with emotion and knowing time had

now grown short, Jody clutched at her heart as her eyes filled with tears of joy for this family. "I'll never forget little Fiona. I'll think of her always." She stood and slowly drifted over to Sarah with her arms outstretched. "Thank you for meeting with us, and thank you for letting me pass her messages on to you."

She whispered in Sarah's ear. "Please go to the doctor. You *are* pregnant."

Jody stood by silently as Jared closed the door behind Sarah and Dallas. When he turned back to her, her forlorn expression as she looked across the room told him everything he needed to know. Her tears flowed freely down her face as she held her hand up in a silent farewell to Fiona.

"Do you think you'll ever see her again?"

Weary from Fiona's journey, she absently shook head. "No."

He crossed the room and drew her into his arms, needing the embrace as much as she did.

Chapter Seventeen

Even though the reunion with Sarah and Dallas had been a resounding success, extreme exhaustion left Jody completely disabled. Her mind wanted to shut down and reboot. Her body found the simplest motor skills almost too difficult to execute. All of her concentration focused on putting one foot in front of the other, each step taken without falling a small victory. If her rubbery legs cooperated long enough, she'd eventually make it back to her room. Thankfully, before they'd gotten too far, Jared noticed her struggling and put his arm around her waist for added support.

By the time they made their way to the elevators, her body felt as though she'd run a marathon. Once inside, Jared steadied her against the railing and punched the button.

While not a small elevator by any means, the space inside felt as if it were closing in on her. When Jared turned to Jody, the intensity of his worry rolled off of him in waves and felt as though she'd been smacked across the face. He'd been such a huge help to her. She wanted desperately to alleviate his concerns, but in this weakened state, she just didn't have the resources to even try. Every ounce of energy had been used to allow Fiona to speak with her family. At this point, the only thing that would make her better was food and rest.

As if he'd read her mind, Jared stated in a manner

there'd be no argument, "I ordered a meal. It should be in our room by the time we get there. I want you to eat and then go straight to bed."

She opened her mouth, but before she could offer her gratitude, he held his hand up. "This is non-negotiable. Your energy is completely depleted. You can hardly walk. I insist."

In response, she managed a feeble nod. She would've offered Jared a smile but no matter how hard she tried, she couldn't seem to make the muscles in her face work. She felt like a stumbling zombie. Hell, she probably looked like one too.

The elevator doors opened, and before Jody could budge, he bent down and picked her up. His satisfied murmur let her know it pleased him she didn't argue about the offered help. When she laid her head on his shoulder and allowed him complete control of her care, his cheek nuzzled the crown of her head. "It's going to be okay now. I've got you."

Once inside the suite, Jared placed Jody in a chair at the table where the meal he'd ordered had been set up. He removed the cloche in front of her to reveal a beautiful gourmet fare. The meal looked and smelled divine, but she'd passed the point of being able to savor it hours ago. Each bite she managed to take served to fuel her body. Beyond that, her state of fatigue made it impossible to enjoy.

They ate in complete but comfortable silence. When he noticed she hadn't taken a bite in quite some time and only stared at her plate, he slid her chair out, picked her up, and carried her to the master bedroom. Attentive to her every need, he sat her on the bed, strode to the closet, and picked out a plush hotel robe for her.

Jared pointed to the door behind him. "That's the master bath if you need it." Jody nestled the luxurious bathrobe in her lap, absently rubbing the soft material. "Don't worry about taking the time to find something to wear in your bag. Just slip into the robe. You'll be comfortable and warm in it."

Somewhere in the back of her mind, the extent to which Jared fussed over her clicked. Jody had no choice but to allow him to make the decisions about what she ate, what room to sleep in, and what she'd wear. Up until this point in her life, outside of her mother, Nathan and Terry were the only people who'd ever treated her so sweetly and so lovingly. Certainly, no other man had lavished her with such attention.

Now that she had food in her belly, the heaviness of exhaustion started to overtake her quickly. Clutching the robe, she responded to Jared's gentle instruction with a nod of understanding. He left the room, leaving the door slightly ajar behind him. She knew he had done that to give her some privacy, but he'd still be able to hear her if she needed him.

****

To ensure he didn't disturb her sleep, Jared waited until the lights had been turned out and a full thirty minutes had passed before pulling his phone out and calling Nathan. He'd had several text messages and voice mails from both him and Terry, all concerning Jody and how she'd held up during and after the reunion. He didn't particularly want to make the call, but as close as they seemed to be, he knew her two friends would be worried sick about her until they heard something.

Nathan picked up on the first ring. "J.D., how'd it go?" his voice strained with anxiety for his friend.

Trying to ease his tension, Jared closed his eyes and pinched the bridge of his nose. "It was the most incredible thing I've ever witnessed in my life." He hoped the admiration in his voice spoke volumes.

Nathan's sigh expressed his experience in the matter. "Jody and her gift have that effect on people."

Jared couldn't help but smile. "Yes, apparently they do. I was just calling to tell you she's sleeping, and she's okay. Little Fiona has moved on and shouldn't bother her again."

"Good. Tell Jody I've called her work and told the staff she'd be out for about a week. I told them there was an emergency she had to deal with out of town. They're taking care of everything, so she's not to worry about getting back."

"I'll make sure to tell her. She's so exhausted that she may sleep for a week."

The intensity of the long pause on the line had Jared squirming. He knew beyond a shadow of a doubt Nathan didn't believe he was good enough for Jody. He'd prove him wrong, but it would take time. Right this minute, there wasn't a single thing that could be said to sway Nathan to his corner. Learning early on that words were meaningless, he'd have to *show* Nathan he was a changed man. Jody had done that for him. She brought out a softer, more caring side to him he wasn't even aware had existed—a side Nathan had certainly never seen before.

Looking at the situation objectively, he understood the apprehension Nathan felt on behalf of his good friend. On paper, Jared and Jody were worlds apart, two independent personalities which should never work well together. But in his heart, Jared knew they would mesh. He'd do whatever necessary to make her happy and safe. However, right this minute, there wouldn't be any way to persuade Nathan his feelings for Jody were heartfelt, so he didn't even try.

"J.D., about Jody…"

Jared interrupted by quickly speaking over Nathan. "I know we need to talk, but after the exhausting day we've had, I just can't have this discussion right now. I'll talk to you when we get home." He hit the end button to avoid the inevitable confrontation regarding his feelings.

Not knowing what to do with himself as the evening progressed, Jared sat in the living room of the suite and pondered what he'd witnessed today. Knowing he'd had a small role in the Hinton family healing had him feeling overcome with joy.

What Jody did with her abilities and how she used them was beyond his comprehension. He'd watched her closely enough to know her gift was one of those anomalies in life which would remain a mystery forever.

To his surprise, what had impressed him the most today had been her courage in facing off with Dallas Hinton. Clearly twice her size and out of his mind with grief, the man could've easily gone into a rage and killed her. Jared shuddered at the thought of what might've happened had he not been there. As it was, Jody hadn't left the meeting with the Hinton's totally unscathed. The guilt twisted in his gut when he thought of how her wrist had been badly bruised when Dallas threw the phone at her. He couldn't help but wonder how often spirit messages put Jody in dangerous situations like the one he'd witnessed today.

Working as a private investigator, Jared had seen firsthand how emotionally distraught people reacted so easily with violence. The destructive, aggressive behavior would usually occur during a confrontation which would end his client's marriage or their life as they knew it. All because the person he'd investigated had made poor choices and been caught in the act of violating the trust of someone else.

He knew full well the comparison between his apples and Jody's oranges was a stretch, but for the moment, it was all he had. With his limited *personal* experience in this area and absolutely no spiritual experience, he had to fall back on what he knew. It all came down to fear. Fear always presented itself as anger.

He felt a sense of pride for Jody because even when physically attacked, she never once considered giving up. She had information she knew would help Dallas and Sarah Hinton. No matter what the consequences to herself, she'd been determined to deliver those messages so they'd be able to heal and little Fiona could finally rest. Never once had she considered disengaging as an option, making her, by far, the fiercest person, male or female, he'd ever come across. Knowing she'd surely deny that quality had him smiling. She amazed him. He wanted her more than he'd ever wanted anything and certainly anyone else ever before.

As the day's events rolled through Jared's mind, a sudden unexpected movement in his peripheral vision caught his attention. Believing Jody had woken up and wanted something had him sitting up and at the ready to get whatever she needed. Peering at the door across the room and seeing no sign of her left him baffled. The bedroom door remained only cracked as he'd originally left it. *That's weird. I could've sworn she was standing right outside of the bedroom door.* With some confusion, he continued to watch the slightly open door expecting her to come through it at any moment. Instead, as he waited for her, he saw a light go on in the bedroom. Since she was awake, he took that as his cue to check on her.

He gently knocked on the door. "You okay in there?"

No response.

Curious, Jared opened the door and peeked in to find Jody curled up fast asleep in the big, soft robe. She hadn't even made it under the covers. Moving his attention to the bathroom door, he found the source of light he'd seen go on from the other room. He was positive he'd seen it go off earlier while sitting in the lounge area of the suite.

Being careful not to wake her, he slipped stealthily across the bedroom and peered into the spacious bathroom. Nothing seemed to be amiss which left him scratching his head in bewilderment. *Maybe she's a sleepwalker.* That didn't feel right to him, though. She'd been so exhausted she barely had enough strength to stumble to the elevator. *I must be losing my mind. The light was probably already on, and I just didn't notice it.*

Filled with an indefinable stirring of discomfort, he reached out and flipped the bathroom light off. He'd never been susceptible to seeing things before, but he wrote it off to his lack of sleep. Jared quickly accepted the fact that he'd obviously been more fatigued than he originally thought, which made him feel a little more comfortable.

As Jared turned away from the bathroom, a cool breeze brushed across his face. The cold air blowing through the room had him trembling and cursing himself for forgetting to check the thermostat. When he realized it registered at what should be a comfortable seventy-eight degrees, he vigorously wiped his dried out eyes to make sure he wasn't seeing things. Even more peculiar, he couldn't explain where the cold air was coming from since the air conditioner didn't appear to be running.

His first concern being for Jody's comfort, Jared moved silently to the bed and tucked the comforter around her to keep her from getting chilled. Turning to leave the room, the sound of her slurred voice stopped him dead in his tracks. Afraid he'd woken her, he held his breath as she continued to mumble. Leaning down, he realized she was still in a deep slumber. Her forehead creased, and her features, which should be soft with sleep, were instead filled with tension.

His heart went out to her. Even in rest, she got no peace. He bent down and moved her hair from her face. "Sh-h-h, baby. Everything's okay. No need to worry yourself. Just get some sleep." Pleasure filled him as her face softened with the sound of his voice.

Jared had never before experienced taking care of someone like this. He gently kissed her forehead and whispered, "You're changing my life, Jody. You're opening doors which were sealed tightly shut, and I'm grateful for it."

She looked so peaceful lying there as he gently encouraged a dreamless sleep. He stood and ran his hands up and down his crossed arms trying to warm the chill. "Damn, it's cold in here."

He started to leave but then worried he wouldn't be able to hear her if she needed him. *What if she wakes up in the middle of the night and is confused because she's not at home?* Fear she may come to some harm while he slept settled his internal debate. He grabbed an extra blanket out of the closet and walked back to the bed. Fully clothed, he climbed on top of the covers. Wrapping his arms around her to keep her warm, Jared finally closed his eyes, willing the much-needed sleep to come quickly.

As a peaceful slumber started to overtake him, the darkness beyond his eyelids suddenly filled with light. Heavily seduced by sleep, he grunted and forced his eyes to open. As he laid there just this side of sleep, he found himself looking through a mist which seemed to be flowing back and forth on a current of air. Unable to comprehend the anomaly in front of him, Jared continued to watch without fear as if it were a dream. The dense mist moved, revealing the bathroom door.

Slowly coming out of his sleepy stupor, he realized the light in the bathroom had been turned on again. He looked at his arm across Jody and knew she hadn't moved a muscle.

"What the hell?" his words no more than a mere whisper. Feeling a bit unsteady, he gently rose on an elbow while trying not to disturb Jody. His peripheral vision caught movement in the room. He reared back as he watched a woman appear out of the mist. She approached the bed and looked down at his peacefully sleeping Jody. There was a dream-like quality to her which Jared's fuzzy mind refused to allow him to comprehend.

Quickly tightening his grasp on Jody, he encircled her with his body to protect her from whomever or whatever this was. A shudder having nothing to do with the cold passed through him. The woman standing only a foot away wasn't a living, breathing person. She was a fully-formed spirit. Just like the pictures he'd captured of little Fiona, he could see right through her. It surprised him how quickly his usually hyper-rational mind had suddenly adjusted to a more open, illogical scenario and accepted it wholeheartedly. Maybe the fact he was scared shitless had something to do with the ease of acceptance.

"Who..." Jared's mind went blank leaving him unable to finish the thought. Not trusting what his eyes plainly saw standing in front of him, he covered his face with his hands. *I'm dreaming. Of course, I'm dreaming!* He'd spent so many hours focused on little Fiona that his resting brain would need to sort it all out through dreams. After all, this was the first chance he'd had to sleep since he'd met Jody.

When he found the courage to open his eyes again, he felt as though his body had been immobilized. The spirit woman stood beside the bed gazing at Jody. His lack of experience with the supernatural realm had his mind reeling with questions. Was this a *good* ghost? A *bad* ghost? How the hell do you tell? He'd have to make a point to talk to Jody about it. While he'd become somewhat comfortable with the idea of spirits like Fiona, he wasn't ready to *see* them. He wanted to run as far and as fast as his feet would take him, but couldn't leave Jody behind.

Not sure what to do, but ready to spring into action at the first sign of danger, he watched as the full-bodied apparition bent down and kissed Jody's forehead. This loving gesture had him relaxing. After all, would a malevolent spirit be capable of such a tender act? No. At least he didn't think so. This spirit seemed to be expressing love for Jody. He had no clue what connection the two women held, but he could feel it, effectively nullifying any remaining fear he had toward the uninvited guest.

Now that he'd been able to put his emotion aside, Jared's highly developed power of observation kicked in. Unlike the pictures of little Fiona, this woman was a ghostly pure white. Her clothes, devoid of the vibrant pinks and blues Fiona sported, were various shades of gray. He could see through her, but most important, he felt no threat of danger from her. *Thank goodness for small favors.*

"Who are you?"

The woman's attention moved to him. They stared at each other for several seconds when a smile blossomed on her ethereal face. *"The dark scares her. She needs the light on."* He heard every word she said but never saw her mouth move.

"Why is it that I can see you? I've never seen a ghost before. Why now?"

The specter's head tilted as she considered his words. *"You've opened your heart. Do not worry. You're seeing me because I'm allowing you to. Jody trusts you. Therefore I trust you."*

Surprised he'd received and understood the answers coming from someone who clearly no longer lived, left him unable to speak further. He acknowledged the ghost with a feeble nod. Seemingly placated by his acceptance of her message, the woman slowly disappeared in front of his eyes.

As his grip tightened on Jody, he felt the fast paced beating of his heart as it sped to what seemed like at least a thousand miles a minute. He couldn't help but speculate at the great personal fortitude the woman he held in his arms had to possess. The thought of enduring years of these visits without going stark, raving mad left him marveling at her inner strength.

He laid his head back down on the pillow, finding it difficult to relax enough to close his eyes. "Holy fucking shit."

Chapter Eighteen

The pilot's voice broke the silence shortly after takeoff from DFW. "Mr. Bastion, you and your guest may now unfasten your seatbelts. The weather is clear all the way home. We should be arriving at Phoenix Sky Harbor by o nine hundred. As requested, the attendant will be serving your meal in the lounge area of the plane."

Jody giggled. "I don't know how anyone could possibly get used to this kind of treatment, *Mr. Bastion.*"

Jared's eyebrows rose with delight. The smirk on his face revealed his mischievous side. "If you've got it, flaunt it." She liked this playful side to him and knew he wasn't the type of man that showed it often. He stood and held his hand out to her. "Let's go and get comfortable. I've asked the attendants to serve a champagne breakfast to celebrate your definitive success with the Hintons."

They strolled to the lounge area and got comfortable on a plush leather sofa. As Jody sat, she pivoted to face Jared and put her leg under her. In doing so, they faced each other and could talk in a more casual, personal manner.

"I don't know how to thank you for everything you did to make it possible for Fiona to speak to her parents. If it weren't for you, I never would have found them."

He grimaced before looking away from her. "I have to be honest with you. I've been paid handsomely for helping you."

She thought back to the brief discussion of his fees the first night they'd met at the gallery and remembered Terry had paid them with a canvas. After a few uncomfortable moments of silence, she cringed and asked, "What canvas did you and Terry agree to?"

"*Solitude*."

"Really?"

Sheepishly, he nodded. "He wouldn't sell it to me. I offered him a lot of money for it, but no matter what number I offered, he refused to sell. I'd like to tell you I feel bad about taking it, but I don't." Her laughter at his confession brightened the air around him and had him visibly relaxing.

"Remind me to thank him when we get home. You were invaluable to Fiona and me. No matter what the cost, having your help was worth every penny. I'll make sure he knows that."

Jared reached out and took her hand, gently playing with her fingers. The wheels in her mind spun as she tried to figure out why such a small gesture seemed to feel so much more substantial than it actually was. Each time physical contact occurred between them, no matter how slight, a kind of shared commingling of spirit seemed to take place. While the physical thrill of a new attraction was most certainly a part of what she felt, the experience went much deeper than that. His touch evoked an emotional response and had her stodgy mind-set lighting up as bright as a Christmas tree. She'd never felt a personal blending like that before with anyone.

The expression Jared's face sported as he intimately touched her hand fascinated her. By the way he fumbled with her fingers she could tell he wasn't comfortable with demonstrative gestures such as this. His clumsy attempt with personal contact was endearing. But no matter how awkward his actions were, her body delighted with the possibility of more affectionate contact with him. Would that be heightened as well? Almost instantaneously, a rush of adrenaline coursed through her landing smack dab in her southern regions.

Jody stiffened when she realized the train of thought her mind had suddenly taken and how quickly her body had responded. Shocked by how easily Jared evoked those sensual longings had her feeling the need to take extra steps to close her heart off.

The way Jared looked into her eyes made it clear he felt something for her, but the other men in her past had feelings for her too. In the end, that hadn't mattered. She'd always ended up hurt and alone. Seduction wasn't an option for her. A romantic relationship just wasn't compatible with her lifestyle. The best possible outcome for everyone concerned would be just to leave the friendship they'd been able to forge together as it was—a friendship. Anything more would be disastrous.

Exceptionally skilled at reading people, Jared knew she had an internal struggle going on in her head about him. The way she stiffened as he held her hand had been a dead giveaway. *Is there another man in her life?* He didn't think so, but that thought produced a highly uncomfortable jealous streak within him that he'd never encountered prior to meeting her. Then again, he'd never had so much at stake before. He didn't like the feel of that particular riotous emotion one bit, but he'd deal with it until she became his because she was worth it. He had no qualms about fighting dirty if she was the prize. He wouldn't allow anyone to come between them.

Currently lacking the emotional foundation needed for easing her mind about them as a couple, he had to approach this relationship business the only way he knew how. For the time being, he'd use the tools at his disposal to help her accept the forward progress of their relationship.

Being an analytical person had its perks in these situations. He ran through the different scenarios in his head until he figured out the most advantages path to take to get her to accept him as a lover and life partner. He would accept nothing less.

First, he needed to make her comfortable with the transition leading to a more personal one-on-one level between them. Second, she had to be put at ease with the prospect of them as an exclusive couple before anything more intimate could be gained. Jared was already so far beyond this phase of their relationship. Yet, he knew he'd have some difficulty slowing down to let her catch up. But he'd just have to keep his eye on the prize. She was more than worth the wait.

So far, for the most part, our relationship has consisted of three main people—her, me and little Fiona. Before they could move forward, it would be imperative to change that dynamic. She'd have to see their relationship in terms of just the two of them. No spirits.

Thinking back to the visitation of the night before,

he understood the dead would always be there, hovering, or whatever the hell they did to kill time. But he and Jody needed a strong foundation between the two of them as a starting point. Once that groundwork had been established, nothing would be able to come between them. She had to understand she could trust him with anything. In turn, he'd always be there for her in whatever capacity she needed.

"Can I ask you a question?"

"Of course." She tensed. Biting her lip was a dead giveaway her anxiety level had just elevated. *Interesting.* Jared knew she'd probably thought he'd be making a pass at her now. For his plan to work, he'd have to throw her off balance and put her more at ease by asking general questions. Once she became comfortable, he'd hit her with a more personal conversation.

"How did you start talking to ghosts?"

As he'd expected, she visibly relaxed with the unanticipated question. He could read her expressions like a book. They were screaming loud and clear that she struggled with her feelings for him. A tingle of excitement ran through him. *If she's struggling, that means there's interest.* As that realization came to fruition, he knew there was no way in hell he'd leave her an opening to back away from him.

Little tremors full of promised thrills ran through his body as her fingers softly stroked their joined hands. With her mind focused on his question, he knew she didn't realize she'd been gently caressing him. It delighted him that her gesture hadn't been contrived, but instead purely spontaneous and natural. The unexpected familiarity drove him crazy. He wanted more. The anticipation of their lips coming together had his pulse racing.

"When I was little, I saw them all the time. They never hurt me, but sometimes…" her voice trailed off as she remembered what must have been a living nightmare for her. "I guess you could say they scared the hell out of me." Jody laughed, but the tremble in her voice helped him understand how deeply she'd been affected by those memories. "I look back on it now, and I understand the spirits were just drawn to me somehow. They knew I could see them, and they wanted to talk, to tell their story." She shrugged. "I was just too scared to listen."

She piqued his curiosity. Jared imagined her as a little girl lying in bed, terrified of very real monsters. The mystery woman who showed up last night had appeared human enough to his adult eyes, but there was also a part of him that had seen a specter or ghoul-like quality to the ghost.

Being so very young when those visitations occurred had to have influenced Jody in an adverse way. He didn't believe for a minute that he'd have been able to endure that phenomenon in his childhood as well as she'd obviously coped with it. And yet, she'd been able to turn those frightening experiences around and make the best of them. Somehow she'd turned the nightmare into something beautiful. Once again his heart swelled with pride for her.

Genuinely interested, he had to know more. "How did you go from being so scared of ghosts to approaching people and passing messages along for them? That's a big leap to take."

Her face crinkled with disbelief. "Are you sure you

want to hear this?"

"Yes." Ensuring their joined hands remained so, he clutched her hand a little tighter. He made a production of getting comfortable while settling in for the story.

Her head tilted, and her eyes squinted slightly. She appeared to be sizing him up to determine how much of her story to tell.

"You're not going to laugh at me, are you?"

"I would never," he joked with a pretense of shock. He knew full well with Jody's change in demeanor she was about to disclose a significant life-changing event. Something had happened that changed the way she looked at the paranormal abilities that had plagued her young life. Anxious to hear her response and wanting to encourage her to continue, his hold on her hand tightened.

"Okay. You asked for it. I was about twelve when I watched a documentary on scientists who were observing monkeys in the wild. They were at the edge of a desert—a sand dune type climate—that had been cursed by many years of drought. It wasn't the typical kind of environment you'd think a chimpanzee would live in, but it was their home. The narrator mentioned over and over again how intelligent the monkeys were. Because of that, the scientists had to take extra precautions to lock up all of their food and water. If they didn't take the time to secure those essentials, the monkeys would be tempted to come into camp and steal whatever they could.

"The documentary was so interesting and chock-full of statistics that I couldn't wait to learn more about the inner social structure of chimpanzees. They loved and lived just like people do." The more she spoke, the more animated and excited she became about what she'd seen. The documentary obviously had an enormous impact on her, and he couldn't wait to hear the full story.

"The scientists talked about the familial organization and bonds within the chimpanzee lifestyle. All of the monkeys looked out for one another and appeared to have great affection for each other."

When Jared felt her grip on his hand tense, and Jody's face hardened into a grimace, he knew the story was about to take a turn for the worse. He just couldn't imagine how a documentary about chimpanzees, of all things, could've changed her life as it did. He couldn't wait to hear how this tied in with her.

"One morning, the researchers woke to find several of the female monkeys had given birth." She smiled, but the tears which had pooled in her eyes weren't happy tears. "The scientists had long range cameras, so they were able to get close-ups of those babies. They were hanging onto their mothers and nursing. It was beautiful." Her head shook from the wonderment of it, as her tears started to fall silently down the curve of her cheeks.

"Because of the drought, the females didn't have enough water to sustain their breast milk production. Once it got to that point, their supply dried up. As a result, the babies started to die one after the other until there were none left. I didn't understand why the researchers didn't give them water." She brushed the tears away only to have more fall in their place.

"The researchers said they were only observers. They weren't authorized to interfere with anything that happened, no matter how horrible. They weren't allowed to change what would've happened had they not been there. They said they had to collect complete, unaltered data. If doing so meant having to watch those babies die, then so be it."

As she relived that horrible scene, disgust for the scientists had her shaking from head to toe. "I was horrified. The momma monkeys carried their dead babies around with them for a month. They never let them go, even after the little ones had mummified."

Seeing the world through Jody's eyes had him taking a deep breath. If Jared had watched the documentary prior to meeting her, he probably wouldn't have thought twice about it. But being this close to her and *feeling* how it affected her, compelled him to open his heart. She'd forced him to comprehend the devastating message that people, even neutral scientists, could be a part of such an atrocity and have the ability to distance themselves from the ugliness. She humbled him.

She took a moment to gather herself. "All I could think about was the fact that they were there. They *could* have saved them, Jared." The pain of her words cinched around his heart. "They were blinded by what they were supposed to do and what was expected of them. They never once stopped to think that maybe the real reason they were there was to intervene. Perhaps, since they were there at that exact moment in time, they had been put there to save those babies. All they had to do was give them some water. That one small gesture would've made all the difference in the world. Those small, innocent creatures would have survived."

She sniffled and looked down at their joined hands. "It got me to thinking, maybe that's what the spirits around me wanted. They wanted me to intervene on their behalf—to pass their messages along to their loved ones. To help ease the pain and grief and start the healing process so their family members could continue on with their lives. Maybe when I show up at a random place at a random time, it's not so random after all. Perhaps, in reality, I'd been drawn there to help someone who needed help. How could I go on with my life knowing I could help someone heal and then choose not to?" She shrugged her shoulders as if what she did with her gift was no big deal. "So, that's how it began."

Moved by her revelation, he lifted her chin. Something within him had churned and rearranged how he looked at life. Jared wanted her to view for herself how deeply she'd moved him. He poured every ounce of compassion she'd made him feel into his gaze. He opened up his deepest, darkest places for her through nothing more than a glance.

Jared moved in slowly and kissed her tear streaked cheek. He pulled back just enough to look into her eyes as his lips gently brushed hers. He'd tested her to see if she'd push him away. *Please don't shy away from me. I need to touch you.* When she didn't back away, he moved in for a tender kiss. Her arms went around his neck, and he tucked her into his lap. A passionate sigh escaped her lips through the kiss, and he thought he'd go mad. Her tenderheartedness and sympathetic nature were the complete opposite of his. Those qualities within her made him melt inside.

The touch of her lips made him weak. The contented little murmurs she uttered as he kissed her filled him with power. As tender as the kiss was, it sent electricity shooting through him, making his body come alive.

He'd been hopelessly lost before he'd met her. With her in his arms, he felt as though anything and everything would be possible. For the first time in his life, the world around him made sense. His thoughts became clear and sharp.

As he broke the kiss, a sudden realization hit him like a ton of bricks. *I didn't want to go to the art show. I hated things like that and avoided them at all costs. I felt compelled to go as if something had drawn me there. Now I know just what that something was. Jody.*

She nuzzled his neck as he gently ran his fingers through her silken, golden locks. Jody took a breath as if she were going to say something but remained quiet. He didn't push her. He waited patiently for the words he'd expected to come.

"I can't get involved with you, Jared."

He squeezed her tighter, sharing his unwillingness to let her go. "I think we've moved past that, Jody." She tried to free herself from him, but he refused to break his hold.

"Tell me why this won't work," he demanded.

Rather than fight face to face, a resigned sigh escaped Jody, and she relaxed back into him. It would be easier to tell him if she didn't have to look into his eyes. If she did, he'd see how much he affected her, and she couldn't bear that.

"Jared, I was engaged a year ago. He broke it off because he said I made him feel like he didn't matter. Anytime we went out in public, a spirit would show up. I'd be distracted until I could get away and talk to the people the spirit needed to contact. It's a part of me. It's who I am. I think it would kill me if I stopped."

Jody waited for him to tell her that he understood, and he'd back away from her. In her heart, she knew he would. She just hoped they could remain friends. Even though she'd only known Jared a short period of time, it wouldn't be possible to give him up all together just yet.

"He was a fucking idiot."

His surprising response had her body jerking upright, leaving their faces so close they were almost kissing again. She looked deep into his eyes questioningly, trying to figure out if this was his idea of a joke.

"Was he ever involved in anything like you and I were with Fiona and the Hintons?"

After thinking about it for a moment, she shook her head in response. "No. He never got close to me when I channeled for people. He always distanced himself." She shrugged her shoulders to convey she hadn't expected any more than that from him. "I think my gift might have embarrassed him, or maybe it was just me that embarrassed him."

His sarcastic smirk had her doing a double take. "He was one stupid piece of shit. If he loved you, he would've seen you for who you were, not who he wanted you to be." He shrugged as if that was all that needed to be said and squeezed her possessively. "His loss. My gain."

Jared's cockiness had her giggling. Jody had to regain control of this situation. She gave him what she hoped would be her most compassionate expression. "Jared, I don't want to hurt you. You don't..."

He stopped her with his mouth. His lips caressed

hers with feather-light kisses. His teeth nipped at her playfully, leaving all of her coherent thought in the wind. "I'm not backing away from you, Jody." His confidence rang loud and clear through the kiss.

She wanted to believe him, wanted it badly, but being hurt in the past had her emotionally withdrawing from him. Finally able to gather her wits, she put her hand on his chest and pushed herself away before it was too late.

"Jared, we need to take this slow. You need to know what you're getting into with me. You have no idea. Everywhere we go, we'd never be alone. There'd be constant interruptions."

Just by looking at him, Jody could tell there wasn't a thing she could say which would allow her to stomp on the brakes. She'd never be able to stop the momentum of whatever this was that had been happening between them. The determination she saw in his stance was clear. He might slow down for her, but she sincerely doubted he'd give up the pursuit altogether.

"Let's make a deal. I'm willing to start out slow for you. We can date. We can get to know each other. I'll be there to see for myself what it's like being with you. Does that work for you?"

She was struck by a myriad of emotions—fear being the most identifiable.

"If it doesn't work, it doesn't work. I'm telling you that this feels right to me, Jody."

She melted when he gave her a beautiful smile full of promises. "I think you're my monkey." It took a moment for the seriousness of his statement to connect in her mind.

"What did you just say?"

"I felt *compelled* to go to that art show. I hate those things with a passion, but something told me I couldn't miss that one. I was being drawn to you. You're *my* monkey, Jody. I'm stepping outside of my box. I'm doing the unexpected. I want to give you water."

His expression conveyed such intense sincerity that it left her stunned. Her only reaction was to stare at him with her mouth gaping open. He'd softened the moment by showing her a glimmer of humor at his comparison, which after some thought had her laughing harder than she had in ages. He'd used her own life changing moment against her, and it was working.

When she recovered from the giggles, she tried to school her body language so it wouldn't scream how badly she wanted to kiss him again. Deep in thought and biting her lip, she walked to the other side of the lounge. She didn't want to get his hopes up, but, God help her, she couldn't let him go either.

"What are you afraid of, Jody?" He'd set all humor aside. She recognized the serious nature of his question in the timbre of his voice.

Unable to look him in the eye, her gaze moved down to her hands as she fidgeted with her fingers. She spoke in such a quiet tone, she knew he probably couldn't hear her. Suddenly, Jared stood in front of her, tenderly lifting her chin up. "What are you afraid of? You can tell me. You can trust me with anything."

Trying to gather the courage needed to open herself up to him, she took a deep breath and held it for a moment. Finally feeling as though she had the fortitude required to hold her ground, she looked deep into his eyes. Within those rich, dark black eyes she lost herself.

She just couldn't lie to him. If she were forthcoming about her misgivings, she'd decided he would surely back down.

"You could break my heart, Jared Bastion, and I don't think I could recover from that."

His eyes softened at her confession. "I'm asking you to trust me, Jody. If you can't do that yet, then trust your heart. What is it telling you?"

With their gazes still locked, she looked for any indication of his emotions. "We'll take it slow?"

A victorious smile crossed Jared's lips. His eyes conveyed the truth Jody was looking for. "We will take it one day at a time, and only move as fast or slow as you want."

Jody reached up and cradled his face in her hands. She pulled him down to her and accepted his offer with a tender kiss.

Chapter Nineteen

After Jared dropped her at home from the whirlwind trip to Dallas, Jody hardly had a moment to digest her all too brief time with him before Nathan arrived voicing his concerns. Weary from the one-sided bitchfest about Jared's vastly different personality, she ushered him to the door and kissed him goodbye. She loved him dearly, but sometimes a friend had to learn when to stop preaching and go with the flow.

Just when she thought he'd finally be on his way, the front door's momentum came to a stop as his hand shot out, putting a halt to closing the conversation. *There's nothing like beating a damned dead horse.* She did her best to restrain her frustrated exhale but couldn't quite keep it in.

"Please think about what I've said, Jody. You're more important to me than anyone, and I don't want you to get hurt. You know I love you, and it's not my intention to cause you any pain. But I need you to think—really think about everything I've said before you make any rash decisions about J.D. The man I know is incapable of love. If you let him into your life, it's not a matter of *if* he hurts you, but when he hurts you.

"For your sake, I can't back away from this. J.D.'s actions have left me no choice in the matter. As your best friend, it falls to me to set you straight about the man and his ways. J.D. *isn't* a long-term kind of person—hell, when it comes to relationships, he isn't even a short-term kind of person.

"It's common knowledge in the security industry that J.D.'s best attribute on the subject of interacting with others is that he doesn't discriminate. Sweetheart, it doesn't matter if you're a man or a woman. It may take him some time, but he'd do everything in his power to bring you to your knees. Where J.D. is concerned, people are dispensable. He throws them away as carelessly as he disposes of garbage. He won't even give it a moment's thought.

"J.D. has *never* been interested in anyone's company but his own. If he is interested, you can bet your ass there's an ulterior motive behind it. The man *never* goes out socially, not even with his office staff for a quick lunch. He's proven time and time again to be a secretive bastard at heart, the polar opposite of you."

She'd had enough. To her way of thinking, there was no one more secretive than herself when it came to those around her. Her angry expression spoke volumes.

"Don't give me that look. I know you have your secrets, but other than your gifts, you're an open book. I can assure you, there isn't a living soul who could give you five personal facts about J.D.

"Baby doll, he'll only end up hurting you. When that time comes, as your best friend, I'd be obliged to step up and give J.D. the ass-whuppin' he so richly deserves."

Jody knew Nathan's intentions came straight from his heart, but that fact didn't make them any easier to swallow. She loved him because he'd always been honest with her. He'd never do or say anything to deliberately hurt her. But she was a big girl, and he had to understand that she couldn't allow anyone, not even him, to make those kinds of decisions for her. Just as he wouldn't permit that type of interference if it were his life they'd been discussing.

To take the sting out of their conversation, Jody walked into Nathan's arms and squeezed him in a tight hug. "I love you, Nathan. I value your opinion, but you have to let me see this through in my own way. I'd like you to do something for me." Continuing to hold him, she patiently waited until she felt the nod of his head.

"I've listened carefully to everything you've said. The man you're talking about is J.D. Bastion. The man I know is Jared Bastion. Before you make any rash decisions, please get to know him as I do. Get to know Jared."

After a few moments of tense silence, Nathan kissed the top of her head and moved Jody far enough away to look into her eyes. "I'll respect your wishes as long as you promise me you'll come to me and talk to me about anything. No matter what happens I'm still your friend, and I'm here for you." He tugged her securely back into his body for another quick embrace before turning to leave.

****

After Nathan left, Jody couldn't sit still. The next several hours were spent keeping her mind occupied by puttering around her home doing laundry, ironing and watering plants. She should dust, but decided to put that particular dreaded chore off until next weekend.

Jody sat down heavily on the chair. Unable to think of anything other than her conversation with Nathan, she absently chewed her fingernail down to the quick. She loved and respected him, but couldn't help herself. Her mind kept circling back to Jared.

She stared at her phone as if it were taunting her. *Should I call him?* Reaching for the phone, she stopped herself in mid-motion. Settling back into the chair, she struggled with the internal war going on between her head and heart.

She couldn't dismiss Nathan's advice lightly because he did, after all, know Jared better than she did. Jody just preferred to trust her heart in this matter. Following that logic had gotten her in trouble before with men, but some kind of unexplainable momentum had been drawing her toward Jared at every turn. She felt compelled to give him a chance.

Jared had introduced a side of his personality to her which he'd obviously kept close to the vest with everyone else. That being said, she'd become acutely aware of his secretive side through their discussions. When the topic of conversation would turn to him, he would flawlessly manage to steer the dialogue in a different direction. As Jody thought back on it, he'd camouflaged the maneuver so well she'd never realized their conversation had been redirected.

She thought, perhaps, over a lifetime, he'd erected a hard, outer exterior to keep people at arm's length. If time was on her side, Jody felt certain she'd be able to break through whatever barrier Jared had erected, and hopefully get him to open up about himself. That thought brought a smile to her face. She could be a real pest that way.

Jody glanced at her phone again. *It wouldn't be weird if I called him, would it?* Musing over Jared, she absently picked at her cuticle which now came dangerously close to drawing blood. Was he missing her as much as she missed him? He'd only just dropped her off at home this morning. It hadn't even been a full day. *No, I'm not going to call.*

"I have to stop this." She stood and crossed the room to the closet, assuring herself she'd be able to put Jared somewhere in the back of her mind for a while. The door creaked as Jody flung it open to pull her vacuum cleaner out. Before plugging it in, she pivoted to glance at the phone which hadn't rang once in the hours since she'd been home. *I could call him. What would it hurt?*

Lost in the thoughts of hearing Jared's voice, Jody jumped when the doorbell rang. Expecting another round with Nathan had her spouting a curse. To keep her favorite, comfy house shoes from slipping off as she walked, she dragged her feet on the floor as she crossed the room. Ready to let her friend feel the brunt of her anger, she growled as she swung the door wide open only to be startled when a stuffed monkey holding a beautiful, long-stemmed rose greeted her. Peering upward, she saw the face of the man about whom she couldn't stop thinking. Her heart did a little happy dance.

Jody knew the broad smile that lit her face would be a sure sign she'd been thinking of him, but she didn't care. She wasn't one to play coy. For the first time in well over a year, a man she couldn't stop thinking about was standing on her doorstep, and that pleased her very much. She wouldn't run from this relationship. She couldn't. When all was said and done, there'd been one determining factor she just couldn't deny—Jared made her feel too good. She hoped her heart didn't get broken in the end, but she just couldn't think like that. For the here and now, her heart was too busy falling in love to care, and there wasn't a thing in the world that could be done about it.

"I was just thinking about you." Stepping toward him, Jody took the monkey and the rose. The meaning behind the stuffed toy hadn't been lost on her. He'd paid attention when she'd told him about the very personal moment that had transformed her life. Jared had found a parallel and related it back to them, making it their story now. Her heart melted at his thoughtfulness. Jody's smile continued to broaden as she moved in for what she really wanted—her lips on his.

Jared pulled her into his arms and kissed her forehead. "That's good," he said, bending down to taste her lips again. "I haven't been able to stop thinking about you at all." The tingles which always seemed to be present when he touched her had her smile brightening more by the minute.

Jody pulled away and reached for his hand. "Come in,

"Why don't you sit here at the kitchen counter while I find a vase to put the flower in?" As if he'd been starved for the sight of her, she could feel his eyes on her as she moved through the kitchen. Looking through cupboard after cupboard, disappointment set in when there wasn't a single vase to be found. Jody finally gave up the hunt and filled a drinking glass with water to put the flower in.

When she turned back and found his gaze still glued to her, the heat of embarrassment pricked her face. Jody could only guess at the impression Jared must've gotten when she didn't even have a simple vase in her home. *Loser.* She tried to shrug it off. "I must have gotten rid of all my vases."

Everyone who knew Jody seemed to think of her as a plant person. She'd always been the practical friend. People never took into consideration the fact that sometimes she just wanted a rose, or a daisy, or some other beautiful flower. Not even old boyfriends had seen her as the type of woman who longed for a fanciful posy now and again. In the short amount of time she'd known Jared, he'd already given her flowers on two different occasions. That thought squeezed her heart a little tighter and made her insides turn to jelly.

Every time she found herself this close to Jared, something about him compelled her to walk into his arms and stay there in a perpetual embrace. She chuckled under her breath. *Yeah, right.* If she were completely honest with herself, what she'd really wanted was to put her hands all over him and hear him beg for more. *Slow down!*

Since the decision had been made to allow the relationship to advance, she couldn't trust herself to keep her distance, or more importantly, her hands off of Jared. Knowing this, Jody moved to the counter and stood on the kitchen side. In doing so, she placed a cold, hard barrier between them.

"I was wondering, are you busy tonight?"

His grin was full of the devil. "I am now."

"Do you like baseball?"

"Who *doesn't* like baseball?"

Consoling herself with just a small touch, Jody reached for Jared's hands and started playing with his fingers as he'd often done with her. "Nathan's having a big get-together over at his house tonight. He's going to barbecue and turn on the game. I was wondering if maybe you'd like to go with me?"

Anticipation had her holding her breath as he moved purposely around the counter, never losing eye contact with her. Jody could tell by the gleam in Jared's eye that her need for his touch would soon be satisfied. *Oh, Lord.* He rested his hands on her hips and pulled her to him.

"Well, I don't know." His voice was so seductive that she could have melted into a puddle right then and there. He ran his hands up and down her back, clearly enjoying the game right here in front of him. "Are you an American League fan or a National League fan?" Twisting his head to look at her sideways, he smiled playfully. "This is important, Jody. Think *very* carefully about how you answer."

After regaining her senses, she smiled crookedly at him. *Two can play at this game.* She brazenly ran her hands up his chest. His muscles tensed with her caress, and the little whoosh of breath he involuntarily released as her touch became more sensual had her internally squealing with delight. Jody's hands came to rest on his shoulders as she offered him her best teasing grin. "I'm going to have to go with the National League all the way, sweetheart."

Jared opened his mouth to speak, but she placed her finger over his lips to quiet him. Instead of looking him in the eye, Jody kept her gaze brazenly glued to that beautiful mouth under her finger. Breathlessly, she said, "If you say you're an American League fan, I'm going to have to boot your ass out of here."

He playfully nipped at her finger. "I like a woman who knows her baseball."

She couldn't contain her giggle. *Under that tough exterior, he's playful. That's a great big plus.*

"Why don't you sit on the couch, and I'll get us something to drink?" She started to move away, but he drew her back to him. He didn't seem willing to let her go just yet which pleased her very much. Jared placed a sweet kiss on her nose in a way that shouldn't have stirred her up, but his lips were like magic. When they touched her, the tingles she'd been feeling had quickly grown into sparks. Jody did a little happy dance in her head. Was it really just a few short days ago she'd believed it would be impossible to open up enough to another human being to feel those burning, lustful sensations again?

As Jared released her, the loss of contact between them left her feeling empty. She took a much needed moment to catch her breath and watch him walk away. *Now that's another great big plus.*

"What would you like to drink? I've got just about everything from beer to water." She hoped her voice didn't sound as shaky to him as it did to her. Those sparks in her body were quickly growing into a slow burn making her a bit wobbly.

"Don't go to any trouble. I'll have whatever you're having."

Jody put their soft drinks on the coffee table and sat next to him on the couch. After getting comfortable, she couldn't help but notice his goofy grin.

"What?"

He answered with laughter.

"I don't get it. What's so funny?"

Jared reached for her hand and brought it to his mouth. His kiss, no more than a gentle caress on her palm, left her feeling lightheaded. If he didn't stop soon, she'd end up embarrassing herself by jumping him and taking that mouth for another test drive.

"Every time we sit together on a couch, you turn your body toward me and pull your leg up under you. When you do that, it makes me feel like I'm the only person in the world. You always give me your full attention and make me feel like my thoughts and opinions count for something. No matter how benign the subject, having a conversation with you always turns into something special."

Stunned by his admission, Jody could only sit there and stare at him with her mouth gaping open.

"What makes it even more extraordinary is that you don't realize you do it. It's endearing."

Beside herself that he would notice something as simple as the way she sat with him, had her taking a moment to come up with a response. "I guess I didn't realize I did that." Leaning into him, she kissed the side of his mouth and then put her hand to his cheek so there'd be no mistaking her opinion of him. "You *are* important to me.

"Talk about a perfect segue." Her nervous giggle escaped before she could catch it. She made a show of clearing her throat to cover the embarrassing chuckle.

"So I thought that since we are in the," she threw some air quotes out into the air, "getting-to-know-each-other phase of our relationship, maybe you'd like to tell me a little about yourself. I don't know anything at all about you."

Jared's hand reached out, his finger gently tracing

Sandy Wolters

patterns on Jody's leg. As he teased her with his touch, it took every ounce of self-discipline she had to keep her thoughts on the conversation.

"I was kind of hoping to find out more about you."

Recognizing his none-too-subtle tactics for what they were, Jody tilted her head toward Jared questioningly. Her forehead furrowed, indicating he wouldn't be getting off the hook this time. "I think you know enough about me for now. I don't know anything about you."

"Okay. You win. Ask me anything you want."

He'd been uncomfortable opening himself up to others, so his response pleased her. At least he seemed willing to try for her. That was a big deal for him, and she gave him kudos for allowing it. Witnessing Jared's hesitancy of giving up personal details propelled remnants of Nathan's earlier conversation to run through her mind. *Why on earth doesn't he want to talk about himself? What could possibly be so bad?*

Deciding the best way to get him to open up would be to start with the ridiculous, Jody inquired, "Have you ever killed anyone?" Her eyebrow wiggled the way she'd seen cops do in old movies when interrogating gangsters. The corner of her mouth lifted, all but betraying her jest.

A sparkle of humor lit his face before throwing his head back and laughing. "Not even with kindness."

"Hmm." She tapped her finger to her lips as if she had no idea what to ask next.

"Do you ever lie?"

Jared chuckled and reached out quickly to playfully pull her onto his lap. "You're asking that to make sure I'm telling the truth about never killing anyone, aren't you?" He did his best to copy her eyebrow wiggle. "Smart girl."

She gave him a playful huff. "The smartest."

Leaning into him, Jody laid her head on his shoulder. Sitting on his lap gave her the warm and fuzzies and had her stomach doing somersaults. With all that going on, it became difficult to concentrate on the task at hand.

Still aiming to keep the conversation light, she thought she'd be able to draw him out with another playful question. "Tell me something about your childhood. What was the one thing you did as a child that got you into deep trouble, but you never regretted doing?"

Instantly she felt his body constrict beneath her. The hand which had previously been stroking her arm momentarily stalled. A strangled cackling sound came from deep within his chest. A telltale sign she'd inadvertently touched on a sensitive subject. The tone of sarcasm in his laugh hadn't escaped her.

"That's easy. I was ten. My parents were out of the country, and I was scheduled to leave for boarding school in Switzerland before they got back. I wanted to see them before I left, so I went to the garage, climbed into my dad's favorite little sports car, and proceeded to total it."

Appalled, she sat straight up. Unable to hide her dismay, her eyes widened, and her chin dropped to her chest. She didn't know what shocked her more—the fact his parents had left him behind when he was only ten years old, or the fact they'd shipped him off to a foreign land at such a young age.

He tried to downplay the emotional pain by

shrugging his shoulders as if the neglect he'd suffered was nothing out of the ordinary. "It was the only way to get their attention. They came back in time to get me out of the hospital and send me on my way."

His admission staggered her. The tension of the past mistreatment encircled them both, leaving the air around them thick with melancholy. He'd tried to act as if what he'd just told her had been the most normal thing in the world. His voice and mannerisms told her differently. He'd tried to conceal the pain of his words, but hadn't been successful. Now she understood why he'd never spoke of his past.

The abuse he'd suffered in his childhood was a huge admission for him. She felt privileged he'd been honest with her and shared his story because she was certain he'd never told anyone before—not even jokingly.

He'd always been cordial around her. It was evident to her, though, he wasn't comfortable letting go and just busting a gut laughing or showing joy of any kind. *Maybe he doesn't have anything in his life to be joyful about?* As soon as that thought raced through her mind, she wanted to weep for him.

As Jody reviewed what she did know about Jared, it had been plain to see he had a habit of dismissing any emotion, with the exception of amorous ardor of course. He seemed to appreciate touching her and receiving her caresses. *Thank the good Lord above for small favors!* Come hell or high water, she resolved to teach him how to let go and really enjoy himself.

Experience with channeling spirits had shown her that when dealing with other people's misery, the best way to handle it was through laughter. She'd do that for him now and hopefully make it easier for him to tell his story in the process.

"Okay." She dragged the word out for several seconds. "I was thinking more along the lines of shoving a dead frog in the face of some bratty little girl, but your story sounds interesting, too."

To diminish the sting of the past, she cradled his face and lightly kissed his lips. "Tell me about it."

Jared pulled her back into his body and held her tight while he told her about his miserable childhood. He'd never spoken of it to anyone else, but felt a deep-seated need to tell her.

He was sure Nathan had already cornered Jody about his concerns regarding his personality, or more accurately, lack of personality. He knew Nathan had told her never-ending stories of his darker, more reclusive side. He felt compelled to let her know why he behaved the way he did with others. Hopefully, in doing so, it would shed some light on Nathan's opinions of him.

"The condensed version is that I come from an extremely wealthy family. The wealth started building generations upon generations ago, growing by leaps and bounds over the years. Each of the Bastion men made their own considerable contributions to the family coffers." He unleashed a laugh, but it contained no joy. "It's much easier to make loads of money when you already have it."

Reliving the past had him carelessly shrugging. "As a child growing up, I was raised, clothed, fed, and educated by paid employees. I rarely saw my parents. When I got old enough, they sent me to be educated as far away from them as possible. Child rearing has never been a priority in my family.

"My father died when I was twelve. The last time I saw him, I was in the hospital. I was ten at the time." His snicker was laced with sarcasm. "He was so pissed at me for wrecking his antique car and making him come back to the States from their home in London that he couldn't even look at me.

"After that, I learned to depend on myself for everything." Jared couldn't maintain his cynicism. Even he could feel the air surrounding him becoming dense with pent up sorrow.

"For as long as I can remember, I'd been raised to believe emotion and dependency on anyone else was a form of weakness. Those qualities were certainly not something a Bastion man would submit to. In other words, I come from a long line of assholes. I learned to depend on myself for everything. I kept myself busy so that I wouldn't miss companionship in my life."

Surprising him, Jody jumped off of his lap and started pacing the floor. She turned and yelled, expelling the anger she felt toward his parents. "How dare they treat you like that? That's the lowest form of child abuse I've ever heard of and believe you me, I've heard some horrible stories."

After several more moments of rage filled pacing, she pivoted to face him. Every muscle in Jody's body was taut with anger. Her eyes were wild and full of fire. She pointed at Jared and punctuated her words by stabbing the air with her finger. "That's it! You and me. Together we're going to show you all about the power of love. We're going to teach you about the power of friendship and what exactly can be accomplished when you share those emotions with others."

Jared couldn't fathom what was happening right in front of him. On his behalf, Jody had worked herself up into a frenzy, and it made him feel good. No one had ever cared enough before.

"I'm going in there to get ready to go to Nathan's house. You get your ass up and prepare yourself to have a little fun with friends tonight."

Excitement building for no other reason than having Jody in his life, Jared couldn't take his eyes off of her as she stomped from the room. Her solicitude had somehow lightened the heavy load of his childhood which he'd carried around with him throughout his life. Afraid of breaking the spell of the blissful moment, he sat motionless, glued to the chair.

When she suddenly came barging back into the room, what he saw had him doing a double take. "What are you wearing?" His lighthearted laughter rang throughout the room.

Jody did a little pirouette for him, showing off her favorite baseball attire. "This, fine sir, is a Diamondback jersey, and this," she said as she tapped her hat, "is a Brewers baseball cap."

"You're rooting for both teams?"

"Of course, I am!" She stated as if he were an imbecile. "The D-Backs and Brew Crew are my two favorite teams. I thought you said you were a baseball fan. Haven't you figured out yet that the best games to watch are the games where you like both teams? It doesn't matter who wins. You end up happy either way."

She was adorable. It was no wonder he'd had such a hard time concentrating on anything but her since they'd met. Somehow, Jody had worked her way through his defenses in the snap of a finger. While it made Jared a little uneasy, he was pleasantly surprised he'd actually fallen head over heels in love. If he wanted to keep her in his life, he'd have to work on opening himself up. He had to be willing to share the good and the bad about himself. This relationship business was all new to him and he'd be the first to admit he was, at best, stunted in the feelings department. He prayed he'd be able to give her what she needed emotionally.

He crossed the room, dipped her backward and lavished her with a sloppy kiss. "You're wrong. It doesn't matter who is playing. If you're there watching the game with me, I'll be euphoric."

Jody threw her arms around his neck and purposely cocked her head as if he'd just stated the obvious. "Damn straight, and don't you forget it, sweet baby. And by the way, Jared, I'll have you know that *I* would have burned the whole damn garage down." Before giving him a chance to react, she pulled herself from his embrace, opened a drawer, and retrieved a huge plastic Diamondback toy rattle. She shook it at him with force. "Now get your ass in gear, and let's go have some fun."

He grinned and bowed. "Anything you say, Monkey."

Chapter Twenty

They'd just finished singing a boisterous rendition of *Take Me Out To The Ballgame* for the seventh inning stretch when Jody felt the hair on the back of her neck rise. Through shuttered eyes, she peered at Jared and warmed with pleasure at seeing him enjoying himself. She mentally crossed her fingers and hoped the spirit who had just shown up didn't ruin the evening for them.

The time had come. Their budding relationship was about to undergo the first test. Now Jody would see how Jared would react to her dropping everything in the middle of a date. She'd have to leave him to pass a message from a spirit to some random person who needed to heal from their loss.

Unable to keep from fidgeting, she looked around the room to see who'd just shown up. *There.* Jody spotted a young woman talking with a group of people by the food. Beaten and bloody, the ghost stood behind her reaching out across the veil trying to get her attention but having no luck.

The condition of the spirit's image served to dial Jody in on just how difficult this off-the-cuff reading was going to be. Jared, ever aware, alerted to her sudden change in mood. In a manner she knew meant to calm her, he gently ran his fingers down her arm. Leaning in to nuzzle her neck, he whispered, "What's wrong?"

Unable to mask her troubled expression, she turned her attention back to him and looked apologetically into his eyes. "You see that girl with the long, red hair standing at the counter?"

The tone of her voice had him sitting up a little straighter. Casually, he looked over his shoulder. "Yes."

"I have to go and talk to her." All gaiety had disappeared, as her outward appearance had dramatically changed to one of all business.

"Do you see a spirit standing around her?"

As she continued to watch the ghost's sad efforts to get the woman's attention, Jody's nod of affirmation had been almost imperceptible.

As he'd done before with Fiona, he lifted his phone and held it out to take a picture. Jody gently covered the phone with her hand and pushed it down to his lap. Not wanting to be overheard, she leaned into him. "I don't think she'd want to see the condition this particular ghost is in. Besides, we don't have permission to take a picture."

Laced with gravity, her words had Jared cringing. "Baby, I'm so sorry. It's so damn unfair that someone as gentle as you has to witness such horrible things. But I don't understand. If you don't have a picture, how are you going to get her to believe you?"

"Sometimes people believe me and listen to the message. Sometimes they don't and walk away. All I can do is try to pass the spirit's communications along."

Her response prompted frustration to flicker across Jared's face. "Would you like me to go over with you?"

A grateful smile crossed her lips. "If you're up to

it, then yes. Judging by the gory appearance of the spirit, the reading is going to be difficult."

He leaned in and kissed her gently. "Let's go. I'll be right there if you need me."

They slowly made their way across the room and approached the people at the counter. Jody zeroed in on the young woman and the ghost who wanted to communicate with her. Before even having a chance to introduce herself, she started receiving frantic messages from the spirit. Ever so slightly, she raised her hand to calm the spirit and acknowledge her story would be told.

"Excuse me. You don't know me. I'm sorry to interrupt your conversation, but I'm a medium. There's someone here who would like to speak with you." The woman visibly paled.

Without giving her the time needed to make a quick getaway, Jody started. "Your sister, Megan, is stepping forward. She wants you to know she loves the tattoo you got in her memory." The woman's trembling hand lifted to her mouth.

As difficult as it was to look into the mutilated eyes of the battered ghost, Jody couldn't back away. Sensing the importance of the impending conversation, the redhead's friends started to gather around her. Willing to protect their friend, as a group, they made their presence known as they watched Jody receive more information with a skeptical eye.

Thrilled at finally getting the opportunity to get her message across to her sister, Megan's spirit spoke quickly. Trying her best to keep up, Jody absently nodded at what appeared to be nothing more than a void space in the room. "She's mentioning something about

M&Ms, green M&Ms," Jody smiled at the spirit's humor. "She said you keep finding them everywhere you go. You were right to believe she'd left them for you."

Visibly shaken from this encounter, the redhead dropped hard on the stool behind her and started to sob. "My sister loved green M&Ms," she wailed through her hands. "She used to pick them out of the bag and give me the rest of the colors. She'd smile and tell me the other colors weren't up to her standards." The woman swallowed hard before adding, "It seems like every time I turn around, I'm finding green M&Ms. It doesn't matter where I am. They just always seem to magically appear."

Giving the redhead a moment to ponder this new information, and a bit of time to compose herself, Jody smiled reassuringly at her. The spirit's message was about to turn serious.

"Megan wants to apologize to you for not listening to your advice." To garner the strength to get through this reading, Jody breathed so deeply her shoulders rose with the effort. She hated these kinds of messages but understood how important they were to the living who received them.

"Your sister said that you were right all along. She should have stayed away from him. That bastard did end up killing her just like you said he would. He lost his temper and beat her to death."

Ghosts had an uncanny ability to use every sense to get their messages across. Megan's spirit had saturated the inside of Jody's mouth with the coppery taste of blood, leaving her fighting the urge to throw up. Without being too obvious, and hoping to alleviate some of that lingering sensation, she reached out and grabbed a napkin to wipe her lips. While she made it a practice to pass all information along during a reading, there were just some things people didn't need to know.

Focusing her attention back on the spirit, who now, thankfully, appeared without injury, allowed Jody to relax a bit. *The rough part of the reading had concluded. It's time for the healing to begin.* "She wants to tell you that you need to stop thinking about those last minutes of her life. You have to stop reliving them in your mind. She's in no pain, and she's finally free from him."

As the spirit continued the conversation, Jody's eyebrows creased together in full concentration trying her hardest not to miss any part of the message. "She wants me to remind you of the fight you and she had in grade school about a boy named Ben." Megan's excitement at finally speaking to her sister had her rambling but in a frenzied manner. Trying to keep up with her was a chore in and of itself and left Jody scrambling. Not sure she had interpreted that last part right, she inquired, "Does that make sense to you?"

The woman's brows furrowed together as she tried to remember something which had happened so long ago. Suddenly, recalling the childhood spat left her gasping and nodding her head affirmatively.

"Megan says there was nothing you could have done to keep her away from the man who killed her. Just like she couldn't keep you away from that little prick, Ben, in fifth grade." The redhead laughed through her tears at the memory now front and center in her mind. She had indeed fought with her sister over that boy so many years ago.

As silent tears streaked through her makeup, the woman locked gazes with Jody. "Why do sisters do that? Why is it so hard to agree on anything? One day you're fighting like cats and dogs and the next day it's too late to tell her how much she's loved."

Jody offered a compassionate smile. "I think it's..." A horrific vision flashed in front of Jody, shaking her to the core. She visibly cringed from it and took a step back. To steady her, Jared firmly put his hand on her back to let her know he stood beside her offering whatever strength she needed.

"I'm sorry. I don't mean to change the subject on you. Your sister is insisting I continue with her message. She finally has your attention, and she's not backing down. Megan wants you to know that after he had beaten her to death, while in spirit form, she watched as he shot himself." The redhead's mouth opened wide, but no words came out.

"Ah..." *Oh jeez. Megan is one pissed off spirit.* "Okay. There's no way around this, so I'm just going to say what she told me. She said the fucker pissed himself and missed the first time, shooting a hole in the wall instead." The redhead nodded somberly, acknowledging the facts behind both causes of death.

"Megan says it's important for you to know, he didn't go easily. He didn't die right away and suffered more than she did as he ended his life. He paid, and is still paying dearly for taking her life. You need to stop dwelling on it. You need to release the bitterness and move on. You need to enjoy your life. Have some fun."

Many people had now gathered around and watched Jody as she held a conversation with thin air. She tried to contain herself but couldn't hold back the bubble of laughter. "Your sister is very funny. She said you were recently going through her trinket box, pissing and moaning about what an idiot Megan was in life. She was there to hear the whole bitch-fest." Jody leaned in close to the woman. "Her words, not mine."

"As you were working yourself up into a tizzy, flailing your arms around, she had to keep dodging your fists." The woman threw her head back and laughed through her tears at the memory which had just occurred hours ago. "Megan says that every time you go through her personal things in that box to reminisce, she'll be with you."

Momentarily distracted by the spirit's unique sense of joviality, Jody wasn't aware the audience around her had grown. "She's telling me she left something for you and can't believe you haven't found it yet. She covered the inside lid of her trinket box with red felt."

"Oh, my God! Yes! She did," the woman exclaimed, unable to contain her excitement.

"Megan wants you to pull the felt fabric away. She left something for you there."

"I will!"

Appeased her message had been delivered, Megan started to disappear slowly. Jody watched her blow a kiss to her sister before she vanished for good.

Jody reached out to the young woman and embraced her. "I'm sorry for the interruption, but it was important for her to let you know it's time to move on. It's been a privilege to speak for Megan."

As if she were holding onto her sister, the woman wasn't willing to release the hug just yet. "Thank you," she whispered. She started gleefully jumping up and down while still holding Jody in her tight embrace. It became apparent that the weight of the world had lifted from her tired shoulders.

Finally, she pushed Jody to arm's length. "I want to show you something." She turned around and tugged at the waistband of her pants. She exposed a tattoo of the sexy, green, female M&M with the marketing tagline, *'What is it about the green ones?'* She'd also added her sister's name.

Chapter Twenty-One

Spending time with Jody opened up new worlds for Jared. With her by his side, it didn't take long to discover being sociable had its perks. Her laid-back, loving and carefree nature seemed to bring out the best in him.

Everyone at the party enjoyed having fun whether they were rooting for their team, telling jokes, or breaking out in lip sync battles. He'd even had an animated conversation with Nathan and Terry about which teams would end up in the World Series this year—each man so sure of their picks that bets were placed. While Jody's best friends still had a long way to go in trusting him, he'd vowed to do whatever necessary to gain their acceptance. Willingly being a part of a large, rowdy group of people—an entirely new experience for him—had him smiling his fool head off.

For the first time in his adult life, Jared felt as if he belonged someplace. With one hand on the steering wheel and the other holding hers, he couldn't help but smile when he thought back on the evening. While he still found it difficult to open up to people, with Jody's help, that would come in time. She made him feel whole as if he were an active participant in life instead of a voyeur. He couldn't remember a time in which he'd laughed as much as he had tonight. Doing so left his psyche feeling richer and lighter. Something inside him had shifted which allowed his love for Jody to brighten his life. It felt wonderful.

During the party, he'd watched her carefully as she mixed with people. It didn't matter if she knew them or not, she'd been open and caring with everyone at the barbecue. Throughout the evening, she had stayed close to his side, either holding his hand or sitting next to him. She'd done everything in her power to ensure he'd been comfortable in this new role. But in the end, it was nothing more than her touch which had eased any discomfort he'd felt.

Her goal for the evening seemed to be making sure he had fun, and she'd succeeded beyond his wildest dreams. Indiscriminately, she'd sought to make certain all of his needs were met. This allowed him to let loose a little and enjoy the evening. No one had ever fussed over him the way she had tonight, and it made him love her all the more. What he thought and how he reacted to people around him mattered to her. He had his very own angel, and just having her presence beside him made him feel like the luckiest man on earth.

Without a second thought, she'd let him into her world. When a spirit showed up and had an important message to give, she'd looked into his eyes and asked him to join her. When she knew the message would be a difficult one, she'd trusted him enough to be there to support her. It had quickly become his mission to assist her with whatever she may need. Never again would she have to endure the complications her gifts created in her life alone.

To witness firsthand how her messages from deceased loved ones healed people, leaving them lighter and happier felt like a miracle to him. And for all of that, she asked nothing in return. *Nothing.* Her purity of heart and genuine concern for strangers left him in awe.

Breaking the comfortable silence, she laughed under her breath. Jared gave her a sideways glance. "What's so funny?"

Like a child, she puckered her lips as her shoulders bounced up. "It's more ironic than funny."

The uneasiness which tinged her voice had him squeezing her hand, a gentle reminder she could count on him for whatever she needed. "What is? What's wrong?"

Knowing she probably needed time to arrange her thoughts, he waited patiently as his questions hung in the air. As the silence persisted, bright red flares started going off in his mind. Something had her upset.

"It's nothing really. I was just thinking about little Fiona." As he drove, she struggled to turn her body toward him but had been hindered by the seatbelt over her shoulder. Completely out of character for her, frustration manifested as anger when she reached up and gave the restraint a rough tug. He knew her irritation had been brought on partially because she'd been denied the intimacy she enjoyed so much when they faced each other as they conversed. Finally accepting she'd be stuck looking forward, she clenched her teeth and growled.

"There have been certain times in my life when my abilities evolved to the next level." Looking at him without craning her neck had proved impossible, so she gave up trying altogether and finally just leaned her head against the headrest. He felt a rush of unease when he realized her mood had quickly shifted to brooding. The vibrancy had all but drained from her voice. "I was stupid enough to think that since the experience with Fiona had been so difficult, maybe…" She broke off, trying to figure out how to put her thoughts into words.

"Maybe?"

"I hope you don't think I'm griping about this—. Damn. I guess I am bitching about it." Jody slapped her legs which built the tension within the car to a whole new level.

"I thought since what I experienced with Fiona had been so difficult that I'd finally paid my penance, and the gift would retreat. Do you understand what I mean?" The words tumbled from her mouth at a feverish pace. She didn't pause long enough for him to answer. "I started to believe that channeling for Fiona might be the final act or closure to something that interfered with my personal life for so many years. It felt like Fiona was my closing evolution and perhaps the conclusion to that part of my journey in this lifetime."

Positive she had more to tell him, he waited patiently through the long silence until she was ready to finish her thoughts

"I'm scared, Jared."

Not a minute too soon, he pulled into her driveway and turned the motor off. Hearing her confession of fear tore him apart. He wanted to hold her. He wanted to make everything better for her as she had done for him.

"Tonight proved my instinct had been wrong. A spirit showed up as usual."

As much as she tried to hide it, the trepidation in her voice rang out as if she'd used a bullhorn. Jared reached out and ran his fingers gently over her cheek relaying the foundation of his support. The silent gesture offered his strength for anything and everything that troubled her.

"What has you scared, Monkey? From what I understand, spirits have appeared to you your entire life."

Accepting everything he offered, she pressed his hand to her cheek and leaned into it. "Yes. But there was a definite shift in my abilities dealing with Fiona. Rather than the hibernation I had hoped for, my gift is more powerful. I could tell the difference when I channeled Megan tonight. What does that mean for the future? What have my gifts evolved into this time?" The unknown had her grimacing. "What's the learning curve going to be this time? I have no idea what's coming, or how to deal with it when it finally happens. It *will* happen, Jared. Something has changed within me. I can feel it, and it scares the living crap out of me."

Without wavering, he looked deep into her eyes and tried to relay his unshakable belief in her. "Whatever it is, I'll be here with you. I'll be holding you and offering you strength. You won't be alone ever again. You have my word on that."

Even in the darkness, her timid smile did nothing to stop the fear which blazed behind her eyes. Trying to distance himself from his own alarm that her statements had provoked, Jared forced his features to relax. While her proclamation terrified him, he stilled his thoughts so she wouldn't be aware of his concern.

She looked for any sign of insincerity of his offered support as she scanned his face. It pleased him that she'd found what she needed in his gaze.

"Kiss me, Jared."

Slowly, he started to move toward her but

unexpectedly jerked to a stop inches from her mouth. He tried again to get closer, but his seatbelt had locked on him. A slow, angry growl left his throat as he released the obstruction. His aggravation broke her surly mood as her laughter rang through the car.

Frustrated, he opened the door and sped around the vehicle. He hoped the damn seatbelt hadn't ruined their tender moment. As soon as he opened her door, Jody slid from the car into his arms. The contented sigh she'd released into his mouth was a thing of beauty. As she melted into him, he wrapped her in a secure embrace. He felt the shift of her fears as they dissipated while her lips lingered on his. They clung to each other, neither one wanting to be the first to let go. Unable to quench their need for one another, the kiss quickly turned from languid to urgent.

"Come inside with me?"

His hands fisted in her silky hair, and Jared pulled her head back to look into her eyes. "Are you sure?" The anticipation of her answer had the breath seizing in his chest.

Flashing him a dazzling smile, she pulled away before holding her hand out. "I'm more sure about this than I've ever been about anything in my life."

Once the front door closed behind them, he moved swiftly. He had Jody's back against the door with his lips brushing kisses along her neck. His body was on fire, and he'd only find relief when he sank deep within her.

Each pass of her lips and nip of her teeth sent fireworks spiraling through him and drove him to the edge of reason. She pulled his mouth to hers and started an exploration with her tongue which left his mind numb.

Unable to break contact, he breathlessly murmured as he kissed her, "Be sure about this, Monkey, because you'll never be rid of me once I take you. You'll always be mine."

She forcibly pushed him away, leaving him momentarily startled. Her expression turned to one of unadulterated lust. Leaving an arm's length between them, she reached out and roughly grabbed the front of his shirt. Enticing him with her smoldering look, he followed along as she pulled him into her bedroom.

She roughly pushed him on the bed. Wanting a clear view of everything that was about to happen, she hit the light switch. Standing stock still, she faced him. "What would you say, Jared, if I told you I am falling in love with you?"

A slow, arrogant grin moved across his face. "I'd say, it's about damn time, Monkey."

Happy with his answer, she seductively leaned back against the door and smiled. He stood and took a step toward her, but her hand flew up to halt his progress. "Stop!" Her finger shook at him in an I-don't-think-so manner. "I didn't say you could get off the bed, sweetheart."

Her playfulness at a time like this had his eyebrows shooting up into his hairline. As he sat back down, his broad grin served as a dead giveaway that the show couldn't start fast enough for him. She made sure he paid attention as her hands moved seductively up her body, finding and undoing each button on her Diamondback jersey along the way. The garment slipped from her shoulders and landed in a pile at her feet. She kicked the jersey to him and watched as he brought it to his face, deeply inhaling her scent. Enjoying his reaction, she patiently waited for him to refocus on her.

Jody toed her shoes off and unbuckled her belt. Before she moved to unfasten her shorts, she noticed Jared's nostrils flaring as his breathing became visibly stilted. She delighted in the knowledge he had started to come unhinged without even touching him yet. *Well, you're not the only one, sweetheart.*

Her hips moved in a seductive, swinging motion, causing her shorts to fall at her feet. Taking one step back, she kicked her leg out launching the shorts toward him. As they hurled across the room, he caught them in mid-air.

She knew his excitement had built to a point which made it impossible for him to sit any longer. He stood slowly, bringing the shorts to his face. Waves of heat ran through her body as he deeply inhaled to imprint the scent of her sex in his mind. The deeper he inhaled, the more frenzied he became. His eyes glazed over and had turned dark with passion. The gentle man she'd known slowly disappeared in front of her eyes. That made her damn happy. She didn't want the calm, cool, and collected Jared at the moment. She wanted to see him lose control. She wanted his wild, dominant side which he'd kept carefully hidden from her.

Her body burned for him as she watched him transform into a more animalistic version of himself. His movements slight but taut with tension proved his readiness to pounce on her the first chance he got. Barely hanging on, she could hardly wait for the moment when she'd finally allow him to catch her.

His gaze moved from her face to her tight tank top

which did nothing to hide her erect nipples.

"Do you like what you see, sweetheart?"

When he answered with nothing more than a tightly clenched jaw, she knew she wouldn't be able to hold him at bay much longer. Turning her back to him, she seductively pushed her hip out to accentuate her curves. Slowly, painstakingly, she pulled the tank top over her head exposing her bare back to him. Glancing over her shoulder, she watched him moving toward her, his demeanor and pace no less dangerous or primal than that of a tiger stalking its prey. His eyes were riveted on her butt.

Since her exhibition had teased him mercilessly, she expected him to be a little rough with her—at least that was her hope. There would be time later for gentleness. For now, it had been over a year since her last sexual encounter which made her want him fast and hard. Instead, he surprised her by moving behind her and running his hands gently down her back, branding every inch of her with a feathery touch. His caress so light and unanticipated, she thought she'd go mad as shivers visibly shook her body. Not only had she worked him into a frenzy, but she'd done a pretty good job on herself as well. Knowing this treatment was his payback, if need be, she'd beg to make him move faster. That prospect made the fire within her burn even hotter.

Tilting her head back, she pleaded for him to come closer. *Didn't he know she needed him to touch all of her? Now!* His fingers found their way around her waist and moved toward her aching breasts only to come to rest at the upward curve beneath them. His touch, still light as silk on her skin, drove her insane with need.

223

Surprising her with his sudden movement as he closed in behind her, his fingers reached up and pinched her taut nipples. His teeth sank into her neck, shooting tendrils of lust throughout her already overheated body. Shocked to realize she'd come very close to having an orgasm, her legs buckled as she screamed his name in delight.

His voice, gravelly with lust, commanded, "Don't you dare move, Monkey. I'm going to touch every inch of you, and then I'm going to taste you."

His words created a manic hunger within her, making each breath a challenge. If she weren't careful, she'd pass out.

"Put your hands on the door," he demanded in a powerful alpha voice that relayed he'd be taking full command of this encounter.

Complying with his orders, she spread her arms in front of her and arched her back, silently begging him to move faster. His fingers slid slowly down her back until he got to her barely-there panties. He traced along the edge of the lace, making her wiggle beneath his touch and groan for more.

Bending to his knees, he hooked his thumbs in the frilly barrier and slowly pulled them down to her ankles. Offering an open invitation to do as he pleased, she spread her legs and thrust her butt out. Still teasing her with a gentle touch, he slowly ran his hands down her backside to her inner thighs. For the second time in a matter of minutes, she felt the weight of an oncoming orgasm. His magic touch had her body vibrating with a primal need.

"Are you ready for me, Monkey?"

"Please, Jared, please. I don't think I can…" Her

words trailed off. She'd lost the power to think as he leaned forward and nipped her butt with his teeth.

"What do you want, Monkey?" The slick folds of her overheated sex started contracting. *Oh my God! That fucking sexy all-male timbre of his voice has my girly parts starting without him!*

"Touch me, Jared. Oh God! I'm begging you. You're driving me crazy."

He stood and moved his hands around her hips. Still behind Jody, he pulled her naked bottom tightly against his still-clothed body and ground his erection into her backside. His hands moved to her belly and continued their journey down the front of her body, torturing her with each leisurely inch. His fingers slipped down and grazed her swollen nub, the touch sending her over the edge with a powerful orgasm. As her scream ripped through the room, she opened her stance and wrapped her leg around his, brazenly pleading for more.

In one swift motion, he lifted her and placed her on the edge of the bed. His eyes took a slow torturous journey over every curve. "Lean back on your elbows and spread your legs, Monkey. I want to see what I've just claimed."

Still reeling from her orgasm, she did as she was told but decided to add a little encouragement. To fulfill Jared's request, she slowly reclined on the bed, seductively sliding her hand from her throat to her nipple. She rolled the rosy nub between her fingers and arched her back. His approving, low, rumbling groan encouraged her to go on.

She spread her legs displaying herself for him. Her body jerked with the remaining tremors of her orgasm.

Just as the last blissful contraction faded, she opened her eyes and found him naked. Every muscle in his body was strung so tight from sexual need that she could see them vibrate. The sight of him had her licking her lips.

He dropped to his knees so fast she didn't have a chance to react. His tongue found her, devouring her as if she were his last meal. Ecstasy had her squealing his name.

Shooting her hips up, she reached down and grabbed fistfuls of his hair, encouraging him to explore every inch of her. The vision of his head between her legs and the way his tongue glided and teased her most intimate spot had her body primed again in no time at all.

His tongue had the folds of her sex swelling and ready to explode. The ministrations he lavished on her had her seeing stars. His lips clamped down and sucked her tender sex into his mouth. He released the hard nub just as quickly only to pull that most sensitive and private place of hers back through his lips. The pulsating sensation proved to be her undoing and shot her over the edge.

Her lust filled screams encouraged him on as he inserted a finger and watched as her body clamped down around it.

Proudly, he stood in front of her. "Look at me, Monkey."

Unsure how much more she could take, she opened her eyes and found him between her legs, holding his erection. He sheathed himself with a condom. "I'm going to take you now, and when I'm done, you'll belong to me and only me."

She raised her knees in invitation and held her arms out to him.

"Say it. I need to hear you say it."

"I'm yours, Jared, and *you're* mine. I'll never let you go."

He pinned her knees to the bed, sliding himself over her sensitive nub. Unable to restrain herself, his name shattered the air as she cried out again.

Still standing, he took her with one quick thrust, her body eagerly accepting his full length. The feel of their joined bodies had them both groaning with desire. She wrapped her legs around his waist and clutched at the bed above her head. Through passion filled eyes, she watched as he stood over her, pounding into her. His fingertips dug into her hips to hold her in place. Rotating his hips in circles made the ride even more pleasurable for both of them. Wanting to prolong her climax, she squeezed her eyes shut but knew it would be impossible to hold off.

She felt his body collapse on top of her and his movements stalled. She opened her eyes in protest and found him staring at her. He began to stroke slowly, prompting her core to tighten once again. Her eyes lost their focus.

"Look at me, Monkey," he demanded. "I need you to see what you do to me. I want you to feel what you do to me. You…" Unable to finish, his words trailed off. The muscles in his neck bulged, and his face tensed. She reached out and pulled his lips to hers, accepting his cry of passion into her mouth.

Knowing full well he didn't have the strength to move anymore than she did, she finally felt his body relax. As his breathing slowed, he lifted up on one elbow and nibbled at her neck. He gently bit her chin and moved to her mouth, leaving her dazzled with his sweet attention.

She played with his hair and cooed blissfully. "I hope you're planning on staying the night because I think I might find a need for you in a few hours."

Because their bodies were still joined, him on top of her, she felt his laugh start in his belly and make its way up to his mouth. With strength she couldn't believe he possessed after the tumble they'd just taken, he pulled her up with him. Standing by the bed, she wrapped her legs around his waist as he continued to hold her. Neither one of them were willing to pull apart just yet.

"Would you like to take a shower? It's big enough for two."

Crossing the room, he turned the bathroom light on and cracked the door. Jared nibbled at her shoulder while he turned the bedroom light off. Moving to the side of the bed, he pulled the covers down. Still joined from lovemaking and never releasing his embrace, he sat on the bed and laid down with Jody cradled into his body. "I don't want to wash what just happened away quite yet. I want to feel our slick bodies, smell our mixed scents. I want to hold you and sleep with you. We can shower later."

It didn't take long for their breathing to become synchronized. Almost asleep, a sudden attack of the giggles hit Jody. Jared's hand came up and gently stroked her hair. "What's so funny?"

Unable to stop herself, she giggled again. "I can finally get rid of that damn dildo. It's not nearly as good as the real thing."

"I say, keep it. You never know. We may find a use for it later."

Each drawing comfort from the other, sleep finally found them through their laughter.

****

Several hours later, he awoke with an erection that was almost painful. He found her between his legs, softly running her fingers up and down the length of his cock. She puckered her lips and blew a steady stream of warm breath on his now tight balls. She never took her eyes off of his erection as it engorged and readied itself for her. Desire coursed through his body as he reached out for her.

"Not so fast," she stated entirely too calmly. His thick sex jumped as he watched her pour a creamy lotion into her hands. Never breaking eye contact with him, she slowly rubbed the silky lotion between her hands warming it for him. "You got lots of pleasure out of torturing me earlier. It's my turn."

Her hands moved to his erection, stroking him, increasing the pressure and then decreasing it. His knees involuntarily slid up so he could pump hard into her skilled hands. She reached between his legs and squeezed his tight sack. "Oh fuck, Monkey, that feels so good." He was so close, so damn close, when she suddenly stopped. His hands clenched the blankets as he tried to calm his disappointment.

Creating an all-new sensation, she lowered her body to him and squeezed her breasts around him. All control lost, he started thrusting into the cocoon she'd created, pumping faster, harder until his body tensed beyond the point of no return. The orgasm came fast and hard leaving him dizzy.

Moving to the shower, they took their time washing each other. Soapy hands glided across wet skin, each committing the other's body to memory through touch.

Jared pulled her close and held her under the warm spray of water. Cradling her he conceded that she was the most cherished person in the world to him. He felt a powerful need to open up to her again—to share another guarded secret.

"That night in Dallas—our first full night together—it was the first time in my life I'd ever spent the night with another person. Even as a child, there was no one."

With Jared's confession, she pulled away just far enough to gaze into his eyes.

"Don't get me wrong, there've been women, but never for more than an hour here or there and never in my personal space. At no time in my life have I ever wanted anyone by my side. You changed all of that for me, Jody. I can't imagine not touching you, not talking to you, not being with you."

He touched his forehead to hers. "It scares me. I've never been this committed to anyone or anything. I don't know what I'm doing, and I'm terrified I'm going to do something to screw it up and push you away."

Jody opened her mouth to speak, but he put his finger to her lips to stop her. "Promise me that if I ever do something stupid or hurt you in some way, you won't just leave me. You'll talk to me first and help me understand what I've done wrong."

Pulling his face to hers, she kissed his nose, the side of his mouth, his chin and then his eyes surrounding him with the love he'd never had. Tears caused by his insecurities washed away with the spray of the shower.

"You have my word."

Chapter Twenty-Two

Lazing around on a Saturday with his girl had quickly become the most coveted reality in Jared's world. He had a hard time believing they'd already been together for three wonderful months. Time spent with his little monkey sped by in the blink of an eye.

Jared now understood why people dreaded Mondays. When the beginning of the week rolled around, their work separated him and Jody for nine long, grueling hours a day. Luckily, a few weeks ago, he'd been able to convince her to move in with him. *Who am I kidding? I got down on my knees and begged her to share our living arrangements.*

As usual, they were sitting at his favorite spot in the house. He faced her on the couch, and she faced him, their blue jean clad legs entangled somewhere in the middle. Jared had propped himself up on his side of the sofa, reading the paper on his tablet. Jody sat directly across from him, reading what she called an important, completely necessary piece of literature for women called *The Mighty Highlander.*

When her foot casually rubbed his thigh, he couldn't contain his smile. Jody had no idea she did it, which made the tender gesture all the more special. Even unconsciously, they felt the need to reach out to each other in one way or another.

Looking over his tablet, Jared recognized that the

current book had transported Jody off to some other world. All but swooning, she tightly clutched her shirt over her heart. Remembering the reaction this particular novel received when they were in the bookstore, left him chuckling under his breath. She'd literally fanned herself, blaming her flushed appearance on the romance and not the smut.

Every moment he'd spent with her proved to be precious. Even times like this when they wound up doing their separate things, they always ended up on this couch together. He'd promised himself never to take this feeling of togetherness for granted. Far too many empty years had passed him by, making him acutely aware of the importance of their relationship.

His gaze roamed up the wall behind her and landed on the portrait responsible for bringing them together. *Solitude*. They'd come so far since that first night. They were now so deeply ingrained in each other that if one of them were taken out of the equation, the other didn't have a chance in hell of surviving. They'd quickly become each other's lifeline.

During his investigations, he'd recently found himself in dangerous situations. Threats to his safety weren't anything new or out of the ordinary by any means. But since Jody had become a part of his life, his approach to that aspect of his career had changed dramatically. Instead of going out on a case without thought and guns blazing, as had been the norm in the past, he now thought of Jody and backed away from the danger. The thrill-seeking cowboy in him had disappeared forever. With this extraordinary woman in the forefront of his mind, he preferred to choose a more practical approach to his work. Over the course of these last few months, she'd become too important to him to let her down by not being more careful and potentially not coming home to her. She'd become that little piece of sanity in his mind and the determining factor in many, if not all, of his decisions these days. He liked that fact very much.

Over the past few months, he'd witnessed firsthand how Jody's gifts had grown since Fiona had come and gone from her life. The evolution she'd initially feared and spoken of early on in their union had finally made itself known. He thanked his lucky stars it hadn't been truly tested yet. They simply weren't ready. He knew in the back of his mind, though, it would only be a matter of time before the new ability became a factor in their lives.

Somehow, Jody had learned to embrace her ramped up spiritual gifts instead of fear them. She'd managed to come to terms with knowing something big would happen one day that would demand her participation. Accepting that fact without reservation, she'd told him time and time again, her fear was suppressed because of his offered help. *'Together we can fight any battle and come out alive.'* Jared had replayed her words in his mind a thousand times, and they still carried both joy and terror. He wished he shared in her confidence.

Initially, her new gift had been so foreign she'd had to look it up to see what to call it. *Psychometry*. The word rolled through Jared's mind. Ever since little Fiona had jumped into her body, she'd felt as though her empathic abilities had been heightened as well.

The empathic abilities didn't surprise him in the least. To some degree, he believed they'd probably been there from the beginning and just hadn't been as strong or well developed. Psychometry, on the other hand, totally wigged him out.

On more than one occasion, he'd feared for her safety when other people's emotions snuck up on her and hijacked her body. She'd had to learn not to touch anything belonging to someone she didn't know. Even something as inane as picking up a stranger's accidentally dropped car keys had proven to be catastrophic. Depending on what was going on in the owner's life, Jody would become overwrought with emotion. Many times, she wasn't able to break the spell of being up close and personal in that person's experiences. Those occurrences left her completely overwhelmed. When they found themselves out in public, he stayed close to her for the simple reason that she may need to be reined in.

As soon as she realized objects held in her hand provided her with the owner's life story, he worried constantly. Psychometry couldn't make the distinction between an innocent baby or someone who sported a more nefarious nature. The thought of her accidentally touching something which would unwillingly lure her into the life of a dangerous person, such as a criminal or serial killer, scared him shitless.

To get them both more comfortable with this new ability, Jared made sure they worked on conquering the mechanics of the psychometry together on a daily basis. Practice made perfect. They'd devised some exercises which facilitated not only reliability of the new gift but protection as well. When the time presented itself to act, he hoped it would be second nature for her to listen to his voice and use his strength. The only way to keep her safe would be for him to guide her through the process.

Through trial and error, they'd found the bookstore a great place to practice psychometry and used that method of exercise often. When she picked out books to read in this manner, she'd get a quick and safe insight into how accurate her impressions had been.

Sometimes they spent hours in the bookstore for her to choose *just the right read*, as she called it. Before entering the store, she would blindfold herself with a scarf. Jody wanted to touch the spines of the books, feel them without being influenced by the cover or blurb. Needless to say, the peculiarity of her actions ended up drawing the attention of other shoppers. While most people moved quickly out of the way, there were some that curiosity got the best of. That's how they'd met Greta, an aging woman that dressed as if she belonged in the fifties and wore enough perfume to anesthetize an elephant.

"Oh, dear heart, have you injured yourself? Can I help you, child?"

Unaccustomed to dealing with little old women, Jared moved protectively to Jody's side and answered to avoid any further attention. "That won't be necessary, ma'am. We'll just move out of your way and you can continue shopping."

"Pfft." An aged hand flew into the air. "Name's Greta, son. I'm old enough already without being called ma'am. You're sure a strapping young boy."

Blindfold still in place, Jody's laughter rang through the store while Jared couldn't help but beam at the compliment.

Pulling the scarf down to her neck, Jody surprised

Jared when she held her hand out to the old woman. He started to step forward but she winked at him to let him know she had the situation under control. Greta appeared to be at the very least ninety years old. Jared wasn't sure if that would prove difficult for Jody and her gift or not.

"It's a pleasure to meet you, Greta. I'm Jody and this is Jared." Even at Jody's petite height of five-foot, two inches, she had to bend down to the older woman. "He *is* strapping, and he's all mine."

Greta cupped her ear. "What's that, dear? I'm a little hard of hearing."

Jody straightened and wrapped her arm around Jared's speaking loud enough to be heard throughout their aisle. "I said, I'm one lucky woman, Greta."

The old woman nodded as a smile filled with sunshine lit her face. "So tell me, dear, what is it you are doing with a scarf around your eyes when you're in a bookstore? I can't for the life of me figure it out."

Jared enjoyed watching the interaction between the two women. The old gal reminded him of his grandmother.

"Well, I'll tell you, Greta. I'm an avid reader."

"Amen, sister," Greta acknowledged.

"But I get overwhelmed looking at all the book covers. Half the time, I end up purchasing a book I don't want just because of the cover."

Greta's lips pursed together. "Yep. I've done the same thing myself more times than I can count."

"This is probably going to sound odd, but I put the scarf on and touch the books. When I come to one that feels right, I hold it tight to my chest to decide if it's a book I would enjoy."

Greta perked up. "Well, bless your heart, child. I should have known! You have the gift of touch, too. Normally, I recognize those things right off in people. You poor thing. I know what a tribulation it can be. I'll say a little prayer for you." Greta's unruly eyebrows met in the middle of her face. "I must admit, I've never thought of using my touch gift in a bookstore before. That's brilliant!" The little old woman rested her cane on the shelf and opened her purse. She pulled a bright red scarf from her bag and held it out to Jared.

Not sure what to do, Jared grabbed the fine piece of silk. "Young man, I have a difficult time reaching above my head. Would you fashion the scarf around my eyes like your lovely wife's was, please?"

Overlooking the wife remark, Jared knew full well, the fragile woman would stumble and felt obliged to confess his misgivings. "Greta, I don't think it's safe for you to walk around blindfolded." She stopped him with a raised finger.

"Harry! Where are you, cupcake? I need you!" Greta's booming voice moved Jared back a half step. "Go ahead and put the scarf on, dear. My Harry's a little slow, but he'll be here in no time at all."

Just as Jared finished tying the scarf around Greta's eyes, a man not much taller than her turned the corner. The coke bottle glasses he donned made his eyes look as big as saucers. He wore baby blue polyester pants that were cut like jeans and rode so high Jared couldn't figure out how the family jewels weren't crushed.

"Young man! Get your hands off of my woman!" Feeling as though minutes passed before the ancient man made it to Greta's side, he was clearly prepared to defend his wife. The old geezer's gumption impressed

Jared.

Since being blindfolded, Greta's hands were held out in front of her, one still grasping her cane. "Harry, stop that nonsense right this minute. This young woman taught me how to pick a book out by using my touch skills. Let's scoot, old man. I'm excited to get started."

Harry grabbed Greta's arm and lead her off. "Take me to them big print books, sweetie."

Jody pulled Jared into an embrace and giggled into his chest. "That's going to be us in about sixty years, *dear heart*."

Another training method which seemed to work in honing her skills had been bringing items home that belonged to his consenting employees. They'd recorded Jody's responses and found that she'd been hitting an accuracy level of right around ninety-eight percent. Jared's interaction with Jody when using this practice method was invaluable. They'd created a process in which Jared guided Jody through and helped her maintain a safe distance from the person's emotions.

They did anything and everything that could possibly be done to give her an edge. Resulting, hopefully, in keeping Jody from getting lost in the tornado of someone else's life when touching other people's things. Unfortunately, because the ability had yet to be tested in a pivotal circumstance, Jared had remained nervous they'd be unprepared when the time did finally arrive. There were just too many variables they couldn't possibly foresee.

This new gift of Jody's wasn't merely harmless images flashing through her mind when she touched an object. Along with seeing the owner's life story as a movie, she'd *feel* the owner's emotions as if they were her own. If that weren't terrifying enough, she'd also feel that person's physical pain which scared Jared to death.

When touching an object, she would become lost inside those experiences as if she were a part of that particular event. Sometimes he could pull her back easily and help guide her through what she was seeing. But other times, generally revolving around more traumatic events, she went so deep into a trancelike state that he had difficulty bringing her out of the vision.

Lost in his never-ending doubts, Jared jumped when Jody suddenly sprang off the couch and started pacing. She tightly clutched the book to her chest and continued to read. It quickly became apparent that the author's adventure had clearly captured Jody's imagination.

During the time they'd shared with each other, he'd learned that an inventive author could have her so involved in the characters and storyline, she'd be compelled to move around as she read. Her subconscious felt the need to help the characters out of whatever mess they had been written into.

Considering how worked up she seemed to be getting, the author of *The Mighty Highlander* must have done a good job putting the brazen Highlander hunk and his sassy trollop through the ringer.

Jody's breathing quickened. She stood in the middle of the room, one hand held the book, the other covered her mouth. Her shocked expression spoke volumes as her eyes grew to the size of saucers and filled with tears. "No," she cried out animatedly. "No! No! No!" As a sign of her dismay, her head shook with such force whipping those beautiful blonde tresses through the air. The Highlander characters had obviously started to misbehave.

He shifted his weight and got comfortable for the show. His little monkey made everything personal, including a trashy novel.

She held the book at arm's length, never taking her eyes from the page. "What the hell?" she gushed with pure disgust over the character's traitorous actions. "That can't be! You better pull your head out of your ass right now, Aileen, or you're going to get him killed!" As if the hussy, Aileen, were standing next to her, Jody's hand shot out for emphasis. "Stupid bitch!"

Jody's reaction to the misbehaving characters had Jared grinning from ear to ear. He knew for a fact that the Highlander had already established himself as a particularly amorous fellow. He'd even been the grateful recipient of some of the brazen Scotsman's more outlandish sexual escapades which Jody had enjoyed sharing with him. That being said, the possibility of makeup sex would be coming quite soon in the book. *That's good for me.* His grin grew to a full-blown smile.

****

Nathan and Special Agent Jursic jumped from the car and ran into the park. Men from two other vehicles followed their lead. Nathan had been working closely with the FBI on the protective duty detail for Lincoln Spurl and his family. Spurl was a prominent businessman and one of the richest men in the world. There had been recent credible chatter about kidnapping one of their family members for ransom.

Spurl's daughter, Margaret, had died just a few

short months ago. That left the old man, Lincoln, and his wife, Jessie, to care for their granddaughter, Mikala. Starting even before his daughter's death, Spurl had fought a long legal battle to get Mikala's biological dad out of the picture.

The lowlife ex-husband had abused the old man's daughter. The bastard only wanted custody of his granddaughter for the money he would receive from the family on a monthly basis. The ex-husband didn't care anymore for his own child than he had for Margaret, his wife. They were his income, his paycheck, and nothing more. Spurl had put an end to the loser's meal ticket and made a dangerous enemy in the process.

The powerful man had contacted Nathan for security purposes six months ago, requesting special guard duty for his family. Now one of his best men, Kane Welter, the granddaughter's assigned bodyguard, had missed his call-in time and wasn't answering his phone. Nathan had promptly located him with the GPS set up for all of his bodyguards. Tracking devices were mandatory for all personnel. In the event something happened to them, and they were out of reach for any length of time, they could be quickly reached.

Sirens could be heard in the distance as the men ran into the park. *Dammit!* Local cops tended to get pissy when other people moved in to try to take control of a crime scene. Nathan thanked his lucky stars he'd brought a cavalry of feds with him to take the lead should the need arise.

They spotted a group of people gathered around a tree and headed in that direction. As the other agents flashed their badges and tried to move the gawkers aside, Nathan and Jursic were finally able to break through the crowd. They were greeted by an empty stroller and a random bystander frantically doing CPR on Kane.

Nathan bent down and felt for a pulse. *Nothing.* He was gone. Doing his best to control his panic, he thanked the woman who'd worked so hard to save Kane. To get the good samaritan out of his way as fast as possible, he directed her to speak with the on-scene FBI agents.

Jursic disconnected the call with Mr. Spurl. "The nanny got sick and didn't come with Kane and the girl to the park. We have people looking for her." Reviewing the murder/kidnap scene to get a quick snapshot of what had happened, Nathan looked first to the empty stroller and then back at Kane's body. Jursic knelt beside the corpse to inspect the bodyguard's wound.

A course of action quickly formed in Nathan's mind. He knew beyond a shadow of a doubt, the little girl's life had been put in grave danger. It didn't matter if the deed had been done by the kid's estranged father, the nanny or someone else. Whoever had taken her had no compunction about killing to get to the child.

Nathan needed to act fast. He didn't care what Jursic and the others thought of him. He'd do what needed to be done to get Mikala back.

Leaning back on his heels, he started urgently speaking to the void above the bodyguard's corpse. "Kane, I don't know if you're still here, but if you can hear me, I need you to come with me. I'm going to talk to someone who should be able to see you and hear you."

Looking at Nathan as if he'd lost his mind, Jursic's

eyebrow rose a fraction of an inch. Ignoring the FBI agent, Nathan continued to plead to the dead man's spirit. "Kane, I know you saw what happened here. Please come with me, and you'll be able to tell me everything that happened. I swear it."

Nathan quickly stood and crossed to the stroller. Jursic grabbed his arm and roughly spun him around. "What the fuck are you doing? We can't leave. We have to stay and talk to these people. They're our only hope of finding the kid."

"I can't explain right now, Jursic, but I know someone who can help. Leave some of your men and bring a few with us. I'll explain everything on the way. Hopefully, we're not too late."

Nathan broke Jursic's hold and grabbed the blanket from the stroller. Without looking back at the chaotic scene, he trotted to the vehicle silently praying Kane had heard him and followed.

Chapter Twenty-Three

Since reading had turned into a morning of calisthenics, as Jared had predicted it would, Jody took a much-needed break. Trying to concentrate on his newspaper, she playfully tapped her foot on his thigh. "I'm in the mood for a Dr. Pepper." Glancing over his tablet, he offered her a warm smile. He'd never had the courage to try a Dr. Pepper until he met her. He had to admit, the sweet, soft drink she enjoyed so much had become a guilty pleasure they often shared.

"Would you like something from the kitchen while I'm in there?"

"I might consider a few sips of your drink."

"You got it." Jared slapped Jody's ass for good measure as she walked by before returning his focus to the tablet.

Mere seconds later he heard a quick intake of air as if she'd been startled. Jared shifted his attention and saw Jody. She hadn't quite made it out of the room but managed to turn back toward him. She stood stock still with one foot in front of the other as if glued in place. She'd gone pale. Her eyes had clouded over and appeared unfocused while her hands fisted tightly at her sides. Her breathing came and went in short, raspy gasps.

The peace he'd felt moments ago had been ripped out from under him, quickly giving way to anxiety. He *knew* the signs. He *knew* what he was seeing. His little monkey had somehow been caught up in the grips of something paranormal. Something or someone had invaded her mind's eye. This episode, whatever it may be, had come on so quickly she hadn't had any warning at all.

Jared hustled across the room and reached out to Jody's hand, but she jerked it away. "Monkey, tell me what's happening," he cried, trying desperately to take control of the uncontrollable.

Just then the doorbell chimed followed by an insistent rapping on the front door. Knowing instantly something vile had just shown up at his doorstep had fear clamping its razor-sharp teeth into his gut.

To help Jody, he had to find out what had happened. He didn't want to leave her alone for a second, but he had to. He ran to the foyer just as Nathan screamed Jody's name from outside. As soon as the door opened, he rushed in followed by several men Jared didn't know, all of whom were visibly upset and obviously federal agents.

Jared reached for his throat as panic partially closed his airway. "What's happening?" he managed to croak.

Nathan pushed past him. "Quick! Where's Jody?"

The men rushed into the living room, where they found Jody on her knees, holding her chest and gasping for air. Still unaware of the dire circumstances which had reached out from beyond and claimed Jody, Jared knelt beside her and latched onto her hand. Unwilling to let her pull free, he clutched her arm tightly with his other hand knowing full well his rough treatment would leave bruises on her delicate skin.

Jared's bellowing voice belied his fear and commanded her attention. "Jody, listen to my voice. Don't get pulled in all the way. Listen to me. Tell me what you're seeing."

Not having a clue what to expect, the strangers nervously gathered in a semicircle. Nathan yelled orders. "I need everyone in the room to take your phones out and video what's happening. Keep your cameras trained on the woman. Make sure audio is on."

Jody's eyes were so wide open they almost hurt. Her chest heaved as she desperately tried to get much-needed air into her oxygen starved lungs. Somewhere in the distance, she heard Jared pleading.

"You've got to separate yourself from the event, Jody. Listen to my voice. Tell me what you're seeing. Tell me what you're feeling."

The room went dead silent as everyone waited for her response.

"There's a man." Trying her best to keep her wits about her and analyze what she felt and saw, had Jody tilting her head slightly to the side. "I think I know him. I'm sure I've seen him somewhere."

Her body violently jerked as if she'd been punched. Looking down at her chest, she removed her hand from where the blow had landed. Blood ran through her fingers making her stomach heave with the need to wretch. For a moment, fear had gripped her in its clutches and removed all cognitive thought leaving widespread panic in its wake. The shock from being gravely injured left her whimpering and unable to speak. Finally, she found a way to force the words from her mouth. "I've…I've been sh…I've been shot!"

The men who'd invaded their home started

speaking in hushed but urgent tones.

"No, Monkey, you have *not* been shot. There is *no* blood. Do you hear me, baby? *No* blood. You're here with me in our living room."

Jody's body begin to quake as if she were going into shock. Jared grabbed her shoulders and shook them hard. "Back away from him, Jody! Back away from the man that's been injured. *Now!* Push him out of your body if you have to, but get rid of him! You're feeling his pain, not your own."

Her breathing came so fast, she'd be hyperventilating soon if she couldn't slow it down. To try to control her body's reaction to the spirit who'd jumped her, Jody slammed her eyes shut and squeezed them together with all of her might. Somewhere off in the distance, she heard Jared screaming at her. She couldn't quite make out what he said, but she instinctively knew to move toward his voice.

All but breathless, she finally forced herself to speak. "He jumped me like Fiona did. He's hurt. He's bleeding. He's scared. Oh God, Jared! He doesn't know he's dead." Beckoning the strength to get through this mess, she squeezed Jared's hand as hard as she could. The man's fear and sorrow swamped her. "I think he's been shot. The wound hurts so bad, I can hardly breathe."

Nathan got on his knees next to Jody. "Kane—is the man you're seeing Kane? He was the person protecting Mikala. Is it Kane?"

Jody thought she heard Nathan somewhere in the distance. She couldn't take the chance of splitting her concentration at the moment. Barely being able to hold onto the essence of herself, had her focusing on Jared's touch and voice alone.

Persistent as always, she recognized the fact that Nathan proceeded to scream at her. He was doing everything he could to get her attention. Somewhere deep inside her, though, Jody knew her survival of this attack depended on doing what she and Jared had practiced. She couldn't take the precious time needed to try to comprehend what her friend was saying. She couldn't risk averting her attention long enough to talk to him, not yet. The spirit of the injured man was systematically draining all of her precious energy and had her fighting her own battles.

"Look at me," Jared snapped, shaking her again to take control of the situation. He forced her head up, and what he saw in her eyes scared the hell out of him. Her eyes were dead.

Still not knowing the cause behind this psychic event, but at least having a name to go on, Jared issued orders in a way a man like his ex-military employee, Kane, would understand. "Kane, if this is you, you *must* leave her body. She can't help you when you're inside of her. You *must* leave. She'll be able to talk to you when she's free of you."

A loud popping noise, accompanied by a sudden shift in the room's air pressure had everyone jumping back. Fear gripped the FBI agents who happened to find themselves mixed up in this freak fest. They all took a long nervous step away from the woman who appeared possessed.

Physically spent after the domineering spirit had left her body, Jody collapsed where she sat. Suddenly limp, Jared managed to carefully pick her up and put her in his lap. As they had practiced, he poured every bit of his strength into her. He visualized the power within him flowing into her depleted body. Needing confirmation that Kane's spirit had left her personal space, he kissed her cheek and asked barely above a whisper, "Concentrate on my voice, Jody. Is Kane still here?"

One of the unknown men bent down in front of Jody and spoke barely above a whisper. "Ma'am, I'm Special Agent Jursic. I'm not sure what's going on here, but Nathan told me you might have information on the kidnapping of Mikala Spurl. She's the granddaughter of Lincoln and Jessie Spurl."

Her eyes fluttered open. "Yes, Kane's here." She spoke as if she hadn't heard the stranger's voice. The only answer forthcoming was to Jared's question.

Jursic opened his mouth to speak again when Nathan forcibly pushed him aside. "Kane, what happened? What did you see?"

Her eyes barely open, and her body still limp, Jared held her tightly tucked into his chest, continuing to transfer his much-needed energy. Her whisper had been so quiet that the agents shuffled closer to hear her.

"He said they came out of the trees at the park. There were people all around, and he had let his guard down. He was sitting with his back against a tree. The stroller with the little girl was in front of him. They were playing peek-a-boo. He didn't hear the shot, but he felt like he'd been sucker punched by someone. He says, he reached down and realized blood was pouring out of his chest.

"There were three of them. One who acted as a lookout. One to grab the girl and one to take care of me." Jared didn't miss her use of the word *me*.

"Jody, you need to separate yourself from Kane." He demanded, hoping his voice conveyed the power she needed to separate herself from the dead man. "Put a little space between the two of you. Come toward my voice, Monkey."

Waiting through the long, agonizing pause for her response left everyone in the room nervous. Jared started to tell her to back away again when she finally began to speak. "He says they were professional. There had to have been a silencer on the gun they used because he never heard the shot."

Jared recognized how hard Jody was working to remain calm when she finally spoke again. "He chased after them."

One of the burly FBI men interrupted the dialog with an angry shout. "This is bullshit! What the fuck are we doing here? The bodyguard was dead. He never moved after being shot. He didn't chase after them. We all know that. Why the fuck are we wasting our time here? We need to move!"

Nathan stood and shoved the man backward with great force. "Leave the room right now." Fuming, the man finally backed down and left.

Nathan moved back to Jody's side. "Jody, baby, did Kane see a vehicle?"

They all witnessed a slight nod of her head. "White…CJK-989." Jursic started dialing his phone immediately to call in the plate number.

"Can Kane describe the three men?"

Blankly, Jody stared off into the corner of the room before finally nodding her head. "Three women."

Shocked, Jursic screeched, "What?"

"He says that's why no one paid any attention to

them when they took the child—it was three women.

"I'm losing him." As Kane's spirit started backing away, her energy depletion had left her voice nothing more than a weak whisper. "He's leaving." Her bottom lip quivered with emotion as her hand rose slightly in an attempt to wish the spirit goodbye. "He doesn't want to go, but he must. His people are here to help him cross over."

The men stood over her and watched in awe as a beautiful smile bloomed on her face.

Nathan bent down in front of Jody and held out a child's blanket which had been speckled with the bodyguard's blood. "Do you think you can get anything from Mikala's blanket?"

Before the personal item could touch her, anger and disbelief had Jared growling and pushing him away. Refusing to let go of Jody, he couldn't put much force behind the shove. "Have you lost your fucking mind? Look at her. She's completely drained. I won't let her do any more right now."

"Jared, be reasonable. We're looking for a four-year-old girl. She could be dead very shortly if we don't get information to act on."

Shaking his head fiercely, he continued to rock the love of his life back and forth like a baby. *This nightmare has to end!* "No!" Immovable in his decision, he had a death grip on her. He was more afraid for her right now than he'd ever been for himself.

Jody reached out and gently grazed Jared's lips with her fingertips. When she had his attention, though weak, her voice held resolve to see this through to the end. "Jared, I know this is difficult, but I have to see if I can help. What if she were our baby? You'd want any help you could get. You'd demand it, as would I."

Having the green light to proceed from Jody, Nathan pushed through Jared's stranglehold to get to her. Before he could give her the blanket, Jared spoke in a dangerously low, rage-filled voice. "I won't forget this, Nathan." The words were spoken with force and held such contempt that Nathan froze for a moment.

"Jared, a little girl's life is at risk. If we don't act fast, she'll be dead. I know it in my heart. I wouldn't put Jody through this if there were any other way."

When it became apparent his plea had landed on deaf ears, Nathan scooted forward. "Here's her blanket. Can you pick anything up from it, Jody?"

Jared saw the fear in Jody's eyes when the blanket came within reach. He also recognized the exact moment sheer determination took over and she stuck her hand out. As her fingers clutched the tiny blanket, her body began to thrash wildly. It became apparent her psyche was no match for the nightmare in which the child currently resided. Her head flew back as a terror filled scream wrenched from the back of her throat, compelling everyone in the room to crouch down out of fear. As if she'd had some form of a frozen seizure, her jaw suddenly clamped down making her screams sound more like a terrified animal caught in the grips of death.

As her body quickly shifted between violent spasms and sudden stiffness, it proved impossible for Jared to hold onto her. Their safety net of physical contact had been shattered. As if possessed, she gained the freedom from Jared's tight grasp and scrambled from his lap, spider walking backward. She backed away from the unseen threat so quickly that she stumbled and landed in a heap on the floor.

Before she could physically hurt herself, Jared tried to regain control by rushing her and forcefully grabbing her face between his hands. She struck out at him, landing blow after blow. Pure terror dilated her eyes. He threw his body on top of her and pressed his nose to hers, screaming at the top of his lungs. "Back away from the emotion, Jody. You have to back away! Listen to my voice. Concentrate on *my* voice only! Come to me, Monkey. Come to *me*."

As her tremors subsided and the fight left her body, he knew she was doing everything in her power to manage not only her fear but that of the little girl's. Finally seeing a slight spark in her eyes, he knew she'd been able to gain a little distance from the child's emotions. Without breaking contact, he sat up and pulled her back into his lap.

Speaking in a clear sharp tone, he demanded her full attention. "Just like we practiced, Jody. Separate yourself from the emotion, and tell me what you're seeing."

"We're in the back seat of a car. We're in a car seat." She reached for her head and winced. "We're feeling so groggy. We think they gave us something to go to sleep. We're holding a sippy cup." Her hand rose as if she were showing the men the child's cup. "We're starting to feel very heavy." Her voice started taking on the characteristics of talking in her sleep. Her words were jumbled and extremely slurred.

"Jody, baby, *listen* to my voice. Move toward my voice. You must step outside of the child."

Her eyes opened a slit, and he knew he was getting through to her.

"Tell me about the car, Jody."

"It's not the same car from the park. It's red and has dark windows. It's newer than the car at the park." Suddenly alert, Jody bolted up and looked to her right. She kept moving her head around as if she were watching a tennis match.

"What are you looking at, Jody?"

"The woman sitting next to me is mean." Jared sighed, knowing by her mannerisms and speech, she'd been pulled back into the child's body again. Her lips thrust out in a pouty manner as if she were a child being scolded. "She's yelling at the other women in the car." She started relaying the conversation she overheard to the men in the room. '*Sharla, stop your goddamn blubbering! You knew what we were doing from the very beginning. You knew what the plan was.*'

Jody jumped in fear. Her eyes became huge as she quickly straightened her head to look in front of her. "The woman driving is beating on the steering wheel with her fist. She's yelling at the woman in the back seat. '*Back off me, Brenda! I'm hanging on by a thread here. Let's just follow the plans on the list and do it without yelling.*'

"Wait!" Jody threw an arm out in front of her. "We're pulling into a parking lot." Jursic bent down and got in her face. "What parking lot? What is the name of the business?"

"There's a big yellow and orange sign. It says Safe Storage." Jody jumped in fear again. She was obviously listening to something because her eyes widened in alarm. "Unit 21."

She started struggling with an unseen assailant. Her arms flailed. Her legs kicked out. She viscously punched and kicked at the air. Her fists pummeled Jared as if she were fighting for her life. Just as it looked as though she'd been somewhat restrained, he'd lost his hold again. Her arms flew above her head in a defensive manner. "No!" her scream heavy with terror, rattled the men's nerves as they watched the scene unfold in front of them. Her breathing became short, panic-filled pants.

She started begging to the captors through her tears. "No! Don't put me in there!" Her body contorted into the fetal position, and her arms went up in the air. "No! Please! I'm afraid! I'm afraid!"

Her fists started pounding at the air above her head. "No!" She pleaded one last time before losing consciousness.

Chapter Twenty-Four

Jared remained on the floor cradling Jody, who still hadn't regained consciousness. His worst fear had just been realized, leaving him terrified she wouldn't come back to him. Everyone except Nathan had quickly vacated their home. Like the jackals they were, they'd all felt the need to move on the information was more important than dealing with the disaster left behind in their wake. Information they'd come by at far too great of a personal cost for both him and Jody.

Nathan was the only person to remain behind. When he reached out to gently stroke Jody's hair, Jared possessively jerked her away. He felt the rage at her so called best friend boiling within for putting Jody in such grave danger.

After several tense moments, Jared finally spoke, but it was through clenched teeth and barely louder than a whisper. "Get out of our home."

"J.D., please understand that I love Jody. What I witnessed today scared the shit out of me too. I just need to know she's okay. I need her to know that I love her. I'm proud of her for stepping in and hopefully saving that little girl. I…"

Jared cut him off. "Enough! If you don't leave now, I'll fucking kill you."

Nathan backed away as Jared bent to kiss Jody's forehead tenderly. "It's all right, Monkey. They won't bother you again. You're safe now."

****

The phone had been ringing off the hook all day, but with Jody in trouble, Jared refused to answer. It had taken over six, tense hours for her to regain consciousness and come back to him. He wasn't ready to see or hear from Nathan just yet.

Through the anxious wait, as a distraction, Jared ran different scenarios through his mind on the perfect and most painful death in which he could personally inflict on Nathan. He would see to it that the jerk-off's demise would be one of epic proportions. Since he hadn't narrowed the choices down yet, he wasn't prepared to see or talk to him.

When Jody's eyelids started to flutter, Jared had never been more relieved. After Nathan had so carelessly brought evil to their doorstep, she'd been forced to fight for her life. The only tools in his arsenal were his voice, touch, and love. He could only hope those would be enough to bring her back to him. His voice had all but disappeared as he prayed she wouldn't be lost to him forever. Finally, his prayers had been answered.

When she'd snapped out of it, he made sure his face was the first thing she saw. Wanting to be certain all of her came back to him, he stared deep into her eyes. He also needed to assure himself that no spirit lurked within her. Thankfully, there had been no sign that a greedy phantom had decided to take up residence as she'd fought so hard to come back to him.

When he saw her own unique sparkle of life return to her eyes, he felt as though he could finally breathe easy again. The moment she recognized him, her beautiful green eyes shone with love. Too overwhelmed to speak, he nuzzled her neck, smelling her scent and feeling her life force in her heartbeat with his lips. Unable to contain himself any longer, sobs violently racked his body as they laid there and held each other.

"I thought you were going to…" he couldn't say the word aloud, out of fear she still might breathe her last breath right here in his arms. "I had started to believe that I had lost you."

Their past experience with Fiona had made him fully aware that it would take some time for her to claw her way through the dark sludge which permeated her mind. She'd remain in a darkened state, making it difficult to speak or even think. When she reached up and ran her hand through his silky hair, he knew it was to comfort not only him but herself as well.

"I don't think I can do this again, Monkey. I've never been so afraid in my life," he murmured into her neck, praying as he spoke she would agree with him. But he knew deep down inside she had no choice in the matter. That distinction didn't stop him from selfishly hoping this would be last time she'd ever put herself in this position again. Realistically, he knew her abilities weren't something she could return like a bad Christmas present. Nor could she turn them on and off at will. There'd be many more times like this in their lives together, but he just couldn't grasp that fact right now. The only important thing right this minute was his overwhelming need to hold onto her and never let go.

"Sh-h-h," she whispered trying to soothe him. "It's okay, sweetheart. I'm right here, and I'm not going anywhere."

Her still weak voice frightened him. *How long will*

it take her to recover from this? Will she ever recuperate completely? After what he'd witnessed today, he wasn't sure she'd ever be the same again.

Trying to regain her equilibrium, Jody held him close. Her sluggish mind left her feeling more hungover than sleep deprived. She still wasn't able to arrange her thoughts and determine what was real and what wasn't. Mentally and physically exhausted, she tried with all her might to piece together what had happened.

Cocooned and safe beneath Jared's large frame, she stiffened as bits and pieces of the previous hours started to come back to her. He rose up on his elbows as some of the terrifying memories came crashing back. Panicked, she grabbed Jared's arms to steady herself. "The little girl? Jared, is the little girl all right? Did they find her?"

To help make her more comfortable, he stacked pillows behind her so she could sit up. Jared's mannerisms, while gentle, belied the anger she sensed just below the surface. She allowed him to tend lovingly to her without pushing for an answer because it helped him calm down and put things in perspective. Several tense minutes had passed before Jared responded. "I don't know, Monkey. I couldn't leave you lying here all by yourself to find out."

Hearing the sharp, angry tone in Jared's voice and seeing the pain in his eyes made her heart break. She realized how hard this experience must've been on him. The guilt she felt for being the person responsible for his pain was unbearable. Reaching out, she touched his cheek to offer him some peace of mind about her wellbeing. "Jared, it was you who brought me back. Your voice. Your touch. You seemed miles away, but I kept hearing your voice and moving toward it. I never felt alone because you were always talking to me. I'm here because of you. Your love kept me safe."

He wrapped his arms around her and held on for dear life. "Oh, Monkey, I didn't think you were going to come back to me. You being lost somewhere out there in God only knows where left me feeling so damn helpless."

She ran her hand up and down his back to console him. "I'm here, Jared. You brought me back. I love you, sweetheart. There are no words I can string together to convey how sorry I am that I scared you."

"I love you too, Monkey."

The chime of the doorbell had him cursing under his breath. He pulled himself from her embrace, wiped the tears from his face first and then dried hers. "I'll get rid of whoever that is. You need your rest."

Overtaken by exhaustion, it took all of her strength to reach out for him. "Jared, please find out about the little girl. I need to know."

She hated the pleading tone of her voice, but Jared had to understand she wouldn't be able to rest and put this behind her until she knew the outcome. He bent to kiss her outstretched hand and nodded his head as he left the room.

As he'd expected, he opened the door to find Nathan and Terry. The unbridled affectation of pain and raw fury Jared openly displayed had them both taking a guarded step back.

Only having part of the story, Terry's concern for Nathan grew as his friend looked down at the ground. His shoulders slumped as if already defeated. He had come along because he knew this problem with J.D.

had to be resolved. Maybe because he hadn't been there, but Terry could see both sides. And it would take someone who although might not be unbiased, when it came to Jody, to be able to try and get J.D. to see Nathan's side also.

"You've got a hell of a nerve showing your face here after invading our home and putting Jody in danger. You must have cojones the size of watermelons."

Knowing that making the first non-aggressive move might be a big mistake, Terry took a moment to gather his courage. He stepped forward, reaching out for Jared's arm. As expected, the big man angrily pulled away while making a sound which could only compare to a rabid creature. Terry's heart skipped a beat at the wholly ferocious display.

Uncomfortable in situations such as this, he allowed his finer, more sharply honed senses to take over. His artist's eye allowed him, not for the first time, to see the deadly predator within this man. This time, however, that dark and angry creature lurked dangerously close to the surface ready to shred him and Nathan to pieces if they made one wrong move.

Before he got mangled, Terry's hands went up in the air in a show of surrender. "How is she?" He spoke in low, dulcet tones trying to tame the beast in front of him.

Jared moved his steely gaze from Nathan to Terry. "How would you expect her to be? She's been lost somewhere within herself all day, and she's just come back to me. She's exhausted. I'm exhausted. And I'm not ready to deal with either of you yet."

"Thank God she came out of it," Nathan said under

his breath.

Jared's attention snapped back to Nathan. "Yes. *You* certainly didn't do anything to help."

Terry appreciated Jared's mindset, but his anger was skewing reality. Since Nathan was in danger of being pulverized, he'd have to be the one to try to make Jared see reason. "That's not fair, Jared, and you know it." Knowing full well he was taking a chance of getting a broken arm, he placed his hand on Jared's shoulder and clamped down so it couldn't be shaken off. He summoned all of the inner courage he could muster to hold his ground.

"We love Jody like a sister. She's our family. Neither one of us would ever do anything to intentionally put her in harm's way. You've got to know that."

Terry waited for an answer, but Jared was so intent on staring Nathan down one never came.

"Look," Terry finally said, taking another tentative step closer to Jared. "If you want to kick *his* ass"—he nodded toward Nathan as he threw him under the bus—"I'm good with that. I'm going inside. When I find our girl, I'm going to give her a hug and tell her I love her." Before Jared's wrath could bludgeon him, Terry pushed his way past him and rushed out of reach so quickly there wasn't a chance in hell of catching him.

Jared's inflexible stare never faltered. His eyes bored into Nathan wanting nothing more than to see him disintegrate where he stood. He would watch Nathan carefully as he groveled for forgiveness, but he wouldn't give the fucker an inch. He'd let him plead his case, but he didn't have a chance in hell to redeem himself. To his way of thinking, nothing the asswipe said or did could get him in to see Jody. On the contrary, Jared felt sure she needed protection from the likes of him.

"J.D.—Jared, I'm sorry. I really am. I would never have intentionally jeopardized Jody. There was a little girl's life at stake. Those women had already killed one of our best men. I couldn't leave her in their hands. Please, try to understand. She was just a scared little girl."

When Nathan mentioned the little girl, Jared's facial features relaxed just a bit. While unintentional, he was aware he'd just offered a small bit of encouragement in Nathan's battle for forgiveness. Yet, he remained silent.

"Look, I don't blame you for being angry. It will be a cold day in hell before I forgive myself for putting Jody through that nightmare."

It took all of Jared's willpower to stand there and listen to Nathan beg for absolution. The man was still fighting an uphill battle with an unknown outcome.

Nathan continued his plea. "Mikala—the little girl, we found her just where Jody said she was. Those bitches had locked her in a box and put it in a storage unit." Nathan's breath hitched in his throat.

"I will see the exact moment Jody channeled the little girl's fight to stay out of that box for the rest of my life. I'll never forget when Jody started struggling with unseen perpetrators. My dreams will be tormented by her tortured screams as she begged not to be forced into the box. Seeing Jody kicking and flailing about as the child had done to gain freedom makes my stomach churn. The thought that my best friend willingly submitted to the fear that sweet, little girl had gone through all because of me, batters my psyche more so than anything you could do to me." He shook his head to clear it and continued to fight his cause. His words were laced with torment. "They were going to leave that child there to die, Jared."

Nathan's statement greatly affected Jared. His body twitched from head to toe giving away another tell that forgiveness was within reach. "We found their checklist in the storage room with Mikala. They were never coming back for her. They were never going to make contact with the family again after they had the money.

"I just left little Mikala. She said she would've been more scared if it weren't for her guardian angel. The protective angel talked to her and kept her calm until she could be found. She said she didn't know how they both fit in that box, but her angel wouldn't leave her. Instead, the guardian angel patted her head and wiped away her tears. While waiting for help to come, they even made up and sang songs together."

Emotionally spent, Jared's body no longer had the strength to keep his muscles taut. Tears pooled and threatened to spill over his already swollen eyes.

"Mikala said her guardian angel's name is Jody."

Jared crumbled. Long gone was the man from a few short months ago. No longer emotionally handicapped and indifferent to everyone around him, Jody's love had broken through his barriers. His hands moved to his face to cover his tears and squelch his sobs—tears which were borne from a fear that would always be present with Jody in his life.

Nathan rushed forward and pulled Jared into an embrace, holding him as a brother would comfort a brother.

"As much as I enjoy hugging you, dude, I need to go in and see my girl." He spoke a moment or two later.

Jared snorted and nodded. "Yeah. Go on in. I'm going to stay out here for a minute."

Chapter Twenty-Five

Since *the event*, as she and Jared now called the kidnapping debacle, Jody hadn't been comfortable leaving the privacy of their home. To maintain her sanity, she had willingly retreated within herself both physically and mentally.

All business duties and responsibilities had been turned over to her capable staff to keep Fur Baby Groomers afloat. Even though Fur Baby was Jody's only means of support, at this point, she had no other choice but to stay away. These days fear had proven to be her guiding force. Trepidation lived with her and mooched off of her just as an uninvited house guest would. No matter what she tried, she couldn't get rid of the depression. The idea of going back to her daily routine anytime soon, if at all, was doubtful.

Jody had faith that Cassi and Kim would keep the doors to her precious business open. They would continue to give her furry clientele the best and most caring service possible. As time went by, it became apparent her employees believed she'd had a mental breakdown. When speaking on the phone, the concern in their voices rang through loud and clear. Unfortunately, their assessment wasn't far from the truth. With each passing day, she removed herself farther and farther from the outside world.

The FBI had informed the Spurls of Jody's

significant involvement in their granddaughter's recovery from the abduction attempt. Nothing had been withheld. The Spurls wanted to hold a meet and greet to offer their gratitude and express their appreciation for everything she'd been able to do. Although uncomfortable with the attention, she desperately wanted to see little Mikala. It was important for her to make sure the child had come through the event unscathed. Jody could only remember bits and pieces of those traumatizing hours, believing the intensity of the fear she'd felt had overridden much of her memory.

By her request, Jared reluctantly set up an after-dinner meeting with the Spurls on a Friday evening. They'd made plans to go out of town the same day which offered the perfect excuse not to stay too long.

If Jared had his way, she'd never meet with them. His best case scenario would be to distance her and himself from anything having to do with the event ever again. He feared for Jody and never stopped worrying about something popping up and sparking another freak fest. It wasn't necessary for him to verbalize how worried he'd been about the potential of her flying off the handle into another crisis. His concern was written all over his face. She loved him all the more for it but started hating herself for putting him through hell.

Stepping up to the front door of the Spurl's home, Jared's hand went out to knock. Hesitating, he pivoted and grabbed Jody's arm. "Are you sure about this? We can always say something came up."

An intense fear had her leaning toward taking him up on his offer. Before she could back away, the front door flew open and a little girl ran into her arms.

"Jody! Jody! You're here! You're really here!"

Mikala's embrace served to soften her heart. The little girl smelled of peaches and cream. If she weren't mistaken, there was also a hint of chocolate. The sweet child's scent and enthusiastic greeting helped Jody relax and absorb the loving warmth of the hug. The soul bond they'd developed during the event couldn't be denied.

Mikala's chubby hands framed Jody's face. "I can't believe you're really here! Can we sing some of the songs we made up together when you saved me?"

Talking about the event made Jody uneasy. Mikala, on the other hand, seemed to think of it as an ordinary, everyday experience.

"Do you remember…"

"Mikala, darling, let me in there for a hug." Jessie, the grandmother, almost knocked Jody down to get her chance at an embrace. Sobs wracked the woman, and all Jody could do was hold on as they swayed.

Not liking being the center of attention, Jody tried not to show her discomfort. Apparently she'd failed. "Jessie, let the poor woman go. You're embarrassing her." After getting his wife to release Jody, Mr. Spurl put his arm around her and squeezed. "Thank you, dear girl, for keeping our grandbaby safe. Please, come inside and have a drink with us."

As Mr. Spurl poured the champagne, Mikala found her way onto Jody's lap. A constant chatterbox, the little girl couldn't stop talking. To Jody's surprise, she relayed stories of how they'd kept each other company when they'd been locked in the box together.

As hard as she tried, Jody just wasn't able to remember much about the actual incident. The experience had been far too distressing. Their demise had been closer than she'd admitted to anyone. If the little girl had died that day, since she had been tethered to her, Jody felt confident she would have died as well.

It frightened her that Mikala had kept those memories. In the end, she chalked it up to there being some reason in the grand scheme of things for that to be so. Jody had learned long ago, not to question the why of things. Someday, the rationale might become clear to her, or she may never get an answer. Only time would tell.

There was a slight rap on the parlor room door before it opened. A handsome man swaggered into the room. Sitting next to Jared, she felt his body instantly tense. He squeezed Jody's hand a little tighter. Before the man could be introduced, Jared quickly stood and pulled her up with him.

"I'm sorry to be in such a rush, Mr. Spurl, but Jody and I have a long journey ahead of us. We really must get on the road."

Obviously taken aback by the abrupt change in Jared's demeanor, Mr. Spurl stood. "Of course. But before you go, Agent Jursic wanted to introduce himself to Jody. He's quite taken with her."

Before the agent could reach Jody, Jared had firmly placed himself in front of her. "I'm sorry. I don't think this is wise. We'll just take our leave."

Agent Jursic only spoke one word. "Please."

Hearing the plea in the man's voice had Jody moving from behind Jared.

"Jody—Ms. Clarke—you probably don't remember me, but I was there the day you gave us the information that saved Mikala. People call me Jursic. I've never believed in psychics before, but what you did that day humbled me. Your gift saved a very special little girl. I'm grateful to you."

"Thank you, Agent Jursic. I'm sorry, but I have practically no memory of the events that happened that day. I'm not really comfortable with the title of psychic, either. I have abilities that can sometimes be used to help people. Nothing more."

His expression softened. "What I witnessed that day was truly a miracle. You *should* know what happened. You should see for yourself. I gave a copy of the video we made for evidence to Mr. Spurl. I'm sure he wouldn't mind showing it to you."

"No!" Jared's voice left no room for discussion.

Jody's attention turned to the patriarch of the family. "Mr. Spurl, If you don't mind, I'd like a private moment with Jared."

"Of course, dear." He started rustling people toward the door. "Before you came, I thought you might be interested in seeing the events of that day. I've got the video cued up on the laptop over there, if you decide to watch." The door closed behind them with a soft whoosh.

Jared crossed his arms and took a firm stance. "No. It's not going to happen."

"Sweetheart, I need to see it. I need to know what happened to me, to you, all of it."

"Monkey, please, I'm begging you. Please, don't watch it. It'll just upset you more."

"You're wrong. I've been worrying about the events of that day ever since it happened. It's worse not knowing. Please, Jared. Don't fight me on this. I have to know." He remained standing in the middle of the room as she hit the play button.

The truth about what the man she loved had gone through during that traumatic event had to be unveiled and brought out into the open. She had to see for herself if it was as bad from his perspective as she thought it might have been.

The entire time the video played, Jared paced the room. She felt his eyes as they remained steady on her.

The tension in the room steadily grew to the point the stagnant air could be cut with a knife. The area surrounding them became dense, forcing her to strain her lungs just to get a full breath.

The event clearly still deeply affected him. That fact served to intensify Jody's guilt. Jared had gotten stuck with what she perceived as the short end of the stick in their relationship. She held herself culpable for the immeasurable distress she'd dropped at his feet and, as time went by, continued to cause him.

Since the event had occurred, she'd been grappling with this new gift of hers. Jody knew all the while there wasn't a damn thing she could do to stop it. For her own personal safety, she did, however, feel a great need to curb it in some way. She'd wrestled with that thought night and day.

As the nightmare continued to unfold on the video, it became apparent the risk wasn't only hers. Jared carried much more of the burden than she did. He'd been very sweet and attentive since that day, never leaving her side. While he hadn't voiced it, she knew he faced the same fear she did. Without question, another event would happen again. It was just a matter of time before it did.

The video made Jody realize that *his* fear had been compounded because he might not be there to help her through it the next time. She could be lost, somewhere out there in the great big universe without the ability to find her way home to him. No matter how wrong that way of thinking was on his part, if that occurred, Jared would blame himself.

Instead of her love giving him happiness, he felt the misery of worry and regret over their relationship. Who wouldn't?

Reflecting on the problem at hand, she realized just how difficult it would be to minimize her risk. She lived in the Phoenix metropolitan area with another four million living people. Add to that number all of the deceased, and her head hurt just thinking about it. With those kinds of numbers, the chances of another event happening very soon had given her more than enough sleepless nights.

****

As they drove away from the Spurl's home, Jody turned toward Jared as much as the seatbelt would allow. Knowing how important this weekend together would be, the decision to get out of town for a break from their worries calmed her.

Reaching out for his hand, she cocooned it lovingly between both of hers. Her worry for him was boundless. Not about his leaving her because she knew now, after watching the video, he never would. Yet, Jody had been horrified to discover that what Jared had gone through during the event was much worse than she could've ever imagined.

Her misgivings stemmed from having dragged him inadvertently into her own personal hell. That was unforgivable.

The thought that her abilities left him more

troubled than her, distressed Jody beyond belief. Truth be told, with everything that had transpired regarding the event, he'd ended up more anxious than her. Knowing his love for her had saddled him with a whole new set of problems, devastated Jody. Love wasn't supposed to be fraught with misery. God knows, in a very short period of time, she'd caused him more than his fair share.

Because of her, Jared's life had been completely turned upside down. Jody saw it in his eyes, in his face, the way he carried himself—he was a constant ball of nerves. *No. It goes far beyond that.* It was fear. Not for himself but for her, which made her guilt all the worse. She'd made him unhappy, and that fell hard on her shoulders.

Selfishly, she'd allowed him into her life, knowing full well it would be hard for him. Granted, upon reflection, Jody's life seemed almost mellow back then compared to now. She had no idea the turn her abilities would take. Those so called gifts were the determining factor in making an inescapable nightmare out of both living with and loving her.

Wanting to keep him close, Jody lifted Jared's hand to kiss it. She'd cherished the time they'd had together. Her eyes started to fill with tears so she shuttered them, not wanting him to know how upset she'd become. She nuzzled his hand with her cheek, getting as much warmth and love from him while she still could.

For the past few weeks, her fear had kept her in a reclusive state leaving her bound to the privacy of Jared's home. Jody was scared to death she'd touch something or someone and snap the tenuous thread that held her together. If that were to happen, Jared would be left to pick up the pieces of her messed up life. He'd do it in a heartbeat. She knew that. He wouldn't complain. She knew that, too. But the realization hit that life with her had become a prison sentence serving hard time rather than the happily-ever-after he deserved. Jared had never left her side and never complained about being shut into their own private penitentiary. It wouldn't be long before he felt like being with her had earned him a life sentence in the deepest, darkest hell imaginable.

The video had sealed the deal. There would be no turning back from the decision she'd finally made. Jared meant more to her than life itself. Jody couldn't and wouldn't continue to put him in situations that brought him nothing but fear and heartache. Life with her just wasn't worth it.

She'd have to find a place to live somewhere away from people. Jody would have to isolate herself—close herself off from the outside world as much as possible. And she'd have to do it all alone. Jared had already given up enough for her. She'd never ask him to leave everything he had built for himself. She wouldn't ask him to disengage from the life he led or allow him to leave everything he was comfortable with just for her. It wasn't fair to him. She'd brought nothing but heartache and worry into his life, and he deserved so much more than that.

As she reviewed their relationship, Jody started to realize just how one-sided it had been. So far, Jared had changed everything in his life for her. The fact that she wasn't capable of doing that for him made her feel like the worst human being on earth. There was no question about it. If she had the power to do so, she'd change in a heartbeat. But the plain and simple truth of the matter was that she didn't have that power. Just because it wasn't within her reach to change, didn't make it any less unfair for him. It had become obvious she'd never be rid of these abilities of hers. And worse, she couldn't foresee ever being able to enjoy her life with the threat of them hanging so heavily over her head. She wouldn't be responsible for dragging him down such a detestable path.

As the realization of leaving Jared fermented, Jody felt a ripping pain in her heart as it broke in two. She wanted to give him this last weekend, make it special for both of them. She wanted to make him happy one last time before leaving. Her heart knew it was the best thing for him. He wouldn't give up on their relationship without a fight. But if she didn't leave, he'd end up regretting ever having met her. She'd never allow that to happen. When he thought of her, she wanted him to reminisce with love. From the moment the video had been viewed, she accepted the responsibility for the look of complete and utter despair on his face as he'd held her and forced life back into her body. She could never ask him to go through that again. Never.

Chapter Twenty-Six

It wasn't until he realized Jody had fallen asleep that Jared could finally relax. Knowing she'd been able to put the video behind her had him breathing easy for the first time in the last two hours. He'd done everything, short of begging, to convince her not to watch it. But in the end, she'd insisted. *My girl is fierce.*

He didn't know what he'd expected, but her calm acceptance of seeing herself so out of control certainly hadn't been on his radar. As she watched the video, he'd hoped Jody would concentrate more on how they worked together as a team rather than what she'd personally experienced. Maybe they could finally put this whole mess behind them now and move on with their lives together.

Since the event, he hadn't been able to pull Jody out of her funk. Jared couldn't pretend to understand what her mind and body had been through that day but could offer support and a shoulder to cry on. Every time he tried to get her to open up, she'd calmly state that she was fine as if a barrier had been constructed to hide her feelings.

Each dawning day seemed to carry Jody to a darker place—a place she wouldn't allow him entry. In the end, he backed off and gave her the space she seemed to need.

Hopefully, this weekend would be a new start for

them. Without Jody knowing, Jared had worked very hard over the last few weeks to put this weekend together. Each night she fell asleep, he would sneak out of their bedroom and worked out the details from his home office. Nathan and Terry had even gotten involved in the planning. All the work would be worth it if she were able to find the peace she so richly deserved.

Knowing there'd never be a moment's rest for her in Phoenix, he planned to convince her she might be safer some place more secluded. Jody needed a safe haven, someplace she could move around without fear of being afflicted by troubled spirits or grieving people, either past or present. She needed a place in which it would be possible to find and heal herself, ultimately gaining her happiness again.

Pulling the car to a stop, Jared turned the engine off. He had to admit, the cabin, highlighted with moonlight, was stunning. It certainly lived up to everything he'd heard about it. The time had come to reveal the real reason they were here. He couldn't help but feel their future happiness rode on the outcome of the next few minutes.

Jared hated waking Jody while she slept so peacefully, but he needed to get her inside. Reaching into the car, he stroked her hair. "Wake up, Monkey. We're here."

He loved the sparkle of life and joy her eyes held in the first moments after waking. But it saddened him how quickly the happiness disappeared once she became fully awake.

She pulled him into the car for a kiss. "Hold me, Jared." He tried to shake off the ominous feeling the tremor in her voice caused.

"Come on, Monkey. I've got a few surprises for you." Pulling her from the car, he wrapped his arms around her and held on tight.

The crisp, fresh scent of pine did more to soothe her soul than any measure of meditation or mantras could. Each deep breath seemed to energize Jody and carry her worries away. There was something mystical and rejuvenating about this place.

"What do you think?"

The beauty of the cabin left her speechless. While Jared's Camelback Mountain estate was the picture of grandeur and opulence, something right out of the pages of Architectural Digest, this rural cabin felt real, felt warm. Above all else the simple cabin in the pines felt more like a home than the Phoenix residence ever could. It was rustic and yet elegant in a purely natural way. The wraparound front porch held rocking chairs and tables, so the occupants could enjoy watching wildlife as they lazed the afternoon away. More importantly this place *felt* safe.

She spread her arms wide, leaned her head back, and took a deep cleansing breath. Opening herself up to the vibrations of the land, Jody tested the waters and received no messages, felt no ghosts. For the first time in weeks, her smile was genuine. "Oh, Jared, it's beautiful!"

Feeling as though she didn't have a care in the world, they walked arm and arm up to the house. He started to put the key in the door but suddenly turned to her and pulled her into his arms.

"Do you love me, Monkey?"

Jody reached out and grazed his mouth with her

fingers, wondering if his skin tingled with her touch the way she tingled with his. "With all my heart."

Her heart swelled with love as he kept the kiss tender. "I've got a surprise for you," he whispered into her mouth, anxious to get her inside. "I want you to close your eyes, and I'll guide you in."

Excitement built between them as he led her through the door. "What have you done?"

"Here." He positioned her and put his hands on her shoulders. "Open your eyes."

Jody blinked a few times until she got her bearings in the semi-dark room. Candlelight softly lit the room, and several dozen roses gave the area a breathtakingly romantic feel.

The gorgeous woodwork drew her attention. Even with the large, open floor plan, the real log walls gave the room a warm, intimate feel. As she turned, the kitchen caught her eye. There, the walls were made of rock with copper embellishments throughout. It truly was the heart of this home and a place where she envisioned the occupant's dreams had been built throughout the years.

His arms moved around her as she automatically leaned back into him. "Oh Jared, I don't know what to say. It's spectacular, more than I ever could have dreamed for a vacation hideaway."

"Come with me. I want to show you something else." Jody couldn't keep her fingers from skimming the roughened logs which made up the walls as they walked to the back of the house. They stopped in front of a picture window large enough to see the beautiful moonlit trees surrounding the home from anywhere in the room. Jared turned the outside lights on to expose a back deck overlooking a large pond with a dock. They moved through the double doors and viewed the beautiful, natural landscape surrounding the cabin.

Wrapping her arms around his waist, she squeezed close into his side. "Oh, Jared, this place feels so peaceful, so serene. No matter how hard I've tried, I hadn't been able to recapture that feeling since before Fiona came into our lives. It feels safe."

Turning her toward him, he held her close to his chest. "I had a priest come and bless the house. A shaman blessed the land. A medium cleared out all the ghosts. I had a local Wiccan coven come and place wards throughout the house and land to make this your sanctuary. This cabin is your safe spot where nothing can hurt you when you're here. This home is our paradise.

"Do you really like it, Monkey?" He held his breath until she reached up and pulled his mouth back to hers.

His sigh of relief was lost in their kiss. "I bought this house for you and me. I can't promise that you'll never be in a situation like you were with little Mikala again or even little Fiona. I *can* promise that you'll be safe here with me."

"You bought this home? You did this for me, Jared? You'd leave everything behind? What about your job?" Barely able to see him through her tears, she looked into his eyes trying to determine the honesty of his answer.

His hands gently moved to her cheeks as he lowered his forehead to hers. "Sweetheart, we live in a digital world. I can have video conferences and do research from my home office. I may have to go to

Phoenix once in awhile, but not often. And besides I'm the boss.

"Oh, Monkey, don't you know I have nothing without you? Haven't you learned that yet? You're the meaning in my life. Before you, I had nothing at all."

Jared guided her to a table where a bottle of champagne chilled and a small black box rested beside it. A gasp escaped Jody's lips. Her hands flew to her mouth as she started to understand the implications of the gesture before her.

"You've changed my life, Monkey. I can't go back to the man I was before I met you. You've given me more in the few short months I've known you than anyone has ever given me before. You make me feel like a whole man for the first time in my life. You've given me love and family. I need you by my side, Jody. Will you marry me? Will you live your life with me here in our own little forest?"

Shock reverberated through her. She searched for the words she didn't want to say but needed to be said. "Jared, I can't ask you to give everything up for me. I've been so selfish when it comes to you. It's not fair to—"

Jared pulled her to him so rapidly she almost lost her balance. "I'm not taking no for an answer, Monkey. If anyone is selfish, it's me. I can't live my life without you. I'm not going back to that bleak existence. I love you too much, and I'll never let you go."

Tears of happiness ran down her face as she molded her body to his. Struck speechless by his beautiful proposal, she could only acknowledge him with sloppy sobs of joy, a runny nose, and an excited nod.

Giving in and letting him take care of her, she allowed Jared to wipe her nose with a tissue, and her tears with his fingers. They sealed the moment with their first passionate kiss on the balcony of their safe haven, looking out at the beauty of their forest.

A few moments later, Jared guided Jody to a bench and sat her down. Opening the little black box, he revealed the most magnificent diamond ring she'd ever seen. Sealing the deal, he slipped the ring on her hand and kissed her forehead.

After popping the cork on the champagne, he offered her a glass and held his up as if to toast. "I have something else for you, Monkey." He stalled by taking a sip of his bubbling wine. The sexy smile he offered held promises of a passion filled evening in their new home. If she were lucky, maybe even right here on the back deck.

Jody's heart sped up and did an excited little pitter patter as his fingers moved seductively to his mouth. The ease with which he turned her on amazed her. Instead of doing something completely erotic with those fingers and tongue, he startled her when a shrill whistle escaped his lips.

As if he hadn't just broken her eardrums, he raised his glass and toasted. "To us."

"What have you got up your sleeve now?" She clinked her glass to his. "To us."

Suddenly, the patter of little feet running toward her could be heard. She turned to find two beagle puppies, ears flopping with each bound, heading straight for her. Dropping to the ground, she patted the deck, enticing the cute little munchkins to her side. The puppies landed in her lap, almost knocking her backward. Jared's laughter rang out as he sat down on the floor of the deck next to her.

He reached out and grabbed a puppy. "This is Fred, and that's," he pointed to the puppy licking her face, "Wilma. I know how badly you've wanted dogs, so I thought we should have a few new additions to our little family. They shouldn't be bothered by any stray spirits here."

Scratching the puppy's back, Wilma joyfully licked Jody's face. At no time in her entire life had she ever known the kind of happiness Jared offered her. She brought his hand to her mouth and playfully nipped at his fingers. "Jared, what have you done?"

"Let's call the house a wedding present and the puppies a prelude to children."

"You were pretty sure I was going to say yes, weren't you?"

The broad grin he brandished lit his face with amusement. Jared's happiness had her heart soaring higher than it ever had before. Nothing else mattered. He was her true gift, and she thanked her lucky stars for him.

In response to her question, he playfully shrugged his shoulders. "When you finished reading your latest literary masterpiece, you left it lying on the table next to the bed. I picked it up and started reading. I learned a few things from the mighty Highlander. I figured if you said no, I'd do what the brawny Scotsman did. I'd sweep you off to my castle, take your clothes off, and tie you to the bed." Leaning in a little closer, he whispered seductively in her ear. "I'd speak in a thick Scottish brogue, and prance around flexing my bronzed, moistened muscles. You'd have no choice but to beg for my throbbing manhood."

His fingers snapped in the air with attitude. "Nothin' to it!"

She let loose with gut-busting laughter.

"Can anyone join this party?" Jody jumped when she heard Nathan's voice. She couldn't believe her eyes when she turned and saw both Nathan and Terry walking toward them, each sporting shit-eating grins. Neglecting the chaise lounges, they grabbed the bottle of champagne and sat on the deck floor next to the new family.

"You know, there are plenty of chairs. I'm not sure why we're all sitting on the ground," Nathan joked.

Jody reached out and kissed her two best friends. Before she could pull away from Nathan, his demeanor turned serious. Looking deeply into her eyes, he asked, "Are you happy, baby doll?"

She glanced at Jared and beamed. "Oh yeah."

"Then we're happy."

"Wait just a damn minute," Terry interrupted, surprising the people around him and garnering everyone's attention.

"I'm happy that *you're* happy." He spread his arms to encompass Jody and Jared. "But there's one thing that's got to happen before *I'm* happy."

Not having a clue what he could possibly be talking about had Jody's brow moving up a fraction of an inch. "What is *that* supposed to mean?"

Instead of Terry answering her question, Jared leaned in to explain. "In exchange for his help with this place, I promised him something."

"Okay." Expecting more information, Jody purposely lifted her shoulders to prompt him to continue. When Jared blushed, she cringed. "Oh God! What did you promise him?"

"Since he didn't get to keep *Solitude*—" Terry interrupted by loudly clearing his throat. When he had everyone's attention, he mocked, "Stick to the script."

Embarrassed, Jared bent his head in shame. "Fine. Dammit. Since Solitude was stolen out from under him, I owe him. He wants to show people what real love looks like. He insisted on using us as the subject matter."

Looking at Terry's winning grin, she whispered under her breath, "Should I tell him there's no way in hell he's going to get to keep that portrait either?"

Jared kissed her head and murmured into her ear. "Nah. Don't spoil it for him."

The sound of his easy chuckle filled her with joy.

Jody lifted her glass to toast. "To troubled spirits. I will be forever grateful to you for bringing Jared and I together. May you all rest in peace."

A word from the author…

I've been an avid reader for years. To my husband's dismay, I have bookshelves full of books, rooms full of books, boxes full of books. My cars have books in them. I just can't seem to get rid of them after I read them. You just never know when you will want to read it again, right? When my husband bought me a Kindle, it cut down on our need for storage, but it opened me up to books that I might never have experienced otherwise.

The biggest transition in my relationship with books occurred, however, when I, much to my surprise, became an author. I had started having dreams about people I didn't know. I started looking forward to my dreams every night. Then I realized that I was daydreaming about these people as well. I'd just be sitting there, and these people and their antics would pop into my mind. Finally, I gave in and began writing their story down, something I had never dreamed of doing. My books invariably feature strong women.

My husband, Michael, and I have raised two strong daughters, Pilar and Shandelle, and they inspire the characters in my stories.

I've had fun with all the books I've written. Inserting real events into my books, things that have actually happened in my family's lives, is like having a private joke.

My romance novels always contain a paranormal twist. I imagine my future writings will always contain romance, strong women and men of character, events that reach beyond what we consider normal, and perhaps seasoned with a little touch of whimsy.

http://sandywolters.weebly.com/

Thank you for purchasing
this publication of The Wild Rose Press, Inc.

If you enjoyed the story, we would appreciate your
letting others know by leaving a review.

For other wonderful stories,
please visit our on-line bookstore at
www.thewildrosepress.com.

For questions or more information
contact us at
info@thewildrosepress.com.

The Wild Rose Press, Inc.
www.thewildrosepress.com

Stay current with The Wild Rose Press, Inc.

Like us on Facebook

https://www.facebook.com/TheWildRosePress

And Follow us on Twitter
https://twitter.com/WildRosePress

www.ingramcontent.com/pod-product-compliance
Lightning Source LLC
Chambersburg PA
CBHW070835280626
47161CB00015B/670

* 9 7 8 1 5 0 9 2 1 4 4 8 8 *